A UNITED FEDERATION MARINE CORPS
NOVEL

BEHIND ENEMY LINES

Colonel Jonathan P. Brazee
USMCR (Ret)

Semper Fi Press

A Semper Fi Press Book

ISBN-10: 1-945743-09-3 (Semper Fi Press)
ISBN-13: 978-1-945743-09-2

Printed in the United States of America

Author Website: http://jonathanbrazee.com
Email List Sign-up: http://eepurl.com/bnFSHH

Acknowledgements:
I want to thank all those who took the time to pre-read this book, catching my mistakes in both content and typing. Thanks to best_editor1 for her editing. Thanks to Alex McArdell for putting together the cover art. You can see more of Alex's work at https://www.behance.net/AlexMcArdell.

Original cover art by Alex McArdell

Cover graphics by Steven Novak

DONKERBROEK
NIEUWE UTRECHT

Chapter 1

Jasper

Jasper van Ruiker gripped the old UKI assault rifle tightly as he stared into the darkness. His thumb fell to the safety which he flipped off, then back on again. He risked a glance to where Ida's boy, Greg—no, that's Sergeant Brusse now, he had to remind himself—stood chest deep in his fighting hole. Greg . . . the sergeant . . . had warned them all to keep their weapons on safe until they had a target.

Sergeant or not, Jasper flipped the selection lever to fire mode. He didn't want to waste even a microsecond when the Tenners assaulted.

I'm too old for this shit, he thought for the thousandth time.

Two weeks earlier, Jasper was harvesting his algae, only his fourth season as a freeman and independent farmer. The new DT-445 Blue was performing better than he'd dreamed, and he and Keela had thought their future was finally secured. He'd never imagined that future would find him in a foxhole, clutching a rifle he'd never even fired, and with only nine rounds to face a Tenner mercenary unit.

He wished he could call Keela, but Maarten, now the lieutenant, had taken all their PAs. "Security" he'd used as an excuse. Jasper didn't know much about fighting and even less about security, but he didn't think a call to his wife would change the course of the coming battle. So, little Amee's PA was now burning a hole in his pocket. His five-year-old granddaughter surprisingly hadn't complained when Keela had taken it from her and slipped it into his pocket last night.

Jasper had been conscripted into the Donkerbroek Militia only five days earlier, but even without training, even without experience, he knew that the 28 of them stood no chance against the professional mercs who were approaching, PA call or not.

"Do you think they're still coming?" Ito, asked in a whisper.

Ito was an outsider, only six years arrived in the village, and Jasper had never reached out to him and his family to make them feel welcomed. But since they were now sharing a fighting hole, things had changed.

"Aye-yah, lad, I think they are," Jasper answered.

"Why are we even fighting? I mean, I don't like the Tenners, but what have they ever done to me? And where is the Federation? Why do they leach us with taxes if they aren't going to protect us?" Ito asked.

"Quiet!" Sergeant Brusse hissed as Ito's voice started to rise in his excitement.

Ito had a point, though, and it was something Jasper had been wondering about ever since the Tenners—the Freedom Consortium troops—had landed on the planet. As a former indentured, or Class 4 employee, Jasper had no love lost for any of the big corporations. They took it to the plebes every chance they had. But they'd been operating in the Far Reaches with relative impunity for a century, and it was only now that the Federation was trying to rein them in.

The politics of it all were beyond Jasper's knowledge or interest. He knew that the fledgling Brotherhood of Servants and some of the independents had their fingers in the mess, but it was the corporations that were the prime players. Their nickname of "Tenners" was based on the ten corporations that initially formed their consortium. And that was about the extent of his knowledge of the situation. Politics might impact his life and that of his family, but he couldn't affect anything at that level, so like most others at the bottom of the social ladder, he was a mouse who scurried around at his own business while ignoring the rumblings of the elephants as they jockeyed for position.

What Jasper did know was that as a freeman, he paid 32% of his income last year in Federation taxes, taxes that were supposed to support the Navy and Marines, among other things. So why was he standing in a fighting hole in the middle of the night, holding a rifle, then? He wasn't a frigging Marine. He was a farmer, providing organics for the fabricators that supported all of human space. Hell, Donbury Ag had been his single largest customer, and they were one of the ten founding corporations of the Freedom Consortium. So, he was fighting for the Federation, who took his income in taxes, against the company that bought his algae. All of this made his head ache.

Maarten, mayor of the village and now lieutenant and commander of the militia, had argued vociferously for loyalty to the Federation, and the rest, albeit some with far less enthusiasm, had agreed. Every adult in the village had reaffirmed their fealty to the Federation. That was before the Tenner mercs had landed, however. Now, there was no turning back.

Some 7,000 mercs had invaded Nieuwe Utrecht, more than enough to take over the sparsely populated planet. If every freeman and indentured joined the various militias, they could create a 50,000-man force, but no one doubted that the well-trained and well-armed merc force could slice through the militias like butter, and even the Marine battalion that had landed wouldn't be enough to hold them off.

But that was the big picture. What mattered to Jasper now was on a much smaller scale. Led by Maarten, the 28 of them were dug in on the crest of Koltan's Hill where they could control the Blue Trail Highway. If the Tenners wanted to take Donkerbroek, they'd need to kick the 28 of them off the hill first. And they were coming. The call from Wieksloot before it fell was sobering. At least 200 mercs, an entire company, had destroyed most of the town and were now heading north on the highway.

"Why do they want us, anyway? We're not rich," Ito whispered.

"Doesn't matter much why, Ito. They're here, and if you want to protect Kara and your girls, you need to fight. You heard what they did to Wieksloot."

The report had been fragmentary, which wasn't surprising given the situation, but the mercs had pretty much leveled the larger town. Civilian casualties had been extremely high.

Political leanings aside, that was the reason Jasper was standing in the fighting hole. Keela was with Carrie Brusse, leading the rest of the women and children back to the Pirate's Cave. Among them were his three grandchildren. Along with their mother—his daughter-in-law, Radiant—they were five of the seven most important people in his life.

He looked to his left, but he couldn't see where his son, Christiaan, was waiting to face the mercs. He'd come to grips with the fact that neither he nor Christiaan would survive, and he had no idea what was the status of Karianne, his daughter, who worked in the capital, but he'd do what he could to keep his grandkids alive. The Tenner mercs would know of the cave, of course. But Jasper was hopeful that they wouldn't bother tramping around the woods and hills to track down non-combatants.

"I know," Ito said quietly.

There wasn't much more that Jasper could add. They were all going to die, he knew, and he didn't feel like lying to bolster Ito's confidence.

I should have kissed Keela one more time, he thought.

But with her rushing to gather the children and him rushing to his position, they'd somehow missed connecting. And now it was too late.

Jasper had accepted his fate. He was far less frightened than he would have thought he would be. More than anything, he was sad. There was so much he was going to miss in his family's life, but this was the gift he was trying to give them. If the militia could delay the mercs even for a few minutes, that would give the rest of the village more time to get deep into the cave.

"Oh, shit, here they come!" Ito said, panic rising in his voice.

Jasper snapped back to the present. Down on the highway below, maybe 700 meters away, a robot was trundling towards them, clearly visible under the light of the twin moons.

The Tenners sure like their tech, he thought as he watched the robot get closer.

Another 30 meters behind the robot, three soldiers advanced, weapons at the ready.

Jasper looked down his UKI's sights. The soldiers were still too far out of range for him, but he wanted to be ready. The plan was to wait until the mercs crossed Brown Bridge over Rustig Stroom, the stream that ran along the highway and through the village. At about 200 meters below them, Jasper thought he should be able to take out at least one of the bastards before they got to him.

That plan was stillborn. The robot suddenly stopped in the middle of the highway. Jasper could see something on top of it spin, then without warning, a stream of lights reached up to them. For a moment, Jasper was confused, and all he could think of was fireflies. Then the rounds started impacting with ferocious intent. Sergeant Brusse stood up mouth open to shout when the top of his head exploded, and he fell back into his foxhole.

"Oh, my God!" Ito shouted before turning to scramble out of the fighting hole. Jasper tried to grab him, to pull him back.

"Your girls, Ito. You've got to fight!"

Ito was kicking for all he was worth, and Jasper lost his grasp. Ito stood up and started to run, making all of one step before most of everything above his hips simply disappeared. A coppery mist fell on Jasper, coating his face.

"You . . . I . . ." he started, staring at the body.

Another round slammed into the dirt half a meter to his side, sending up clods that pelted him. Jasper turned around and ducked into his hole, breathing heavily. He'd been ready to die, but now, this was real. Fear started to creep over him.

He took several deep breaths.

"Come on, Jasper van Ruiker! No time for cowards!"

With an extreme effort of will, he stood up, swinging his rifle to take the mercs under fire, only to immediately duck back. He'd barely a split-second, but that had been long enough to see they were still too far away. With only nine rounds, he wasn't going to waste them on impossible shots.

"Stay down until they're closer!" someone shouted, coming to the same conclusion.

Jasper could barely hear whoever had shouted, given the hammering of the gun from below. He tried to sink lower into the dirt at the bottom of his hole as the merc combat robot tore up the hillside. Scrunched up like that, Amee's PA dug into his thigh.

Screw it. They know where we are.

He pushed out his leg the best he could and fished out the pink Lil' Bunny PA. He only hesitated a moment before keying in Keela. His wife answered after the first chime.

"Are you OK?" she asked, her voicing high and strident the way it always was when she was stressed.

"Aye-yah," he said automatically, before he corrected, "Uh, no. Ito's dead. Tried to run. And the Tenners are down on the highway."

"I can hear the firing," Keela said. "It's . . . there's a lot of it."

"Where are you?"

"At the switchback. I'm bringing up the rear with Marta. Five more minutes, I think."

Jasper breathed a sigh of relief.

More like ten from the switchback. But still, if we can hold the mercs off for a few more minutes, maybe they can make it.

With Keela were over 70 women and children, and if she was in the rear of the group, he hoped people were already pouring into the cave.

"Can you . . . I mean, is there any way you can hold out?" Keela asked.

"I love, you. You've been the best thing in my life," Jasper said, avoiding the obvious answer.

Even if they tried to retreat, the mercs weren't going to let them get away. And surrender wasn't an option with them, not if what they heard from Wieksloot was true.

Jasper heard a gasp on the other end, then, "I love you, too."

The robot below them quit firing, the silence almost deafening. Jasper didn't know if it had been cut off or if it had simply run out of rounds. He craned his head around, but couldn't bring himself to pop up to see.

"Get ready!" someone shouted from down the line.

"Look, Keela, I've got to go."

"Wait!"

"I love you," he said, tears forming as he cut off the PA, dropping it to the bottom of the fighting hole as he turned around, facing downhill.

"Not yet! Wait for my command," the voice cried out.

It sounded like Jan ter Horst, which struck Jasper as odd. Jan was the town drunk, straight out of a Hollybolly-casting. Jasper couldn't imagine him taking over the defense. But without any better option, Jasper was going to obey the commands.

The horrendous tsunami of fire had ceased, but rounds still impacted around them, angry bees looking for a target. Jasper figured it was controlled fire from the mercs themselves, and he knew that if he popped out of his hole, he'd be targeted. Still, the urge was strong to do just that. If he was about to die, he wanted to see his killers. Crouching in the foxhole only heightened his anxiety.

Time barely crept on, but when Jan yelled "Now! Kill the bastards!" it seemed too soon.

"*Kus mijn kloten!*" Jasper shouted, borrowing his grandfather's favorite profanity, as he rose up, rifle ready.

Downslope, at least 30 Tenner mercs were heading towards them, clad in their hardshell armor. Jasper didn't even know if his .30 cal round would penetrate the armor chest pieces, but he had to try.

He aimed in at the nearest merc and fired. He had no idea if he hit the soldier, but he felt a thrill when the merc dove for the ground.

"Take that you—" he started before a heavy fusillade of fire reached out to them from the far side of the highway, and he had to duck back down.

Jasper had thought that the 30 mercs he'd seen were possibly the only ones in the fight, forgetting what Maarten, reading from a downloaded manual, had said about supporting fires or something like that. The 30 mercs were the assault force, but the bulk of the force would be supporting them.

Sporadic fire from the militia reached down from their positions, but not enough. Jasper took another deep breath and popped back up, snapping off another shot. He was sure he hadn't come close to anyone, but hopefully, it would have helped slow them down.

But he couldn't do that too many times. He had seven rounds left, so he had to make sure each one counted.

Someone down the line started screaming in pain—and he kept on screaming. Jasper closed his eyes. That was one of his friends dying an awful death, and he didn't even know who it was. The screaming was getting to him, sapping his will. It wasn't right, it wasn't honorable, but he wished someone would just put the wounded man out of his misery. If it were him in that position, he'd hope that a friend would grant him that release.

The return fire from their positions was petering out, and that should give the mercs more confidence, so Jasper popped up once again—and was shocked to see a merc not 20 meters below him, rushing up the hill. Instinctively, Jasper fired off two shots. The first glanced off the merc's chest plate, but the second shattered the man's face shield. Jasper felt a thrill run through him as the man fell, rolling back down the hill. That thrill was only partially mollified when the merc gathered himself and scrambled for the cover of a depression in the ground. Jasper may not have killed the man, but he sure as hell had gotten the merc's attention!

The mercs on the slope could not get their weapons to bear on them. Maarten, for all his lack of experience, had selected a good position in that regard. The mercs all the way at the bottom of the hill, though, the ones pouring fire onto them, had better angles. Jasper wanted to take them under fire, but he didn't really have anyone he could spot.

The ground just below Jasper suddenly erupted in a mini-volcano of dirt and a loud explosion that set Jasper's ears ringing. He realized that mercs had to be using mortars on them. He was amazed that he was still alive, and he had to give credit once again to Maarten's positioning of them.

A sudden increase of fire from the east end of the line reached him. He wheeled to his left, oblivious to the fact that he was exposing himself. He couldn't see anything—the curve of the hill blocked his view.

"Christiaan!" he shouted.

His son was on that end of the line, opposite his own position, and it sounded like the entire Tenner Army had suddenly appeared over there.

He didn't need to be an Academy graduate to know what was happening. While the mercs below them had grabbed their attention and the ones in the tree line down by the stream kept them pinned, another force had flanked them. And now they'd roll right up their defensive line.

What do you expect, sending amateurs against real soldiers? he thought bitterly. *We never had a chance.*

He'd always known that, he'd already accepted that, but there had still been the tiniest bit of hope, especially when the merc assault had seemingly stalled.

Well, time to take out as many as I can, he told himself.

The sounds of fighting reached him, getting louder and louder the closer it got. He knew that with each moment, more of his militia, his friends, were dying.

With the berm facing downhill, he could see to Barry and Felipe's hole while still protected from the assault force. He wanted to shout to the two of them that he had them covered, but his throat was too dry. Nothing came out except for a croak.

He couldn't even see the mercs when Barry and Felipe shuddered and fell as a buzzsaw of rounds hit them. They never even got off a shot of their own.

It was probably less than fifteen seconds later when a figure dashed up, then dove to the ground. Jasper crouched lower, and when the next merc ran into view, probably intending to bound past his fellow merc, Jasper fired.

This time, he hit the man square in the neck, and the merc dropped like a sack of fertilizer.

"Heck, yeah!" Jasper shouted.

He realized he had only a few more moments to live, but he was damned sure he was going to revel in sending at least one of the bastards to hell first.

From where the first merc had hit the dirt, an arm flung up. Jasper barely saw the dark ball fly towards him. He ducked back into the hole as an explosion, not a meter away rocked him, dirt cascading down the walls of the foxhole.

Jasper immediately jumped up, ready to take the merc under fire when he caught movement out of the corner of his eye. He started to turn, barely catching sight of three mercs who had just flanked him raising their squat, ugly Gescard bullpups to take aim. Jasper started to wheel about, but he knew there was no way he could fire before their bullpups spit a stream of .42 caliber rounds to send him to his grave.

"YAAA—" he started to scream before his entire world erupted into a maelstrom of heat, noise, and confusion before all went dark.

Chapter 2

Mountie

"You are clear, Mountie. Kick some ass for Mutt!" Skeets passed.

Lieutenant Castor "Mountie" Klocek, United Federation Navy, inverted his Basilisk and dove at the center of mass of the Tenner positions. Without known locals in the area, he was weapons free, and his BD-42 was one hell of a weapon. He was going to make the fuckers pay and pay dearly.

Mutt, Lieutenant Pasqual Morthensen-Gable, was his bunkmate and friend, and only two minutes before, the mercs had shot him down with a Piper GTA missile. The Basilisk, known affectionately as a "Lizard" by its pilots, was a heavy bird, able to take an amazing pounding, but the Piper was up to the task. Luckily, they were so expensive that most merc units could only afford one. For them, a fight came down to a cost-benefit analysis, and spending for more missiles wasn't a good business decision when the hope was that even the threat of one would keep enemy air away.

But the war with the Tenners wasn't some local dust-up. This was total warfare, only the second such war since the formation of the Federation. In this situation, the bean counters simply could not be allowed to dictate tactics. Unfortunately for the mercs—and fortunately for the Federation forces—that is exactly what happened, and they wouldn't have anything else that could threaten him.

They would try, though. Mountie's Threat Reader kept up a stream of alerts as the mercs 3,000 meters below threw whatever they had up at him. Nothing mattered. Between his repeller fields and the heavy armor plating on his ugly ride, nothing got through.

Lizard jocks took a perverse pride in their planes' appearance, and the ugly label was lovingly embraced. They may be low man on the Navy pilot totem pole, but the Marines sure liked having them around. A Lizard jock could walk into any Marine club and be sure of more than a few free drinks—something they tried to take advantage of whenever they could.

With a free approach, Mountie brought his Lizard almost straight down. The BD-42 could be released at any approach, but for the maximum attenuation of the blast wave, its trajectory should be perpendicular to the ground.

Mountie wanted the satisfaction of a manual pickle, but his Attack AI could better calculate the optimal release height given the terrain features and ground cover. He wanted to inflict maximum hurt to the bastards, so he was in AI mode. He'd keep his plane in the cone and react to anything unexpected, but the AI would pickle the bomb.

Still, he had to exact some revenge himself. He had only 56 of his 30mm rounds left, the rest having been expended on his flight's primary target. Relying on his HDMS[1], he zoomed in on a field gun. With a flick of the safety lever, he triggered his Forsythe vulcan and sent the 56 rounds downrange in less than half a second. His seat vibrated with the "Forsythe Buzz," but for a far too short duration.

He watched until the rounds hit the target, flashes visible where the depleted uranium rounds hit metal. He knew the field gun normally had a three-man crew, and he was pretty sure he'd just zeroed all three. Mountie felt pure, unadulterated joy in the thought.

His HDMS flashed amber. Mountie could still take over, but he let the AI keep control. After three flashes, it turned to red. His Lizard was a heavy plane, but it lurched as the BD-42 released as if happy to have gotten rid of the burden. Mountie thumbed his cursor to pull *Pretty Gabby* into a sharp oblique climb, out of the path of his 42's shock wave. It wasn't really too serious of a concern, but it was SOP, and frankly, Mountie enjoyed pushing his plane to its limit. He watched the timer count down, and right on cue, a bright flash lit up the air from behind, filling his cockpit with white light.

---

[1] Helmet Mounted Display System

"BDA: I'm getting all four pieces destroyed and damaged vehicles out to 150 meters. Probable Casualty Reading of. . .looks like 83% to 120, 67% to 180. . .hell, Mountie, you frigging nailed the bastards. Good shooting," Skeet passed from where he circled 9,000 meters above the target.

Mountie felt a surge of both relief and dark satisfaction. Relief because with Skeets on angel post, Mutt would normally have been coming in on his run in case the target had not been destroyed. Satisfaction that without Mutt behind him, he'd at least issued a serious payback to the Tenner mercs. It wouldn't bring Mutt back, but at least it was something.

"Roger that," he passed onto Skeets. "And I'm winchester;[2] the cupboard is bare."

"Understood. We're returning to home to get replenished. Come up to nine angels and we'll head out."

Mountie checked his readouts. He was still 20 minutes to bingo,[3] but without any munitions, there wasn't any reason to stay on station. The sooner he could get back, the sooner he could return to the fight. He slowly brought up his Lizard on a wide, sweeping climb until he reached 9,000 meters, coming in on Skeets' seven. Together, the two headed back to the expeditionary airfield at Philips Landing where they would refuel and receive another combat load of munitions.

Mountie tried to keep his thoughts off Mutt, but the more he tried, the more he remained fixated. Mutt was his wingman, and not just in their Lizards. For the last two years, as the squadron's only bachelors, they'd had more than a lifetime of escapades that bordered on court-martial-worthy—if they'd ever been caught and some tight-ass promotion-hungry commander had wanted to level charges. But except for more than a few weekends assigned as the squadron watch officer, they'd escaped their adventures with their careers intact.

Only now, it didn't matter. Mutt would never be using his pilot's wings and ready wit to try and seduce some young honeywa

---

[2] Winchester: out of munitions
[3] Bingo: minimum amount of fuel to required to reach an airfield

at their latest port of call. Anger seethed inside Mountie, and dropping the BD-42 wasn't enough. He had to do more.

The sky above him was crystal clear, with towering vertical columns of clouds that would normally make flying a joy as he wove his way through them on Skeet's tail. But all he wanted to do was to get back, refuel and reload, and return to the fight.

"Victor Flight, stand by for mission," came over Mountie's comms.

"Roger," Skeets responded.

Skeets was the flight commander, so he'd be doing the talking.

"Victor Flight, we've got a militia unit in trouble, and the six wants to know if you can render support."

"What's the Nine-Line?"

"Don't have one. All we know is that a militia platoon is being overrun by a Tenner unit of unknown size and strength."

"Unknown? What the hell good does that do me? Can you patch me through to their commander?"

"Negative on that. The call came through the local commercial comms circuit from the wife of one of the militiamen. The fight is on Koltan's Hill—"

"How the hell am I supposed to know where that is?" Skeets interrupted.

"Roger that. The crest is at CZ85563498, overlay blue. Friendlies are arrayed at the top."

"Patch me through to this wife," Skeets said as Mountie inputted the coordinates on his HMDS.

Thirty-five klicks at our 330, Mountie noted. *Three minutes if we break off now. Still more than enough fuel to make it back.*

"Negative on that. The wife said she's entering a cave, and we've lost contact."

"You copying this, Mountie?" Skeets asked on the flight circuit.

"Sure am."

"No Nine-Line, no comms on the ground, and some 'wife" calling for help and can't be reached?"

Mountie knew what his flight leader was thinking. This could be a Tenner trap. On the other hand, it rang true to him.

"If it's legit, they need us. If it isn't, we can break off."

Skeets was quiet for all of five seconds before he passed, "Yeah, I've got to chance it. I'll meet you back at the airfield."

"No, Skeets, I'm coming with you."

"You're winchester. What good are you going to do?"

"More targets for them. I'm going in first."

There was dead silence as Skeets keyed out his comms. If Mountie took his Lizard in, he'd just be there as a flak magnet. He couldn't take any offensive action. And if this new merc unit still had their Piper, he could get shot out of the sky for nothing. Only it wouldn't be for nothing. That would clear the approach for Skeets.

Mountie waited five, then ten seconds before Skeets opened his comms with squadron ops.

"Roger on the mission. We're on it."

Mountie didn't even wait for the order. He punched the coordinates into the navcomp, then thumbed the cursor to bring his big bird on course for this Curtain or Kollan or whatever-it-was Hill. It was 38 klicks away now, and he peered through the slight haze below, trying to spot the hill where the blue blinking triangle on his visor indicated it should be. Below him, trees stretched to the horizon, but the hills looked like mere bumps and not worthy of the term.

Doesn't matter. I've got you locked in, he told himself.

He didn't know if the merc unit had a Piper, but he wasn't going to take any chances. He punched in a Delta approach, letting his AI take over. The random and arbitrary approach was crap for putting bombs on target, but since he was winchester, that didn't matter. A Delta approach was pure hell on a pilot, but it was better than eating a Piper up the ass.

He started clenching his stomach, grunting as the G's hit. This wasn't the steady G's of a prolonged turn but rather the jerky push and shove as the *Pretty Gabby* juked and jived her way to the target. Mountie blinked up the avatar for the countermeasure release, but he knew his AI would release them at the first sign of fire coming his way.

He tried to focus on the target hill in front of him, but with his head bouncing around his flight helmet like a ping pong ball, that was not an easy task. But he could follow the numbers as they counted down on his visor display.

At three klicks, Mountie overrode his AI, releasing the first volley of flares. If there were a Piper gunner down there, he'd sure just made a good target of himself. Flares gave off intensive heat which could fool a heat-seeking warhead, but the Piper used an alternating active plasma pulse and passive atmospheric-disturbance system. The pulse could be spoofed, but doing so would open up his bird to AD guidance.

Suddenly, the top of the hill came into his view. In a flash, he could see a line of fighting holes. He could also eyeball the signs of fighting, even the shapes of men running across the crest. Whether they were friendly or enemy, he couldn't tell, but that didn't make any difference to him. He wasn't dropping ordnance.

"Skeets, we've got a line of fighting holes along the military crest. There are at least 15 to 20 targets out in the open, and I'm guessing they're mercs," he passed to his flight leader.

He pushed his cursor to overfly the crest. His Lizard kept jerking as it maneuvered, but he knew his navcomp would take him in full view of both forces as he buzzed them.

Unless the mercs had anything to say about it. His alarms went off, his visor flashing red. He felt more than saw his ghosts vomit out of his Lizard's belly ports in an attempt to spoof the Piper which was reaching up into the sky.

Mountie pulled his bird into a hard right as he climbed, hoping to outrun the missile long enough to dive back down under it. The Piper had a big punch, but his Lizard had a tighter turning radius—if he could get some air below him and some speed behind him. Too slow when he doubled back, and he'd stall.

The Piper's approach avatar showed a narrowing gap between them. He had to keep the missile far enough away until he could perform a Dykstra Turn.

Come on, girl, give me more!

But the Piper was closing too quickly.

Fuck it, Mountie told himself. *It's now or never.*

His Lizard had not achieved the speed necessary for a Dykstra Turn, but in another two seconds, it would be too late. He thumbed the cursor all the way to the right and forward, pushing the nose of his bird down and over. She shuddered as she fought physics, her wings struggling to provide lift while turning tighter than her stated specs allowed. Mountie's eyes were locked on his HDMS as the Piper altered course, turning to keep on his ass—and drifting outside of his arc.

"I'm going to do it!" he shouted.

And then the Piper blew up. Its targeting brain could calculate that it couldn't turn inside Mountie's Lizard, so it detonated at its closest approach, about 40 meters off Mountie's eight o'clock.

There was a thunk as a jolt pushed past the shuddering of his Lizard. Mountie held his breath as alarms pounded at him. He was still airborne and not an expanding ball of flame, which was a win as far as he was concerned.

His airspeed was dropping, and Mountie tried to dive to recover some of it. His tail end started to crab to the left. On his HDMS, a schematic of his Lizard appeared. Mountie didn't need the tail end to be highlighted in red. His left vertical stabilizer was gone, and only 25% of his right remained. His AI was making a valiant effort to bring her down gently, but it wasn't going to work. Mountie and his plane were going to crash into the trees below.

Well, hell, was all he could think as the ground rushed up to him.

With more than a little reluctance, Mountie hit the eject. A thousand mules kicked him in the chest and shoulders as he shot up and away from the wreck of his Lizard. Another jerk on his harness about castrated him as his chute opened and caught the air. He looked up to see the glorious sight of a full, intact canopy.

As he looked back down, he could see the top of the hill that had to be their target. It was covered in a rising cloud of smoke and dust.

"Good shooting, Skeets," he said just before he plunged into the trees.

Something hit him hard in the back, and he jerked to a stop as his chute caught in the branches of a tree. He hung there upside-down, wondering how that was even possible, when a loud crack sounded over him. He jerked once, twice, then fell, bouncing off another branch before hitting the dirt with a resounding thud.

Mountie groaned, afraid of taking stock of his battered body. He didn't want to know if he was broken or not.

Gingerly, he stretched out his right arm, then his left. Both seemed to follow his commands. With another groan, he shifted his legs around so he was sitting upright. His right leg was on fire, but there weren't any bones protruding, at least. There, alone and under a tree in the forests of Nieuwe Utrecht, he tried to take stock of his situation.

"What the hell do I do now?"

Chapter 3

JJ

"You ready?" Sergeant Gary Go asked JJ as he looked nervously back into the trees where the recon team waited.

Lance Corporal Javier Julio Gregory Portillo, United Federation Marine Corps, checked his demo vest one more time. He had prepared the six Bunson charges, inserting the detonator caps, which the sergeant had calculated was more than enough to bring down the small bridge. The problem wasn't with the charges, but rather emplacing them.

JJ didn't know if Bridge 2203 even had a name. About 30 meters long, it didn't look like much, but its strategic value was becoming obvious, so much so that Go-man and JJ had been attached to a recon team to take it out. As it spanned a deep chasm and was the only bridge for 20 klicks upstream and almost 47 klicks downstream, blowing the bridge would be a huge blow to the Tenner ability to move troops. The fly in the ointment was that the bridge was deep into bad-guy territory, hence the need for the recon team to escort the two combat engineer Marines to the objective.

JJ took a moment to glance over the railing of the bridge to the creek some 80 meters below him. He wasn't normally afraid of heights, but he felt his nerves were a rational reaction to the situation.

"Ready, Sergeant," he said before stepping over the rail, and onto a narrow ledge.

He leaned back, clutching the rail, looking straight ahead into the distance.

"OK, I've got you," Sergeant "Go-man" Go, said. "Let get on it."

Easier said than done. I didn't see you volunteering.

That wasn't fair, JJ knew. He massed 60 kilos soaking wet. The sergeant probably tipped the scales at 95 kilos. This was the logical course of action.

He didn't have to like it, though.

Bridge 2203 was a fairly typical deck truss type, with the trusses and support beneath the roadway. With a normal truss bridge, the charges could be emplaced from the roadway itself. Between the two of them, they could have set the charges for that within a couple of minutes. With the strength of the bridge below the roadway, however, someone—JJ—had to go below to do the dirty work

Taking a deep breath, he squatted, not committing just yet as Sergeant Go took up the slack of the utility rope that was all that would keep JJ from plummeting to the bottom of the gorge. Intellectually, he knew the one-cm rope was more than strong enough to support his weight, but that part of his brain was having a hard time convincing the rest of him of that.

"Come on, anytime today, Portillo," the sergeant said.

JJ had sunk almost to his haunches, his ass on his heels. The rope attached to his combat harness was taut. He crossed himself, muttered a quick Ava Maria, then shoved off the tiny ledge.

"Fuck, Portillo! Easy!" the sergeant hissed as JJ fell a few meters, his heart jumping for his throat.

The sergeant had him, however, and after a couple of swings where he bounced off the bridge's infrastructure, he managed to grab ahold of a diagonal strut. His heart was still pounding, but at least his feet were planted on something solid.

"You OK down there?"

"Yeah. I'm fine," he got out between breaths. "I'm emplacing the first charge now."

The Bunson charge was one of the mainstays of the engineer community. The small, 1.8-kg rectangle was filled with C6, a nano-thermite mixture that burned much slower than a monomolecular explosive but with extreme power-to-density. That might not bring down a building as well as other explosives in the Marine arsenal, but it was superior in cutting through objects or moving dirt. The little rectangle didn't look like much, but it packed a big kick.

JJ pulled off the slick, exposing the gecko pad. He reached over and slapped the pad on the longitudinal girder where it disappeared into the cliff face. With a quick twisting motion, he could get the pad to release the charge, but it would be almost impossible for any linear force that a man could exert would remove it. With it firmly in place, he pushed the arming switch on the detonator and was rewarded with a single series of three green flashes.

"Charge number one in place," he shouted up to Sergeant Go.

"Why don't you tell the world, Portillo!" the sergeant hissed back.

"Sorry. I'm moving to the first transom," he said in much more subdued voice.

"Roger that. I'm on belay."

JJ was not sure "belay" was the correct term. Maybe the sergeant was absorbing too much of the recon Marines who'd brought them through enemy lines, such as they were, to the target.

Reaching out to the next strut, he made sure his grip was secure before he stepped off and pulled himself forward. He trusted the sergeant to hold him if he fell, but he saw no reason to test that trust unnecessarily.

It took almost two minutes to make it to the first transom. His rope kept getting hung up, becoming more of a nuisance than anything else, and he had to fling it around with one arm, the other in a death grip on a strut or beam, as he tried to free it to move forward with him.

The transom was a good half-meter wide, and JJ was glad for something a little more substantial on which to sit. He pulled out the second charge, slapped in on, and armed it.

Two down, four to go, he thought with satisfaction.

JJ might be a combat virgin, but he was pretty confident of his engineer skills. And when he kept his mind on making things go boom, he almost lost track of the fact that he was sitting under a bridge, 80 meters above a creek, and deep within enemy-held territory.

Almost.

As he started reaching out to move forward, a volley of fire sounded from the approach to the bridge. He stopped dead, spinning around, but under the bridge, he couldn't see anything. He reached for his M90, only to remember he'd given it to Sergeant Go to hold while he played gymnast under the bridge.

"We've got a company-sized unit incoming," Staff Sergeant Bristol, the recon team leader, passed on the team net. "What's your status?"

"Two emplaced, four to go," Sergeant Go answered.

"Is that enough to bring it down?"

There was a moment of silence. JJ knew the two charges would do some damage, but while they would weaken the bridge, the system of trusses would probably be enough to re-route the lines of stress enough for the bridge to remain standing.

"That's a negative. We need more time," the sergeant answered.

The fire intensified, and the low blast of an explosion reached JJ.

"Understood. You'll have your time, but push it. Things are getting hot here."

"You heard them, Portillo! Move your ass!" Sergeant Go shouted from above him.

JJ looked ahead, trying to plan the quickest route to his next position. With all the girders, trusses, and supports, it was like a jungle gym, one where his safety rope was a hindrance to quick movement.

He sidled over to the side to see if that might eliminate some of the obstacles when two rounds hit the plastisteel supports near his head and sending him diving back for cover. His safety line got caught up around a truss, and he tried to jerk it free.

"Fuck, Portillo! Watch it!"

From just a meter or so above him, he heard the familiar staccato stutter of an M90. Sergeant Go was firing back, so that meant the Tenner mercs were getting close.

Crossing himself once more, and before he could remind himself of the torrent of reasons why it was a bad idea, he unhooked the rope from his harness.

"I'm off belay!" he shouted up at the sergeant as the rope drifted out of reach, not caring if that was the correct terminology or not.

"What? Get that back on now, Portillo!"

"Can't hear you, Sergeant! Get some rounds downrange and cover me!"

There was a whir as Sergeant Go fired off another 100 darts or so, then a "Mother fuck!" before the other end of the rope appeared beside him and the entire length fell into the gorge. He could hear footsteps retreating to down the bridge before a final "Get your ass moving!" reached down to him.

Without the safety rope, he felt more maneuverable, but naked. Trying not to think of the fall, he wormed his way forward to the next transom. He didn't even brace himself but slapped the next charge in place, armed it, and pushed forward, only to stop dead in place. The center of the bridge was almost bare, without any of the infrastructure that he'd just climbed through.

What the hell?

A "clean" center was common for swinging bridges or bridges close to the water's surface, but 80 meters up? It made no sense. But crazy or not, that was what faced him.

There were braces under the roadbed, and along each edge and the middle were the longitudinal girders, but there wasn't room for him to climb on top of any of them.

If he'd still been attached to the rope, he could ask the sergeant to pull him up, and he could cross over on top of the bridge. But the rope was now 80 meters below him, and from the sound of it, the sergeant was heavily engaged from the far side of the bridge.

"What's your status?" Staff Sergeant Bristol asked again.

"Still working on it. Maybe five minutes," Sergeant Go responded.

"Too long, you need—" the staff sergeant started before he grunted, and then the comms fell silent.

"You're out of time," another recon Marine broke in, breathing heavily.

JJ didn't hesitate. The girder was a typical H-shaped beam, with a horizontal bottom connected to the top by a vertical piece— from his engineering classes, he dredged up that the horizontal parts were called the flange, the vertical, the web. Each side of the bottom flange extended a good 18 or 20 centimeters out from the web. JJ leaned forward, grabbing each side of the girder, then let his legs fall free. He swung forward until his legs reached up in front of him. Desperately, he tried to lodge his heels on the edges of the girder. His right heel caught, but his left bounced off. Panic almost overwhelmed him, but he forcibly calmed himself, reaching up with his left leg and hooking the edge of his heel above the girder's bottom.

Hanging ass-down like some sort of baby sloth gripping his mother, he wasn't really hooked, though. If his hands slipped, his heels wouldn't hold him, and he'd be in for a long fall.

JJ walked his hands forward, one after the other, about 40 centimeters. Then, gripping as tightly as he could, he pushed with his feet, extending them.

Shit, only 20 more of these and I'm there. Ain't no thing.

Once, twice more, he edged forward. His forearms began to shake, but there was no choice. He had to push across.

There was a crescendo of fire from behind him, but he couldn't pay that any attention. He had five more meters, four, then three. He looked under his arms to see how close he was, and the slight twist of his body was enough to lose his footing. First, the right heel slipped, immediately followed by the left. His body swung down in an arc as he desperately hung on with his hands.

Somehow, he held on, his body swinging like a pendulum. He tried to swing his heels back up, but he could barely get them half way, and each kick threatened to knock loose his grip.

"Portillo, are the charges placed?" he heard the sergeant shout.

He didn't reply. He was focused on the transom a little more than a meter away. It might as well have been a klick.

A line of rounds impacted on the web, centimeters from his hands, spraying his fingers with tiny bits of plastisteel. Spurred into action, he hand-over-handed it forward, reaching the transom where a small diagonal strut braced it against the large vertical post. He swung his feet up, and with them wedged in, he was able to take the weight off his failing hands.

Thank God for lower gravity, he told himself.

Nieuwe Utrecht was at .96 ESG,[4] and even though that wasn't a huge difference, JJ wasn't sure he'd have been able to hang on had the gravity been even Earth-Standard.

He stopped a moment, trying to catch his breath before another line of rounds impacted just above him, and exhaustion forgotten, he scrambled up on top of the transom and back into the guts of the truss system.

JJ's heart was pounding, and his arms ached, but he couldn't stop. He whipped out the fourth charge and slapped it on the middle of the transom. He started second-guessing the placement, but he was already scrambling up and over struts and braces to get to his next point. Without the rope, it was much easier, and within a minute, he slapped one more on the central girder.

"Portillo? You there?" the muffled voice of Sergeant Go reached him.

"Two minutes!" he shouted, unsure if the sergeant could hear him from his position smack dab under the middle of the roadway. He could move to the side and shout up, but that could put him in the line of fire of the Tenner mercs.

The firing behind him was petering out, which could be good or bad. The four recon Marines were about as fierce a group of men as he'd ever met, but the staff sergeant had said they were facing a full merc company. JJ didn't think anyone was that tough. And if the recon team had fallen, the mercs wouldn't be long in coming.

JJ banged his knees as he hopped over and squirmed under the trusses to reach to where the bridge met the far cliff face. Unlike the other side where the cliff was shear, on this side, part of the cliff wall fell away in a more gradual slope for about three or four meters before dropping off more precipitously. As he reached the slope, JJ dropped down, feet on the rocky ground, even while still keeping a death grip on the girder above him. Never letting go with both arms at once, he walked up to the final transom and set his last charge.

Now to get out of here!

---

[4] EG: Earth Standard Gravity

First, before he did anything else, JJ carefully armed the detonator control. He entered 6-9-6-9 into the keyboard, programing it. Without hesitation, he pressed the detonating lever.

Nothing happened, which was what he expected, but still, there had been the slightest nagging doubt in his mind. The code was to program the control into a dead man's switch. If JJ dropped the control—as in being shot—the six caps would detonate, setting off the Bunson charges, and if Sergeant Go and he had been correct in his calculations, the bridge would fall into the gorge.

He started to turn to his right, but he'd taken fire from that side before, so left it was. As he reached the edge of the roadway above his head, he drew his Prokov 8mm. Unlike his M90, the sidearm was a lead-thrower. It was great for close-in defense, but the magazine carried only 12 rounds.

With the detonator in one hand and his Prokov in the other, he ran out from under the bridge and started scrambling up the last few meters of the slope. The final step, though was about a meter-and-half of bridge footing. He knew he was exposed to the mercs on the other side of the gorge, but he had to holster his Prokov to free a hand. He reached over the footing to the roadbed, then tried to pull himself up—when someone grabbed him.

JJ tried to jerk his arm free to grab his Prokov back when Sergeant Go asked, "Are they all emplaced?"

"Shit, I didn't know who you were!" he said as he swung his legs up onto the bridge.

Sergeant Go yanked JJ to his feet, then started bolting for cover.

"Did you get them emplaced?" he repeated, shouting over his shoulder.

"Yeah. All six," JJ said as he rushed to follow.

He flopped down on his belly, facing the other side of the gorge as the sergeant handed him his M90. It felt comforting to have it in his hands again. The range across the gorge was more than he could manage with his handgun.

Across the gorge, the firing was not as intense as before. There wasn't any sign of the four recon Marines.

"When do we blow it?" JJ asked.

"Not until recon crosses."

Almost as if on cue, their comms sputtered, and then one of the Marines said, "Cover me. I'm coming over."

"Is anyone else with you?" Sergeant Go asked.

"Negative. It's only me left."

"Roger. We've got you covered."

With one hand still holding the detonator control, JJ used the raised footing to support his M90. Accuracy wouldn't be as important as volume of fire, and with a cyclic rate of 400 rounds per minute, he could sure provide that.

"There he is," Sergeant Go said as Sergeant Bill Thies bounded down from a small rise, hit the roadbed, and darted down the bridge toward them.

JJ hadn't recognized his voice over the comms, but there was no mistaking the recon Marine's short, but broad-shouldered figure. The heavy-worlder's legs churned as he sprinted.

JJ swept his fire into the trees on the other side. He couldn't see any mercs, but a quick crescendo of fire was proof enough that they could see Bill.

The sergeant took only seconds to reach half-way across, and JJ could clearly see the strain on his face as he put everything into his run—and he could clearly see the look of surprise? regret? as he was hit, the sergeant's right hand moving to the back of his thigh as he stumbled and fell face first onto the roadbed.

"Shit!" JJ yelled while dropping his mag and inserting another.

Sergeant Thies tried to regain his feet, but his leg didn't seem to work. He started to drag himself forward with his arms, pushing with his good leg when a heavy automatic gun of some sort spewed rounds all around him. Chips of the roadbed few up in the fusillade.

"Come on!" JJ shouted, trying to will the sergeant forward.

For a few brief seconds, it seemed as if the rounds were impacting everywhere except on their intended target, but that brief window of hope was quashed when the sergeant shuddered and fell still. The unseen gunner poured more rounds into the sergeant's body, each one a nail to JJ's heart.

JJ knew that Marines would be killed on this mission. He knew the other three recon Marines were already dead. But he'd never actually seen anyone killed before. There, 15 meters in front of him, a Marine's life had been snuffed out, a Marine JJ had only met the day before, but still a man he knew.

A sense of anger boiled up within him, and he had the urge to stand up and scream while emptying his magazine at the hidden enemy.

A hand on his arm brought him back to reality.

"Stay down. I'll tell you when to blow the bridge," Sergeant Go said.

JJ ducked back below the lip of the buttress footing, breathing heavily, the back of his head pressed up against the buttress wall. The sergeant was right. They still had a mission to accomplish.

From the other side of the gorge, a few rounds reached out to the near side, but they seemed to be questing, rather than aimed. Nothing hit near them. The mercs had to know they'd been taking fire from the two of them, but somehow, they didn't seem to know exactly where they were. JJ couldn't guess as to how they hadn't been spotted, but he wasn't going to argue. They were pretty well protected from direct fire by the footing in front of them and the raised roadbed behind them, but a simple airburst grenade would put them in a world of hurt.

"Here they come," the sergeant said quietly.

JJ looked over to where Sergeant Go was holding a tiny hand mirror around the edge of the footing. JJ almost snorted. With all the high tech available, his sergeant was using a hand mirror?

Whatever works, I guess.

"I've got a squad coming down the road."

A squad on the road, and a company in support of them, JJ noted.

"One of them's trying to check under the bridge now."

JJ's breath caught. He'd put the charges towards the middle, and they were designed to be hard to spot, but still, he wasn't sure if the mercs had any dampening capabilities that could block his detonator control's signal.

"If he looks like he sees anything, I'm blowing it," he said.

"Roger that. I'll let you know," the sergeant said, then a few moments later, "No, looks good. He's climbing back up to join the others."

"I think I should blow it now anyway," JJ said, suddenly getting nervous.

"No, I'll tell you when."

JJ didn't think that was the right move. He wanted the bridge gone, and gone now. He looked down to the control still grasped in his hand. A simple release, and the bridge would be no more. He could tell the sergeant that his hand slipped.

But he was a Marine, and the sergeant had made the decision. So he sat and waited.

"They're coming onto the bridge now," the sergeant said, satisfaction evident in his voice.

Duh! Of course that was what he was waiting for, JJ thought as excitement rose within him.

He could bring down the bridge and take out some of the bastards at the same time. He had both hands around the detonator, resting it on his chest. He'd just wait for the word, then release it. Only, he realized that wasn't good enough; he had to see the bridge fall.

Carefully, he turned around onto his belly and pulled his knees in until he was crouching, his head just below the top of the buttress. When the time came, he could pop his head up and watch.

"Get ready," Sergeant Go said.

JJ waited ten seconds, twenty, and still no order.

What the hell's taking them?

Finally, the sergeant said, "Now!"

JJ released the control and popped his head up as a low rumble sounded from beneath the bridge. Two mercs were standing around Sergeant Thies' body, and another ten were behind them. All startled at the explosions, then spread their legs as if trying to retain their balance—all except for two. One of the mercs by Sergeant Thiel started sprinting forward, and one of the others wheeled to sprint to back to the other side.

For a split second, JJ thought the bridge had held. It lurched, but didn't go down. Then, almost in slow motion, the far side of the center, right where the transom was, gave way, and the span seemed to open like a reverse drawbridge with the two sides going down instead of up. Three mercs fell with the span. Several of the other mercs tried to get away, but the opening was only the first break. Like a zipper opening, the next two sections of the bridge fell, followed in turn by the rest of the bridge, one section after the other.

JJ thought that the merc running towards them might make it, and he brought up his M90 to take him under fire, but just before he could make the leap for safety, the final transom gave way, and the near end of the bridge fell, smashing onto the slope beneath it before sliding over the edge and into the gorge. The merc made a valiant effort to save himself, jumping to land on the rocks, but either he never had his balance, or the jolt of the bridge section knocked him off is feet, and he slid, hands flailing, until he went over the edge and disappeared from sight.

The weight of the bridge hitting the slope had another unintentional consequence. It knocked free a good chunk of rock, rock that was supporting the buttresses in back of which the two Marines were taking cover. The concrete buttresses shifted, tilting to the gorge.

Both Marines immediately scrambled up on their hands and knees up to and over the roadway, going flat behind the minimal cover it offered. A few rounds chased them.

"Holy shit!" JJ said, laughing out loud.

If Sergeant Go thought his reaction was weird, he never showed it.

"We're not clear yet. Once they take it all in, they'll know where we are. We've got to get some space between us."

He started low-crawling, using the raised roadbed for cover. JJ immediately followed. He was so amped that he didn't know how far they crawled—one minute he was on his belly, the next, Sergeant Go was helping him up where the road cut back to the left and out of a direct line-of-sight to what had been the bridgehead on the far side.

"On me, Portillo!" the sergeant said as he broke into a trot.

JJ looked back, but the curve in the road blocked his view to the bridge just as it blocked the mercs view to him. He wished he could see into the gorge and spot the twisted mass of junk that would be littered on the bottom.

JJ turned back and broke into a trot that matched his sergeant's. They were alone, in the middle of bad-guy territory, and on this side of the gorge, without a firm plan to get out. Despite that, JJ was on Cloud Nine. He—they—had been given a mission, and they'd accomplished it.

That is what Marines do.

Chapter 4

Jasper

Jasper's neck hurt. That was the first thing he was aware of as his mind started coming back. He didn't know why it hurt, and he didn't know why he seemed to be upside down. He kicked out with a leg, but something was in the way, and he couldn't extend it. He knew there had been a battle, he knew the Tenner mercs had been about to shoot him. . .

Am I captured? he thought in panic as memories flooded back into him with an almost physical force.

He struggled to free himself, kicking out until his head slipped forward and he got a mouthful of dirt. It wasn't until he pushed himself up that he realized his hands weren't tied—he wasn't a prisoner.

Carefully, he poked his head above his fighting hole where he'd been lodged at the bottom. The hilltop was barely recognizable. Trees were shattered into splinters, some sharp shards the only things still upright. The dirt was chewed up, and the mangled remains of bodies, both the Tenner mercs and what was left of Ito, seemed to have sunk into it, almost as if being consumed by the hungry earth.

Jasper remembered yelling, then a blast. The next thing was waking up, head down, in his fighting hole.

The explosion must have knocked me back into the hole, he thought, realizing that had probably saved his life.

From the looks of the tattered remains of the three mercs, nobody out in the open could have survived. He'd been lucky, *very* lucky.

"Christiaan!" he said before biting off his words and ducking back into his fighting hole.

He needed to find his son, but he didn't know who had survived whatever had hit them. The mercs could still be out there—alive ones, he meant. The three mercs near him were no longer a threat to anyone. He slowly raised his head and looked around. Wisps of smoke rose from various spots on the hilltop, seemingly from random spots. There wasn't any movement.

Turning to look down the hill to where they'd been taken under fire, he could see what was left of the combat robot: a smoldering and shattered hunk of synthetics. Beyond the bot, down on the highway, there was nothing. No movement, no figures, nothing.

How long have I been out?

He looked up at the sun, but his mind was still slightly muddled, and he couldn't quite remember what time the battle had started. Early morning? It looked to be about noon now, so he might have been unconscious for a couple of hours.

Keela!

Was his wife safe? He reached for his granddaughter's PA, but his pocket was empty. Panic started to set in, and he wheeled around in the fighting hole searching for it. The tiniest splash of pink caught his eye, and he dropped to dig the PA out of the dirt where it had fallen and been trampled. Brushing the soil off of the display, he felt a sweep of despair when he saw it was blank. He shook it as if that could somehow jolt the molecular state circuits inside.

PAs were almost foolproof. With no real working parts, they tended to work no matter what. As long as they were within the power sphere of a village or even a vehicle, they were connected to the net.

As long as there was a power sphere! Oh, my God!

The village's sphere reached out for almost 20 klicks. If the PA wasn't drawing power, then the power relay had to be knocked out. He automatically looked up as if he could see the Bright Horizon's collector in orbit. That could have been knocked out, too, leaving the entire hemisphere without power, but the mercs needed that power, too, so he doubted they'd have taken it down. It was probably the village relay that was out of commission.

The PA had a short-term residual spark capacity, maybe close to an hour's worth, so Jasper knew he'd been out at least that long. He pocketed the PA. As soon as he entered a power sphere, it should work, and he could call Keela.

His son, though, was up on the hill with him. He had to find Christiaan, and he couldn't do that hiding in the foxhole. He scanned the crest carefully, then like an eel, squirmed over the back edge of the hole. He'd seen enough war flicks to know that was what soldiers did, but it was exhausting, pushing a knee up, then pulling himself forward. By the time he reached his sergeant's hole, he just flopped in—only to immediately jump back out. Both Greg Brussie and Handel Portios laid in a tangle at the bottom of the hole, both very obviously very dead. Jasper scrambled back on his butt in horror, breathing heavily.

There was no way they were alive, but Jasper knew he had to check. He took a moment to steel his nerves, then he bent forward on his hands and knees and crept to the edge of the hole and peered in.

Handel was on top of Greg. His jeans were wet at the crotch, and Jasper didn't need the acrid urine smell to know his body had let loose as he died. His face, pale and sallow, looked almost peaceful. His shoulders and head poking out from under Handel, Greg was face-first in the dirt, the top of his head pressed against the foxhole wall. The back of his head was a bloody mess, and flies were buzzing around, lighting for a few moments before taking off and buzzing again.

Jasper felt the gorge rise in his throat. Handel was bad enough. They'd been indentureds together, both gaining freeman status within a year of each other. But Jasper could almost pretend Handel was merely asleep. He couldn't do that with Carrie's boy. This was Christiaan's friend, his partner in crime when they'd broken two of Tennison Corp's algae tubes while playing holdball where they shouldn't have been—something that had cost Jasper another eight months as an indentured. This was the boy who'd come to their house each Saturday for a year to do odd jobs in payment. This was the boy—no, *man*—who'd been given the position of sergeant when they'd formed to protect their homes from the Tenners. And now he was dead, the back of his head gone.

Jasper still didn't know what caused the explosion that had killed the mercs, but he'd seen Greg killed before that. And judging from the devastated Tenner bodies behind his own fighting position as well as what had happened to Ito's body, he was sure the two had been killed by the mercs before the entire hilltop had been hit.

Handel had an UKI as well, the twin to Jasper's. He leaned into the hole, and trying not to touch the bodies, he pulled up the rifle. He dropped the magazine and checked the load. Three rounds. He slipped the magazine into his pocket and started to let the UKI fall before remembering the chamber. Normally, once fired, all that was left in the breach would be gasses, but there were occasional jams, so the weapon had a charging handle that could be used to extract a recalcitrant round. Pulling the rifle back up, he worked the handle, and the dull grey of one of the jacketless slugs flew up and over him to land in the dirt two meters away. He scrambled to get it, wiping it off before loading it into Handel's mag.

With four rounds in that magazine and the five he had left from his own issue, he was back to nine rounds. They were comforting to have, but they were not nearly enough.

His knee was aching, and his back hurt, so he gave up crawling. He hadn't seen anyone alive, so with a sense of foreboding, he walked to the next hole.

Saul Portios, Handel's nephew, was dead in his position as well. The back of the position was trampled down, as if someone had crawled out, and it looked like there was blood at the spot. Jasper tried to remember who'd been in the hole with Saul. Lyon? Schuyler? He wasn't sure. But the lack of a body and what he could read of the signs convinced him that someone else had survived the fight. His heart lifted for the first time since coming to. Maybe Christiaan had survived, too.

Jasper stepped over two-and-a-half more Tenners. The bodies were mangled, and one was just legs and hips, cut off at the waist. Exposed guts were attracting flies, and the smell of death was heavy in the still air. Jasper looked around, but he couldn't see the top half of the merc. He couldn't imagine where it was, but the numbness that had settled around him dampened any idle curiosity.

The platoon had been spread out over 14 fighting positions. Jasper didn't find anyone alive as he made his way down the line. Most of his friends were dead. Hale, John R., John M., Oman, Dion, Masafumi, Lars. Dion was armed with a UKI as well, but when Jasper checked, he found the old man's magazine empty. Maarten's body was mangled, a good ten meters in front of his hole, his broken Olsen Hyper still clutched in his hand. Ito had bolted when the mercs showed up, but away from them. From the looks of it, Maarten had tried to charge the mercs at the bottom of the hill.

Jasper wasn't a real soldier, and he didn't know the protocol except from the flicks and holos, but he was positive that he was alive only because of Maarten and the fighting positions he'd forced them to dig. He came to attention and saluted the best he could.

The next hole had three bodies in it: Jan ter Horst, Mantei Caesar, and to Jasper's surprise, a merc. Jan's big Buck blade was buried in the merc's neck. Jasper would never have thought the town drunk had it in him, and he suddenly felt guilty for his treatment of the man over the last several decades.

Not all the holes were occupied. One was completely empty, and only Ken Lee was in his foxhole; his twin brother Kev was missing. Including him, Jasper thought that at least five of the platoon might have survived. And that gave him hope.

Christiaan had been in the second-to-last hole. As he rounded the curve in the slope, he saw a body half out of the downhill side of the hole, face first in the dirt. But the body was too big. It was another of Christiaan's friends, Asante. The young man had wandered into the village a few years back, saying nothing about his past. Rumors had run rampant, but he was a steady worker, and Maarten had hired him on. And now, like most of the others, he was dead.

With extreme hesitancy, Jasper crept forward. Even before he reached the hole, he knew what he would find. An arm inside the hole came into view, an arm he knew well, and arm that used to clasp him around his neck until he grew beyond wanting to be carried by his daddy. The arm of a freeman just starting out on his life's journey, a journey that had been cut far too short.

Jasper ran the last few strides and looked down upon his son. He didn't say a word but sunk to his knees, motionless for a moment until his stomach spasmed, and vomit burned its way up his throat and spewed on the ground. He heaved, over and over, even when his stomach was dry as tears cursed down his face.

"I'm sorry, Mr. van Ruiker," a soft voice said, intruding into his grief.

Jasper jumped to his feet, his rifle ready. It took him a moment to realize that the bloody lump of flesh that was Asante was speaking to him. He dropped his rifle and rushed to the young man's side.

"I'm sorry, I couldn't protect him," Asante said.

"I . . . I know you tried. It's not your fault."

Asante was missing part of his face; his right eye was gone. An arm was broken, bone shards visible poking through torn skin. But those were the minor wounds. Something had taken a huge chunk out of his left buttock and side. Jasper could see his spine, and he could see where his spine was missing.

"I can't feel my legs, sir. Are they OK?"

"Don't you worry about that. I'm going to get you to some help."

Jasper was very aware of his son's body just a meter away, but helping Asante was something he could do, something to take his mind away from what he'd lost. He stood up and straddled the big man's head, putting his hands under Asante's shoulders, and pulling to get him out of the hole.

Asante screamed in pure agony.

"Don't, Mr. van Ruiker! It hurts," he begged.

Jasper stopped. When he'd pulled, most of Asante's lower body had remained in place, like it was coming apart. The young man shouldn't be alive with that kind of damage, but he was hanging on. Not for long, though, Jasper was certain.

"I need to get you to a doctor," Jasper said, unsure of himself.

"No doctors up here," Asante said, almost chuckling before that turned into a cough. "No, please, just sit with me, sir, if you would."

"Of course. I'm here with you."

Jasper sat, sliding his hips forward so that Asante's head was in his lap. He stroked the young man's hair, occasionally telling him he was there. He purposely didn't look into the foxhole at his son's body. He couldn't.

He didn't know when Asante passed. The body started to cool, but he didn't move. He sat there, a dead man's head in his lap, his eyes focused out over the forest as the sun went down and darkness hid his grief.

Chapter 5

Mountie

Mountie spun around again, pointing his Prokov in the direction from where he'd heard the noise. He was exhausted and his nerves frayed, and each rustle, each slight noise turned into a company of mercs ready to jump him. Whatever was scurrying around in the grass was too small to be much of a threat, so he turned back, peering through trees in the waning light, wondering if it was safe to proceed.

He fingered his beacon again, depressing the button, but the complete lack of resistance hadn't changed. Somehow, probably during his plunge through the trees, he'd damaged the supposedly rugged device. He'd probably pressed the lever a couple of hundred times so far, but the green indicator light had never turned on. The beacon had no obvious signs of damage, but with the loose button, Mountie was betting that the unit itself was intact—it was just the button that was broken.

With few options, he'd decided to head to the hill he'd buzzed when he was shot down. The hill had friendlies on it, and if Skeets had managed to clear it of bad guys, then the town militia was his best bet. If he could reach them, he could try and contact someone for a pickup.

Mountie felt at home in his Lizard, master of his domain. But down on the ground like a Marine, with only a Prokov with which he was only passably familiar, he was out of his element—and extremely uncomfortable.

He took in a deep breath of air. The smell of expended ordnance and smoke was getting stronger as the slope started to rise. He was fairly confident he was heading to the hill, but he was not confident at all that his route to the hill was clear of Tenner mercs.

But I don't have much in the way of options, now, do I?

As he'd tried to gather his thoughts after landing, he could hear Skeets circling the area, trying to spot him. But with no beacon, Skeets had to assume the worse, and as he'd already been close to bingo, he'd been forced to depart.

Should have punched out sooner, he told himself. *Skeets might have spotted me in the air.*

But what was done was done, and Mountie was now marching through the forest, trying to recall his SERE training. It has been years, maybe decades since a Navy pilot had had to put that kind of training to use, and a young Ensign Klocek hadn't paid that much attention to the training, only doing enough to pass the course and not much more. He was a pilot, not a mudpuppy.

He wished now that he'd been just a little more attentive to the course.

Mountie came to an opening in the trees. Taking cover behind a decent-sized trunk, he searched the other side for signs of the enemy. He knew he should go around, but the sun was going down, and the thought of wandering around in the dark was frightening. No, he had to make contact with the villagers.

Taking a deep breath, he sprinted across the opening, expecting to be taken under fire at any moment. Somehow, he made it across and almost dove into the welcoming embrace of the trees on the other side. His lungs heaved as he sucked in the air, bent over at the waist. If someone rushed him now, he'd be helpless. He realized that he'd have been better off not to making a headlong sprint like that.

It took a few moments, but the growing shadows spurred him forward. The slope started rising as the smell of battle intensified. Flying high above the ground, Mountie had never been around that smell. In countless training missions, he'd dropped enough ordnance to level a city, but he'd never experienced it at a visceral level. And among the aroma of smoke and explosives, there was something else that triggered something deep within his brain, something that had probably been there before man became man. He didn't want to dwell on it, but he knew without seeing that it was death. Men had died up there, and he was walking into it.

He reached the edge of the trees to a wide-open expanse of the hill. Below him, the local highway ran alongside a stream. Halfway up the hill, a shattered piece of war gear lay spread out over four or five meters, wisps of smoke still slowly rising in the still air. And up above him was the military crest. Even from where he was, a good 150 meters away, he could see how chewed-up the area looked.

Mountie looked to the sky in an attempt to figure out how much of the waning light was left. He knew the planet was slightly smaller than Earth (or his home planet of Hobart's World) and had a quicker rotation, but his mind was too tired to try and do the calculations. The sun was barely a speck disappearing below the horizon, so he knew daylight was limited.

For a moment Mountie considered turning and fading back into the trees to try and hide out until the situation on the planet stabilized, but the thought was not too attractive. He wasn't a loner by nature.

And if he got to the top to find mercs there?

The mercs follow the Harbin Accords, right? he reasoned with himself, even as a sense of shame hit him as he thought about being a POW.

That was almost enough to change his mind, but if the mercs were on the hilltop, they were being extremely quiet, and that didn't seem likely. No, he had to at least check out what happened, and hopefully, he could find someone up there who could take him to the other villagers.

Before he could second-guess himself, he marched out from under the trees and into the open. He made no attempt at stealth as he climbed the slope. He wanted to be seen so some militiaman wouldn't take a potshot at him.

Just before the military crest, he almost stepped on a body, or rather, what was left of one. Mountie had never seen a dead body before, and this one was rather mangled. It was clad in mostly civilian clothing, a camouflaged blouse with a blue armband the only nod to having a uniform. A military-style Olsen Hyper lay shattered by the man's side.

The remains had almost been driven into the torn-up dirt, and Mountie knew that no merc weapon had done that. The militiaman might have been dead before Skeets had lit up the hill with his BD-42, but that was what had mangled the body. Mountie hoped the man had already been dead. Skeets had been trying to save them, not kill them.

Mountie felt he should do something about the body. That was what civilized people did, right? But he knew he had to try to find survivors. With a sense of sadness, he stepped passed the body and climbed the last couple of meters to where the fighting holes were dug, and into a scene out of Dante.

As a flight student, he'd seen the results of various types of ordnance carried by his plane. He'd known the immense power a Basilisk could unleash. But walking the ground was different. His feet stumbled in the furrowed soil as he looked at the devastation. Bodies were scattered, but most looked to be Tenner mercs. He glanced into a fighting hole and saw two bodies, militiamen. The bodies were mostly whole, nothing like those of the mercs.

The pilot mind in him calculated lines of force, and he knew that Skeets had come in low before pickling his load. At that angle, men above ground would have been extremely vulnerable to the BD-42 while those in the fighting holes would have had a reasonable amount of protection. This had been a danger close mission, but Skeets had done the best he could to take out the bad guys while giving the good guys a fighting chance.

At least I got the message out to Skeets, Mountie thought. *I just hope some of the militia survived.*

It wasn't looking good, though. A couple of fighting positions were empty, but most had dead militia in them. Only a few had signs of BD-42 wounds, so most had probably been killed before Skeets had been able to make his run.

Darkness closed in as he walked down the line of fighting positions. He pulled out his Vibrotorch, bezelled it to beam, and looked inside each foxhole. The last position in the line was empty with three dead mercs and what looked to be another dead militia out in the open. Mounties hopes of finding a survivor was fading, but he hadn't checked the entire line, so he doubled back past the holes he'd already checked to get to the rest.

It was more of the same: dead bodies or empty fighting positions. That was until he rounded a curve. Ahead of him, in the darkness, it looked like a man was sitting, back towards him, with another man's head in his lap. Mountie couldn't tell of either or both of them were alive, and he couldn't even see if they were militia or mercs. With his Prokov aimed at them, he bezelled his light to fan-mode and lit the two up.

Mountie could immediately see that both men were locals, and that the prone man was long dead. Much of his side was gone, the organs taking on the sheen of drying meat, and his head was canted back loosely on his neck. The sitting man, though, was alive, even if he wasn't moving.

"Sir?" Mountie asked, unsure of what to do.

The man slowly looked up, turning his head slightly as if confused. Mountie lowered his handgun and took a step forward when the man suddenly leaped to his feet, drawing an old rifle of some sort and holding it dead on Mountie, the muzzle never wavering.

Mountie froze, dropped the torch, and shouted, "Don't shoot!"

"Who are you?" the old man asked.

There was enough ambient light from the two moons to see that the man looked confused and tired, but the muzzle of the rifle looked huge to Mountie as it was locked onto his chest.

"Lieutenant Caster Klocek, United Federation Navy, sir. I'm here to help you."

He wasn't quite sure how he was supposed to help the militiaman, but he didn't know what else to say.

"Navy? Federation? You a pilot, I'm guessing? And did you do all of this?" the man asked, one hand waving to encompass the area, the other holding the rifle steady.

Mountie briefly considered trying to raise his Prokov and firing off a shot, but he didn't think he could fire before the old man dropped him, and even if he did fire, he wasn't sure he'd hit the man over the 15 meters or so.

And then there was the little fact that they were on the same side.

"Not me, but my flight leader. We got the call from someone on a phone that you needed help."

The man suddenly perked up.

"You got yourself a call? Like on a PA?"

"Yes, sir. On a PA."

"I bet it was my Keela who made that call. Sounds like her," the man said quietly.

Mountie didn't know if he was speaking to him or to himself, so he didn't respond. But nervous energy bade him speak again.

"I'm sorry if any of your friends were hurt my flight leader's run. I saw. . . well, I saw a few of your bodies."

"Oh, no doubt they were dead already anyways. Or about to be," the man said before he lowered his rifle. "I guess you're not to blame, so no reason for me to shoot you."

Mountie let out a huge breath, then holstered his Prokov. He didn't want to give the man any reason to reconsider.

The man turned to look into the fighting position at his feet.

"That's my boy in there," he said, his voice calm and sounding almost matter-of-factly. "I can't take care of everyone, but I can take care of him and Asante here, at least for now."

Without another word, he took the dead man's legs and pulled him to the edge of the hole and dumped him in. Kneeling, he started pushing dirt into the hole with his hands.

Mountie rushed forward and knelt on the other side to push in more dirt. In the hole, laying in a jumble against each other, was the man who'd just been pushed in and another young man. Darkness hid most of their features. The old militiaman shoved another push of dirt that fell with a dead sound as it hit the bodies.

It took almost 20 minutes of shoving. Mountie knew there had to be a shovel somewhere. The holes had not been dug with bare hands, after all, but he didn't want to interrupt the old man. Together and wordlessly, the two labored to get the men mostly covered.

Finally, the old man stopped. He sat up straighter and said, "Jasper van Ruiker. I thank you kindly for your assistance."

He stood up, slung his rifle across his shoulder, and started walking.

"Where're you going?" Mountie asked as he picked up the old UKI that one of the dead men had been using. "Can you take me to your village? I have to contact someone to come get me."

"No village left, I'm thinking. No power, at least. So, that won't help you. And as to where I'm going, I'm off to find my wife."

Mountie watched Jasper start to trudge up the last 20 meters to the top of the hill. If the village was gone, then it was on to Plan B. But he didn't have a Plan B. He didn't want to be alone in an unfamiliar land, and if this Jasper found his wife, then that was as good a start as anything.

"Wait!" he called out as he rushed to catch up with Jasper. "Can I come with you?"

He pulled up alongside the militiaman and started matching his pace.

When Jasper didn't say anything, he simply announced, "I'm coming with you."

Jasper grunted, but didn't object.

Mountie took that as a yes.

Chapter 6

JJ

"OK, I think we're out of range," Sergeant Go said, taking a knee. "Cover our six while I report in."

JJ nodded, turned, and took a knee as well, M90 at the ready. With the bridge down, he didn't think anyone was going to be coming up their rear like that, but he'd do as he was told.

"Platoon headquarters," the sergeant said into his throat mic.

They'd been on the team circuit, and to reach the company, the sergeant's AI had to sync in with the frequency-hopping combat nets. In peacetime training, the random hopping paradigm caused far more headaches and downed comms than they were worth and was roundly hated by the Marines in the field. Except this wasn't training. This was the real deal, the first full-fledged combat the Corps had faced in over 15 years.

It took Sergeant Go's AI a good 20 seconds to mesh with the battalion combat net—an eternity in AI-time. But once in, it was an almost instantaneous connection to the Engineer Platoon's circuit.

"This is Badger-Three. We accomplished our mission but have lost our escorts. Request—" the sergeant started before being cut off. "Fucking comms!" he shouted as JJ spun back around to look at him.

"Yeah, comms are out. I had the staff sergeant on the hook when this piece of shit squealed, then nothing but static. I'm about . . . squealing? Oh, shit! Run, Portillo, run!"

Sergeant Go immediately jumped up and started sprinting. JJ didn't understand why, but when a sergeant tells a Marine to run, he does it. He pelted after the sergeant as they covered 100 meters, 200 meters. His heart was pounding, but not from the dash as much as a surge of adrenaline. He wanted to ask what was going on, his imagination running wild. Then, behind him, a loud explosion sounded. He turned to look over his shoulder to see dirt just starting to fall back to earth—right at about where they'd just stopped.

Sergeant Go started to slow down, pulling to the side of the road and into the trees before he stopped.

"How did you know that was going to happen?" JJ asked as he pulled up beside him.

"The threat brief? On the *Kildeere*?"

JJ shook his head.

"You were there. In the mess decks? That Navy JG? When he told us about the jamming and targeting?"

JJ vaguely remembered some lieutenant junior grade in an impossibly creased uniform drone on about some of the mercs' jamming capabilities, but not much. He shrugged his shoulders.

"Hell, Portillo. They brief us for a reason, you know. Like, to keep us alive?

"Not that you'd remember your best girl's birthday, but he told us that the mercs listen for comms, and then they jam them before sending a little welcome to light our asses. Only, when they jam us, our comms tend to squeal."

"But aren't we encrypted?" JJ asked. "Didn't they tell us no one can break that?"

"They don't need to know what we're saying. All they need to know is that someone is transmitting. And if we aren't one of them, then they'll know that and send over some arty."

JJ looked back again. A cloud of black smoke was rising into the air. He didn't know what had been fired at them, but from the looks of things, it was pretty lethal.

Sergeant Go grabbed JJ's shoulder and spun him back. He reached up and turned off JJ's comms.

"Until we know what's going on, we're off the net, understand?"

"Roger that," JJ said, totally cowed.

He hadn't paid attention to the brief, and that could have cost him his life. Without Sergeant Go there, he'd probably be dead by now. As a lance corporal, he tended to let others make the decisions. He just did what he was told. But he knew Marines were so effective because anyone could step up into the breach if needed.

Take out the officer, the SNCO took over. Take out the SNCO, then the NCO led. And if the NCO was zeroed, the rifleman did what he had to do in order to accomplish the mission.

JJ had joined a peacetime Corps. It had been his road to life as a free citizen. He'd never really taken his job seriously—it was do his time, then get out and find a job. But now, this was the real deal. The Federation needed him, and he was not going to shirk his duties. Whatever Sergeant Go needed done, he'd be the one to do it.

He looked to the Sergeant, who was taking off his engineer vest. The man had just saved his life. He'd never been in combat either, but he had the wherewithal to adjust. A touch of hero-worship bubbled up within JJ.

"Let's get a full count of what we have," the sergeant said as he started to lay out the various charges, ammo magazines, and grenades he had. "Then we're heading north. Battalion should be about 70 klicks away by now, and it looks like we're going to have to hump it."

"Aye-aye, Sergeant," JJ said as he slid off his vest and started taking an inventory.

Like all recruits, he'd completed the Crucible's final 75 klick hump. This would be behind enemy lines and with only the two of them, but he wasn't concerned. He knew Sergeant Go would get them through it.

Chapter 7

Jasper

Jasper had lived in Donkerbroek for all of his adult life, brought as an indentured at the age of 17 to work on one of Mr. Gorashein's many scattered holdings, then staying on after buying out his contract to start his own algae farm. He'd recognize it day or night—at least he thought he would. What he saw now was someplace different. The village had been leveled. Something big had demolished the center of the village, buildings and rubble flattened and fanned out from a single spot. Jasper didn't know what could do that kind of damage, but it had to be something powerful.

Further out from the center of the devastation, some odd walls stood, then partial buildings. On the outskirts of town, a few homes stood. Harold Cochran's beautiful house looked to have withstood the initial blast only to fall to fire afterwards. The flickering flames clung to life, illuminating the immediate vicinity.

The Brotherhood of Servants way station, right on the highway and with its low, unadorned shape, seemed to be about the only building inside the village left untouched. Donkerbroek wasn't big enough to have a manned posting; the brothers came by once a month to resupply the small refuge for travelers who might not have the funds for the Rustig Stroom Inn, the town's only hotel.

The smell was intense—the acrid sting of some sort of explosives, the penetrating miasma of fire and smoke—but what was missing was the stench of death, something that before yesterday, Jasper hadn't ever thought to be able to recognize. Dockerbroek was gone, but it looked like the people hadn't been there when it was destroyed. And that gave Jasper hope.

"Come on," he said to the Navy lieutenant.

"Where're we going?"

"To the cave."

Jasper didn't mean to be curt. The lieutenant hadn't done anything wrong. In fact, he was alive because the lieutenant's flight leader, some guy that went by the improbable name of Skeets, had wiped out the attacking mercs. But at the moment, Jasper was more worried about finding his wife and family.

No, not my entire family, he thought with a pang. *Not Christiaan.*

He knew he was still in shock, and he knew he had to grieve, but that would have to wait until after he found Keela. He had to hold back until then; otherwise he might break down completely.

The lieutenant seemed to understand. After babbling on about this Skeets and what he'd done, he seemed to realize that Jasper needed some time. For the last 20 minutes, Lieutenant Klocek—"Mountie," he'd asked to be called—silently followed him around.

And now, probably not knowing anything about the cave, he hadn't argued. He just followed, holding what had been Christiaan's UKI.

Pirate's Cave, named by generations of children who'd played in its depths, was a good 30-minute walk past the town and on up a steep trail on the slopes of Mount Varken. Jasper felt a pull, as if Keela was calling him, and he sped up the pace, but at 78 standard years old, he was beginning to feel the passage of time. He knew he had another strong 30 or 40 years before old age really set in, but he wasn't a spring chicken anymore. At the switchback, he had to stop and catch his breath.

This is where Keela was when we last spoke, he realized. *Just a day ago. Twenty standard hours.*

"How much farther?" Lieutenant Klocek—Mountie—asked, stopping beside him.

The lieutenant wasn't breathing hard, which hardly seemed fair. He was a pilot, not a Marine, after all, and Jasper thought they must spend their service sitting on their butts in their planes, not conducting manual labor on the farm.

"Maybe five minutes," Jasper said, remembering when Keela had said the same thing to him.

But he didn't have a passel of kids to herd, so once he caught his breath, it probably would be only five minutes for the two of them. He waited another few moments, hands on his knees before straightening and starting up the slope again. The dawn was beginning to make itself known when he saw the large rock at the side of the trail that marked the opening of the cave.

Pirate's Cave wasn't much of a cave. The opening was small, and a person had to squirm around the Sentinel Rock to get to it. The first passage was only nine meters deep, with the overhead dropping to less than a meter in height. After clearing the constricted space, though, the main passage opened up, partially natural and partially man-made. The main cavern was 20 more meters down the passage. The "Cathedral" was almost 15 meters across, and in the back of it, another innocuous passage, low to the ground, led to a secondary cavern. This was where the villagers were supposed to hide from the mercs.

As they entered the cave, Mountie snapped on his light, for which Jasper was grateful. He hadn't thought to bring one.

There were signs of passage. An entire village couldn't pass by anywhere without dropped wrappers, water pouches, and other detritus of civilization. Where the ceiling dropped to a meter above the passage's ground, a small fuzzy kitten was pushed up against the wall where a child had dropped it. Jasper pocketed the shocking pink toy as he crawled forward.

When his hand hit something hard, he picked it up, holding it so he could better see it in the lieutenant's light. It was a clip of some sort, and he was puzzled for a moment before he realized what its presence signified and almost dropped it. He didn't recognize it, but he recognized the style. It was a military clip, probably designed to attach something to a combat harness. No one in the village had that type of equipment. At least one merc had been in the cave.

Jasper scrambled ahead, anxious to get into the main cavern. He crawled in, stood, and ran to the opening of the second cavern even before the lieutenant could stand up and light the area.

"Keela?" he shouted, knowing the silence was too acute for anyone to still be in the cave.

He waited for the lieutenant by the opening, dreading what he'd see.

"Nobody in here," the lieutenant said as he flashed his torch. "Where would they go now?"

Jasper stepped into the Nave, relief flooding through him. There was a single small shoe on the rocky floor, abandoned, along with a few bits of trash. Keela and the rest were not in the cave. But he hadn't met them on the way up from the village, so they must have left and gone deeper into the hills—or they were being held by the Tenners.

Or, the chimney! he realized.

"Can I borrow your torch?" he asked the lieutenant.

He rushed back into the Cathedral, then over to a small crevice leading away from the main chamber. It rose on tumbled rocks. Long before man settled the planet, rain had eaten its way through the soil and rock from above, finally collapsing a tube of sorts from the surface to the cavern floor. It was a rather restricted space, but children could clamber up the chimney and out into the open air 15 meters above. Jasper leaned his head in and flashed the light. He didn't need to be a Ranger to see that somebody, or rather a large number of somebodies, had made the shallow climb. A child's sippy cup was right at his eye level, and several pieces of clothing littered the route.

Somehow, Keela and Carrie had evidently managed to get more than 70 children and adults up and out the cave via the chimney, which fed into a tiny canyon that led to another trail going northeast instead of the main trail's northwest. But he knew not everyone could have made the climb. The kids, yes. But Barta Jones was older than Jasper by 20 years and massed at least 150 kilos. There wasn't any possibility that she'd climbed out this way, and he could think of another five or six who probably couldn't as well. He even doubted his Keela could, but she might have been able to, given the alternative.

Jasper was tempted to climb after them, but he wasn't the smallest man in the world, and the lieutenant with him was even bigger. He doubted that they could squeeze through. He turned back, handing the lieutenant his light.

"They're gone. Up the Red Rock Trail," he said.

He didn't mention the handful of women who could not have gone that way. He didn't know where they could have gone, and it didn't make sense to speculate.

"So, what now?" the lieutenant asked.

"I need to follow them."

"And what about me? What should I do?"

Jasper looked at the man for a few moments. He needed to marry up with his forces, and they were somewhere to the north on the Van der Horst Plateau. It looked like women and children were heading north as well, so for the time being, their paths coincided.

"Come with me, sir. We're going the same way for now, and I'll get you on your way."

"Can we go the same way as the others? I couldn't see much, but it looked pretty small."

"No. We've got to go back down almost to the village, then hit the trailhead for Red Rock. It'll be a pretty tough go, but it connects in about 25 kilometers to Highway 44 in the valley. From there, you can go all the way through the passes to the plateau."

Jasper had never made the trek before, but he didn't think he needed to mention that.

"OK, sounds good. Let's get going."

Jasper had hoped to find the villagers safe and sound hiding out in Pirate's Cave. They had abandoned it, but with mercs making their way inside as well, Jasper could accept that. Now he just had to find them.

He sidestepped past the Sentinel Rock at the entrance to the cave, turning to tell the lieutenant to watch his step when a voice called out, "Freeze right there! We've got you covered."

Chapter 8

JJ

Marines tried to avoid trails as SOP,[5] but the hills were rugged above the village, and the small road made for much easier movement. This deep in bad-guy territory, JJ wasn't comfortable on what had to be the major route through the hills, and his nerves were on high alert as he led the way up the mountain.

He almost jumped out of his skin when he heard someone stumbling out from what looked to be the cliff wall.

He swung his M90 to cover the old man—an old man armed with some sort of ancient rifle—and shouted, "Freeze right there! We've got you covered."

"We" might seem to be a generous term for only two Marines, but the old man didn't look to be much of a threat.

"You, the second man, get out here, too," Sergeant Go shouted. "Don't make me come in there and get you."

JJ hadn't seen anyone else. He'd barely seen the first guy seemingly come out of nowhere.

"Just lower your weapon, slowly," he told the man. "Then step out here."

The man didn't hesitate. He bent to place his rifle on the ground, then straightened, up, stepping over it to the roadbed.

"You boys Federation?" he asked JJ.

"I said, come on out," the sergeant said, his voice going up a few notches. "Let me see your hands."

JJ was torn between holding a bead on the old man and sliding over to be able to see to whom Sergeant Go was speaking.

"Yeah, Federation Marines. Get on your face and don't move," he ordered.

"Aye-yah. No need to get excited," the man said as he sunk to his knees. "But that's one of your boys still in there."

---

[5] SOP: Standard Operating Procedure

"A Marine? Who?"

"Not a Marine. A sailor. A pilot."

"A Federation pilot?" JJ asked, totally taken by surprise.

"Aye-yah."

"Sergeant Go, this guy says there's a Federation pilot back in there," JJ said to the sergeant who was moving forward, M90 trained forward.

"You in there. I'm Sergeant Gary Go, United Federation Marines. Who the hell are you?"

"Marines? Federation Marines?" a voice called out from seemingly inside the rock face of the hill.

"Yeah. Who are you?"

JJ moved to his right, and he could see that there was a space between a large rock outcropping and the hill itself, and back along the face, there was an opening.

"Lieutenant Castor Klocek, United Federation Navy."

"OK, Lieutenant. Let's just make sure of that. I want you to come out of that hole you're in, hands first," the sergeant ordered, the muzzle of his M90 steady as a statue's.

"OK, I'm coming out. Just everyone calm down."

Two hands poked out of the opening, followed by the unmistakable sight of a Navy flight suit. JJ started to relax. He guessed a flight suit wouldn't be too hard to fake, but that still seemed to be a lot of effort just for some sort of trap.

He still kept his M90 ready to rock and roll, though.

"OK, sir. If you can just come out here," Sergeant Go said.

He may have added the "sir," but JJ caught that he hadn't lowered his weapon, either.

The lieutenant stumbled, but within a moment, he was standing in front of Sergeant Go, looking a little uncertain.

"Can I get up now?" the first man said from where he was lying face down on the road bed.

"Uh, sure," JJ said. "And who are you?"

"Jasper van Ruiker—I guess I'm still a private in the Donkerbroek Militia, not that that means anything now. The Tenner mercs took care of that."

"Donkerbroek? That town at the bottom of this hill?" Sergeant Go asked.

"Aye-yah. That's my home."

"Oh, man. Sorry about that," JJ said.

None of what was being said had been confirmed, but JJ let the muzzle of his rifle fall.

"What's your story, sir?" the sergeant asked.

"Nothing much to say. I'm a Lizard jockey, and I got shot down giving support to Jasper here, he and the rest of his unit. We're heading north now. I've got to get back to my squadron at Philips Landing.

"What about you two? You're a long way from any other Marines."

Sergeant Go seemed to be debating on what to say, but evidently, he made up his mind; he raised the muzzle of his M90 and said, "Had a mission not too far from here. We lost the recon team with us, and now we're heading back ourselves."

"Good," the lieutenant said. "You can come with us. We'd all be a little more secure with four instead of two."

"I . . . we're moving fast, sir. The situation is fluid, and the sooner we hook up with our platoon, the better."

"And you think you know the area, Sergeant? Better than Jasper there?

"Jasper," he said, turning to the old man. "Is this the best way north?"

"No, it isn't. The mercs have gone up there," Jasper said, pointing up the road. "Which is why we'd decided to take Red Rock Trail."

"Red Rock Trail?" Sergeant Go asked.

"Much smaller, Sergeant. Much less chance of running into mercs that way."

"So, unless you've got other orders, I'm taking command here, and the four of us are going to form our own unit to get back."

JJ thought the sergeant was about to argue, but he shrugged his shoulders and said, "Aye-aye, sir. So, what now?"

"Now we head back down the hill, cross over to Red Rock Trail, and then head north."

The lieutenant retrieved his weapon, the twin to Jasper's old rifle. He slung it over his shoulder, then without a word, started back down the slope. Sergeant Go tilted his head at JJ, who took the unspoken order and hurried in front of the Navy officer, taking point.

JJ wasn't sure why the two men had come up the hill in the first place if this was such a bad route, but he had to agree that the four of them might have a better chance than just the two Marines, especially as the local knew the lay of the land.

Still, an old, untrained militia private and a Navy pilot didn't seem to add much to their combat power.

Chapter 9

Mountie

Jasper moved to the side of the trail, looking at something on the ground before quickly looking up and trudging on. Mountie was the third man in their little column, and as he walked by, he saw the empty water pouch, crumbled up and discarded. He'd never heard of Crystal Glacier, but it had to be a civilian brand, and it was almost certainly dropped by one of the older man's friends. This was real life, not some Hollybolly flick, so Mountie didn't have the ability to somehow glean information that would pinpoint how long it had lain there, but at least they knew they were on the trail of the villagers.

"They" meant the two of them. The two Marines weren't in the loop. Mountie wasn't sure why he hadn't told them.

He'd about shit his flight suit when he'd heard the sergeant call out that he'd had them covered, and he'd almost run back into the depths of the cave. But Jasper had become his wingman, and you didn't abandon them. He'd been extremely relieved that it had been two Marines who had the drop on them, not Tenner mercs, and he'd intuitively known that four of them had better odds of finding friendly lines than two of them—at least as far as his situation was concerned. He wasn't sure how far Jasper would take him— probably only as far as it took to find his wife and grandkids. SERE training or not, he was not confident that he could survive alone in the middle of Tenner-controlled territory. The two Marines gave him an immediate boost.

But the advantage wasn't just one-way. He was still an officer in the Navy, and he could be an asset to the two Marines as well. So, he'd seized the moment to take command. Sergeant Go had been resistant, he could tell, but military discipline had kicked in, and he'd accepted Mountie's position.

It came down to discipline, which was somewhat ironic in that, of all the Navy, the small craft pilots and maintenance crews had a reputation for being the most lax in that regard. Crews called the pilots by their call-signs, and military courtesy could sometimes be lacking. The Marines, on the other hand, were sticklers for discipline, and Mountie had counted on that.

Not only had he taken command to keep the four of them together, but he'd changed their route to Red Rock Trail. It had probably been a good tactical decision, but that wasn't why he'd done it. He'd discovered long ago that if he did have to give an order, it was better to give one that his subordinates wanted to follow than one that they didn't. And if he'd let the Marines keep leading them up the main mountain road, he was sure Jasper wouldn't have accompanied them. They needed Jasper's knowledge of the area, and he changed the route to make sure the older man stayed with them for as long as possible.

He turned to look back at the sergeant, who was bringing up the rear. The two Marines were engineers, not infantry, but they both looked like killers. Mountie knew that all Marines served their first tour in the infantry, though, before some received training in other areas, and Sergeant Go could have been out of open casting for the part of the grizzled combat vet. Most of that was in the man's eyes, which seemed to take in everything, evaluated what he saw, and found it wanting—including, Mountie feared, one downed Navy pilot.

The sergeant was respectful, and he didn't seem to resent a Navy lieutenant assuming command of their little group, but Mountie reminded himself not to issue an order the sergeant might not want to obey. He didn't want to put either of them into that position.

Chapter 10

JJ

JJ pulled down on his breastplate yet again. It kept on riding up, pushing his gorget up into his throat. The polydeflexion plates weren't particularly heavy—his entire issue came in at less than four kg—and it was somewhat flexible against the face, but lengthwise, it was stiff, and could be extremely uncomfortable as it dug in along the edges. His body armor had been custom made for him, just as all Marines' armor was, but other than training humps—and those were without full armor—he'd never walked this far. As a grunt, his battalion had never deployed, and as an engineer—well, "why walk when you can ride" was more than just a saying: it was a way of life. Once they were back on Compton Reef, he'd have to see about getting his armor refitted.

He felt a hand on his shoulder, but instead of the old militiaman, it was Sergeant Go.

"Portillo, how about fucking looking back every decade or so? It's not like I can just hit you up on the comms."

Ever since the battery fire they'd taken near the bridge, the sergeant had insisted on comms silence.

"Sorry, Sergeant. What do you need?"

"Next decent spot, pull off and take a knee. We need to take 20, and I'd like to scout out a way to keep off the trail."

"Roger that."

The trail rose around a bend, but the drop-off was steep and untenable. JJ marched another 400 meters before the uphill side flattened out a bit and he could lead the small patrol into the trees. Jasper took a seat beside him, then lay back.

Sergeant Go whispered something to the lieutenant, who nodded his assent. The sergeant stepped past the two of them and climbed the slope,

"He's somewhat forceful," the militiaman said, eyes pointing up into the canopy.

JJ didn't need to know the older man to understand who he was talking about.

"He's a sergeant. They're all like that."

"We had a sergeant. Greg Brussie. I watched him grow up with my boy. Being a sergeant didn't matter much, though, when the mercs killed him."

"It's different, though. Sergeant Go is a Marine, not a militiaman," JJ said, then realizing how that might sound, added, "No offense intended, sir. I'm sure your sergeant did his best."

"Best or not, it didn't make no difference to him in the end, I'm thinking."

Jasper was still breathing hard, his chest moving up and down as he looked up into the canopy. JJ didn't want to dwell on the village militia's fight. The old man had lost his son there, too.

"His nickname is 'Go-Man,'" he confided quietly, changing the subject.

"Appropriate." A few moments later, he added, "And what's your nickname?"

"Don't have one. I mean, a cool-ass Marine name. I've always been JJ since boot camp. My real name's Javier. Javier Julio Gregory Portillo."

Jasper smiled. "Javier Julio. JJ. Not much in the way of imagination, but again, appropriate."

JJ had always wished for something a little more martial, like "Killer" or "Knife." Still, it was better than "Lardo," which had stuck with Corporal Uttley, another engineer in the platoon.

"Where're you from, JJ?" Jasper said, lingering over the nickname as if trying it on for size.

JJ didn't like to talk about his past. He might as well have been written into a Hollybolly flick. Boy from the slums—in this case from San Filipe on Neuvo Oaxaca—using the Corps as a way out of a bleak future. His was the story of ever trope in every military flick ever made. It could only follow the script further if he were selected for officer training.

At least that's never going to happen.

Jasper didn't seem to be the type to hold something like that against him, though, and it wasn't as if he'd had any choice as to where he'd been born.

"Nuevo Oaxaca," he said after on a moment's hesitation. "San Filipe."

"Indentured?"

"My old man was. Is. I hadn't been classified yet," JJ admitted.

"So, you took the Corps as a way out. Going to be a free citizen, right?"

JJ bristled. *So what if I did?*

Jasper might have seen him tense up, because he added, "Smart move. I was I4, too. Took me 53 years to buy my way out."

JJ relaxed. The old man and he had some common ground. He didn't even ask why it took so long for the militiaman to buy out his contract. The law said the maximum indentured contract, an I4, was for 13 standard years, but the law never seemed too concerned with enforcing that, and those who held the contracts always seemed to have a loophole that kept the commitment intact.

JJ looked over to where the lieutenant sat on the ground, his back against a tree. He'd never been indentured, JJ knew. The Corps and the FCDC[6] would buy out a contract if the candidate were accepted into training, and for someone like JJ, an enlistment contract would block a designation as one. Not the Navy. It was entirely made up of free citizens, and the officer ranks came mostly from the upper classes. They didn't even have to serve as enlisted sailors, unlike the Marines where officers were drawn from the enlisted ranks.

JJ leaned forward and in almost a conspiratorial tone said, "Back in San Filipe, we had this guy, Bomba Borisova, he had five I4s. Kept buying his way out only to fall back in debt and getting signed on again. The second time, he . . ."

Military men loved sea stories, and even if he'd only been in a week or so, Jasper had already evidently caught on to that. He eagerly listened to JJ relating tales after tales of this Bombay guy.

---

[6] FCDC: Federal Civil Development Corps

JJ knew that every place settled by man probably had a Bomba, but he was confident his Bomba "out-Bomba'd" most others.

"We're not on a fucking picnic, Portillo," Sergeant Go said in a low voice twenty minutes later as he came sliding back down the slope. "I could hear you two from the top of the rise.

"Fall in on the lieutenant, both of you."

JJ made an exaggerated face to Jasper—behind the sergeant's back. Both men jumped up, however, and followed the sergeant.

"What did you find?" the lieutenant asked as the three walked up.

"It looks like we can get off the trail up ahead. But there's something else. Near the top of the hill up there, I spotted three mercs. They're on a projector of some sort. I didn't recognize exactly the make, but from the dish, I'm guessing it's there as a comms relay."

When none of the three said anything, he said, "If we stay low in the trees, we can march right on past them, providing they haven't put sensors down the slope. But should we? I mean, they're sure as fuck doing something, and something important to the mercs. I'm thinking we should take them out. It's your call, sir, but that's my strongest recommendation."

The lieutenant seemed startled to have the decision placed in his lap. He'd taken command readily enough, but JJ was under the strong impression that he wasn't a natural leader and wasn't used to making decisions. The guy flew a Lizard, and JJ gave him mad props for that, but it wasn't like he actually commanded anyone.

"Well, do you, I mean, can we, you know, take them out, as you say?"

"I don't see why not, sir. We've got two Marines with M90s, and even with those two old UKI's you two are lugging around, we've got more firepower. And we've got the element of surprise. With all due respect, sir, I think this is a no-brainer."

The lieutenant looked at JJ and Jasper, lingering over the older man, and not for the first time, JJ wondered what was going on between the two of them.

"A no-brainer?" he asked.

"A no-brainer. And it's really our duty. If we can zero them, it could cause all sorts of havoc to their missions."

JJ could almost see when something clicked into place in the lieutenant's mind.

"Well, in that case, Sergeant Go, how do you suggest we do this?"

JJ's face broke out into a smile. Their exfiltration had just turned into an offensive mission, and that's what gave Marines hard-ons.

Chapter 11

Jasper

"I've got three of them," Sergeant Go said. "One's on the console of the equipment, and the other two are eating chow."

"Good timing," JJ whispered.

Jasper gripped his UKI tightly, his heart pounding in his chest. This time, though, there was no fear, no sense of futility. His heart was pounding in excitement.

In a way, that bothered him. He was a nice guy. Everyone said so, the kind of guy who would split off a nitro line when a neighbor's supply went empty, the kind of guy who'd put up the Grossman's kids when the two parents were in the middle one of their epic fights. So why was he excited that he might kill a fellow human being in just a few moments?

Yes, he'd lost a son, and yes, he had no idea where his wife and family were, but still, taking a human life shouldn't be a thing of joy—at least he didn't think it should be. But the fact of the matter was that he was not only willing, but eager to kill one of those bastards sitting there 200 meters away.

"So, you two know what to do?" the sergeant asked.

"Yes," the lieutenant confirmed. "Jasper and I are going to stay here. You and Lance Corporal Portillo are going to work your way down to the white and silver rock. When you open up, we're going to fire, too."

"And when are you going to stop firing?" Sergeant Go prompted.

"As soon as either of you reach the dead tree."

"Make sure of that, sir. We don't need to be getting friendly fire up our asses. Remember, don't expose yourself until after you hear us fire. That should be in 20 minutes. But don't hold us to that. You go on our firing.

"Any questions?"

Jasper had lots of questions. Who should he fire at? Should he expend all his rounds? What if they run? But he kept quiet.

The plan was pretty simple. The two Marines were going to maneuver closer to the merc position. When they opened fire, he and the lieutenant were to open up as well, putting the mercs into a crossfire. As soon as the Tenners were down, the Marines were going to rush the position—and he had to stop firing as soon as they reached a dead tree 15 meters from the mercs—and then destroy the equipment there. If anything went wrong, then it was everyone for himself, splitting up to make his way back to what Sergeant Go called a "rally point," in this case, a bend in the trail about a klick back.

In the flicks, battle plans were full of subterfuge and feints, one surprise after another. This was extremely straight-forward. Jasper wondered if that was because of the lieutenant's and his own lack of infantry training or if this was more of what really happened in war.

"OK, then. If there's nothing else, let's get it done," Sergeant Go said.

He half-slid down the little slope below their position until he hit a flatter section. JJ gave Jasper a clap on the shoulder before he, too, slid down. On the bottom, he gave the two of them a half-salute, then turned to follow the sergeant. Within a minute, they were around the curve in the hill and out-of-sight.

"You OK, Jasper?"

"Aye-yah, Mountie. "Ready to go."

Neither of the two Marines would call the pilot by anything other than his rank, but Jasper got a sort of perverse pride in using his nickname. A Navy officer was high above Jasper's social status, yet for now, at least, they were on a first-name basis.

"How was it? I mean before, in your fight?" the lieutenant asked.

"Not good, to be honest. We all pretty much knew we had no chance."

"Were you scared?"

"At first, yes," Jasper answered. "But once I accepted it, I was more sad than anything else."

Jasper turned to look at the lieutenant as he spoke, and he realized the man was nervous at best, but probably afraid. That struck him as rather odd. The man was a Navy pilot, one who'd seen combat. He'd made a dummy bombing run, for goodness sakes, without any ordnance. In Jasper's book, that took mighty big balls.

Mountie glanced over at Jasper, and something in the older man's face must have given away his thoughts, because the pilot gave a rueful grin and said, "This is different. I don't have a 20 million-credit high-tech fighting machine around me. Now, it's just you and me and these ancient rifles."

"And the two Marines," Jasper reminded him.

"Well, yeah. You, me, and two Marines."

"I think it's those three mercs who are in a tough spot, not us. And this time, I'm looking forward to it."

"Payback?" Mountie asked, then hurriedly "Sorry, I didn't mean to bring that up."

"No problem. And yes, payback. It won't fix things, but it's sure going to feel good."

Jasper mindlessly stroked the butt of his UKI. He'd already accepted that he was excited about the coming fight. He still wasn't sure why he was, though. Maybe it was because the four of them were taking the action instead of waiting for it to come to them. Maybe it was that he felt better with three Federation military men. Or maybe it was just the chance to extract some revenge. Whatever the reason, he was ready, even eager. He knew he should be finding Keela and the rest, but he was glad the lieutenant had gone along with this.

Is this what Marines feel when they go into a fight?

He glanced at the Seiko chrono on his forearm. Unlike most people with simple PAs, he needed something a little more sophisticated to manage the nutrient and gas flows to the algae tubes. Twenty minutes had already passed since the Marines left them. He wanted to poke his head up over the rise to see if he could spot them, but the sergeant had been very clear on that. They were not to move until they heard the firing.

At 22 minutes, he started to get more concerned. At 23 minutes, he was about to ask the lieutenant what they should do when a staccato of fire reached them. The buzz-saw report of hypervelocity darts was their signal. Both men jumped up and brought their rifles to bear. One merc was already down, but the other two were rushing to take cover from the Marine's fire behind their equipment—and that left them completely open to the Jasper and Mountie.

Jasper was very aware that he had only nine rounds, so each one had to be aimed. He aligned his sights, just as Maarten had instructed them four days ago (was it only four days ago?) He wasn't sure about adjusting his sights to take into account range, crosswinds, and probably a score of other effects, so he centered his sights right at the nearest merc's shoulder. He took a couple of deep breaths, and remembering that he should squeeze the trigger, not jerk it, he tried to take up the slack—and was shocked when the rifle went off.

Buzzard balls! I didn't mean to do that.

He quickly tried to regain his sight picture, and to his great surprise, his target was down, slumped in a heap and leaning forehead first against the console.

Beside him, the lieutenant was firing wildly, but without effect. The last merc had dropped to his belly and was firing down the slope towards the two Marines. Jasper only had a small window if he was going to hit the man, just the top of his head and part of his shoulders.

The Marines were running up the slope. One of them rushed up a few steps, firing his rifle while the other was prone and firing as well. Then the first flopped down and the second rushed forward. It was an impressive ballet of fire-and-maneuver. But they were vulnerable to the merc.

"I'm out!" Mountie shouted.

Jasper took another deep calming breath, sighted on the merc's head, then squeezed the trigger. The old rifle bucked against his shoulder, the dampening system in the stock not enough to keep him sighted on his target. He brought the UKI back on target, and the merc was still there, firing downrange. He hadn't even noticed that Jasper had shot at him.

The sergeant and JJ were getting closer, probably not even 20 meters away. Both the Marine's buzzsaw of rounds and the merc's pop-pop-pop kept on unabated, and it seemed impossible that none of them were being hit. A thousand rounds had to have been expended without effect.

The closing Marines must have finally spooked the merc. Just as Jasper tried to target him again, he stood up and spun around to run. He managed just two steps before he fell flat on his face. He tried to get to his feet again, but to no avail. Down he went again, this time to lay still.

"They got them!" Mountie said, his voice hyped with adrenaline.

Jasper raised the muzzle of his UKI, then watched the two Marines, M90s trained, push forward. Their focus was clear. If any of the three mercs were still alive, and if they made any sort of move, they would be would be ready to riddle them with darts.

The two might have rehearsed this a million times—Jasper didn't know. But it looked like they had. There wasn't a wasted movement or a moment's hesitation. With Sergeant Go covering, JJ checked each body, kicking aside weapons. The merc that Jasper may or may not have shot was still slumped in a sitting position, and JJ's kick flopped him over to his side.

When the last merc was checked, Sergeant Go lifted an arm and waved the two of them over to join them.

"That's it," the lieutenant said a little too quickly before jumping to his feet.

Jasper followed Mountie over the boulder-strewn slope to the merc position. He still felt excited, but more muted than before. He'd thought he'd be jumping up and down with joy after extracting revenge on the three mercs, but while there was a touch of that, there was also an underlying current of a let-down. He wondered if that was just the effect of the adrenaline rush.

"Which one of you was that?" Sergeant Go asked, pointing the muzzle of the rifle at the merc whom Jasper had targeted.

"What do you mean?" Mountie asked.

"Look at his side. That wasn't no dart that did that. That was one of you with your blunderbusses."

The merc had been kicked over to lie on his side. Jasper stepped forward to take a look, and the base of the man's throat was gone, with only a bloody mass of mangled meat left.

"I don't think it was me," Mountie said. "It could have been, but I was all over the place. But maybe I got him."

Jasper knew in his heart that he'd been the one to kill the merc. His sight picture had been perfect when the rifle had fired. He took a step closer, taking in the amount of damage his .30 cal round had made. That hunk of lifeless flesh had been a living, breathing man just a few minutes ago, and now he was nothing but fertilizer for the mountain meadow.

He felt . . . he wasn't sure what he felt. There was a warm glow of accomplishment, but the expected feeling of exultation on extracting revenge was missing. Maybe he needed to take it all in, to let it settle, before things became clear.

"Well, whichever one of you it was, good fucking shooting," Sergeant Go said. "You zeroed him but good.

"Portillo, you ready?" he asked, turning away from them.

"Roger that. Here, help me pull this guy away," JJ said as he joined them.

Jasper bent over to grab the dead merc's left leg, and together, he and JJ dragged the body away from the comms station.

"That's far enough," JJ said, grunting as he stood back up.

"They nailed me twice," he confided to Jasper, pointing at two rents in the cloth covering over his armor. "Bam, bam!"

"But your armor stopped the rounds, right?"

"I'm standing here, aren't I?" JJ asked with a grin. "But a .370 packs a big punch, and I'm feeling it but good. Especially this one," he continued, pointing to the rip just over his right pec. "Gonna have a stupendous bruise there, I'd say.

"I'm just glad the polydeflexion held up. A .370 can go right through it if it hits right," he said as he started walking back to the console.

Jasper stared at JJ's back. The guy had been hit twice, yet he'd kept charging the merc. He could have hit the ground and taken cover, but he hadn't faltered. He and Sergeant Go had demanded the field by pure force of will from the merc, and it was the merc who broke and ran—and died.

Jasper was suddenly glad that the Marines were on his side.

"OK, Portillo, do your stuff," Sergeant Go said.

With a huge smile breaking out over his face, the young Marine said, "You've got it, Sergeant!"

He reached into his engineer harness and pulled out a small, dark green cylinder.

"Wait until you see this!" he said with evident glee. "Brand new to the arsenal. It's an ME-201; we call it a "toad."

He took a moment to look at the console for a moment, then placed the toad right where the screen met the rest of the body.

"Fire in the hole!" he said before popping off a restraining clip, then flipping what had to be an arming lever.

JJ quickly took a few steps back and said, "Mind your eyes!"

Jasper quickly put a hand up to protect his eyes, then as nothing happened for a few moments, lowered them just as a small sun burst into life on the mercs' equipment, sending an actinic glow to light up the immediate area.

"Holy Mother Earth!" Mountie exclaimed. "That's freaking amazing!"

"That's chained-oxythermite," JJ said as the small grenade immediately melted through the metal case, hissing and popping sounds continuing as it sunk into the guts of the console. "It'll about burn through anything. Right through any known armor, if it has to."

Jasper watched, fascinated. He had spots in his vision from the initial flare, but he couldn't drag his eyes away. The toad burned for almost ten seconds, which was more than enough time to destroy the mercs' console and burn its way into the rocky ground below it.

Sergeant Go took a step forward and peered into the glowing hole in the console case. He must have been satisfied because he nodded, then turned back to the other three.

"I'd say that's mission accomplished. Good job, you two. I think we need to get moving, though. Who knows when the rest of the mercs are going to come to check up on them? Uh, that's if you agree, sir," he added.

Jasper could tell that the sergeant felt in command, but was working hard to keep up the military decorum. If Mountie noticed that, though, he seemed willing to let it slide.

"Yes, we need to put some distance between us and here," he agreed. "Lance Corporal Portillo, if you'd resume the lead, we can move out. Wait a sec, though," he added.

Mountie took a few steps to the body of the first merc killed. He dropped his UKI, bent over, and picked up the merc's Gescard. He worked the action, then dropped the long magazine, checking to see how many rounds it had. The merc had four more mags in a pouch, which the lieutenant took and slid into his calf pocket.

"OK, now we can move out," he said.

Jasper turned to look at the bodies of the three dead mercs. The Marines and the lieutenant seemed willing just to leave them lie. He shrugged. Dead was dead, he guessed, and if the mercs wanted to retrieve their men, that was up to then.

His glance lingered on the merc he'd killed for only an instant before he turned and followed in trace of Mountie as they left the small field of battle.

Chapter 12

Mountie

The four men stopped at a rocky outcropping, looking down into the valley stretching out below them. They'd been paralleling the original trail, but up the slope almost to the military crest. Moving down into the valley, though, they'd get funneled back to the trail, something the sergeant had been warning them about. They were still deep into enemy-held territory with thousands of Tenner mercs between them and safety.

"If I'm reading my maps right, down there is the Beneden Merwede," Sergeant Go said, slightly stumbling on the river's name. "Then, we've got the Granger Range, and past that, we've got our forces up on the Van der Horst Plateau. Maybe 50 klicks more. Is that right, Mr. van Ruiker?"

"That's about right, Sergeant," Jasper answered.

"So, I don't see as how we've got much choice, right sir?"

Mountie looked out over the valley. A low-lying level of smoke hung over most of the area, while columns reached up into the sky in at least three places in the distance. The smoke made the setting sun a bright red. It was rather beautiful, but a beauty that disguised the ravages of war.

Fifty more klicks. I could fly that in five minutes, Mountie noted. *But I guess we're going to have to hoof it.*

"Right, Sergeant. We're doing no one any good hiding out up here. But we need to be on our toes. That smoke makes it a pretty good bet that the merc forces are out there, too. So, no hot-dogging. Just nice and quiet."

"Of course, sir. Unless we see another target of opportunity, that is," Sergeant Go said.

"What do you mean?"

"A target of opportunity. Something we take out to further the war effort, sir," the sergeant said as if surprised the lieutenant asked that.

"Well, now I think our first mission is to get back to friendly lines. So, we can live to fight another day and all of that."

"I understand that, sir, but I also understand the Military Code. Clause 4."

Mountie had to quickly mumble under his breath from the first clause to get to Number 4.

"A Federation service member will never willingly surrender, and no matter the odds against him, will fight to deny the enemy his objectives," he finally said.

"Exactly, sir. If we see where we can hurt the mercs, we have to do it."

Mountie had to stop himself from rolling his eyes. He was a trained pilot, someone the Federation had spent over a million credits to train. His best service to the war effort would be in another Lizard, wreaking havoc from the air, not playing commando behind enemy lines. Sergeant Go's ultra-gung-ho attitude, while admirable in many ways, failed to take into account the big picture.

Mountie was grateful for the two Marines' presence. Their assault against the mercs had been a thing of beauty, one moving while the other covered him. But he was in command, and he needed to make the decisions that would affect them all. He'd agreed to take out the merc comms relay, but that was a one-off, as far as he was concerned.

"We'll take that into consideration, Sergeant, if we come up against such a situation. For now, though, unless we want to stumble off this mountain, I think we should rest up here until daybreak. That sound good?" he said, making sure he looked at all three of them, even if he knew he was really confirming it with the sergeant.

A flash of something, possibly annoyance, flashed over Jasper's face. Sergeant Go, though, hesitated only a moment before saying, "Sounds good, sir. We can leave an OP right here, and the other three can back up under the denser canopy right back there. If you don't mind, I'll take the first watch."

"OK, you do that."

Mountie and the other two moved back about 20 meters where the trees gave more overhead cover. He was glad to get off his feet. His pilot's boots were pretty comfortable, but they were not designed for long humps. If the sergeant were right, they'd only covered about 10 klicks so far, and they had a long ways to go.

Mountie was tempted to tell one of the Marines to turn on his planetary positional tracking to confirm where they were and how far they had to go, but the Marine's story of what happened when they tried to communicate with battalion gave him pause. If the sergeant, looking at his previously downloaded maps, thought he knew where they were, that was good enough for him.

He tried to settle down, but something was digging into his butt. Reaching underneath him, he pulled out a half-buried stick. He gave it a toss down the slope where it bounced a few times in the leaf litter. Back at the overlook, Sergeant Go spun around at the sound and then frowned. Mountie acted like he didn't know what had made the noise.

He rolled onto his side, trying to find a comfortable position. This was another reason he was glad he was a pilot and not a grunt mudpuppy. After a mission, he slept in a cot at worst, in a hotel bed at best. He was a "civilized" warrior, and he didn't think he needed to be uncomfortable to prove his warrior credentials.

Lance Corporal Portillo, though, was already out cold. He'd plopped down on his back, grasped his M90 to his chest, and in 30 seconds, was fast asleep.

Mountie turned to his other side where Jasper was sitting. The older man was not trying to sleep.

"You OK, Jasper?" Mountie whispered.

"No, not really. I don't think we should have stopped."

"We had to. Too dangerous to walk around on this hillside in the dark. You and I don't have night vision goggles."

"Neither do my wife and the kids," Jasper said. "But they seem to keep moving."

Mountie should have realized what was bothering the militiaman.

"They had more than a day head start. We'll catch up to them."

"I've been expecting to catch up every turn in the trail down there. There's 72 of them, and they can't be moving very fast.

"And there's something else. Down the hill, where it comes out of the hills, the trail branches out. I'm thinking they're going to split up."

Shit. That means he's not going to know which way his wife went.

"Do you know where they're going?" Mountie asked.

"It's a long ways, but I'm guessing it'll be Spirit Lake."

"Spirit Lake? Where's that?"

"Up there in the Grangers."

"Why there?"

"It was brought up at the town meetings, before the attack. Spirit's a poison lake. It can kill you right quick."

"What do you mean, a poison lake?" Mountie asked, having never heard of such a thing before.

"Part of the terraforming, I'm told. The lake was adjusted to use as a carbon sink, but the CO_2 reacts somehow with the native sulfur, and nothing can live there. It was supposed to have cycled itself out by now, but terraforming is still not an exact science."

"And they're going there?" Mountie asked, surprised.

"Not in the lake. The gasses hang down at the lake level. But up the slopes, there are some caverns. I've never been there, but Roma Teussel goes to take readings every year for the survey. She can lead them."

"Even if they split up like you think?"

"That's what's got me worried, Mountie. I don't think this was thought out."

"Try and get some sleep. Let me try and figure something out," Mountie told him.

"I . . . that's fair. I'm just afraid I'll lose them, too. I don't think I can take that."

Mountie knew that Jasper must be feeling pulled into more than one direction. He had to be worried sick about his wife, daughter-in-law, and grandkids. If he chose to slip out during the night to try and find them, Mountie would understand. Technically, it would be desertion. Jasper was a member of the local militia, and in a time of war, that made him subject to the Federation military. In this case, to one Lieutenant Castor Klocek, UFN.

If Jasper did run, Mountie wasn't going to do anything about it. With thousands of mercs between him and his airfield, he had more important things to do than to run down an old man who only wanted to save his family.

Chapter 13

JJ

A rush of noise off to his right made JJ swing his M90 up, ready for anything. Further down from the hills, the brush was thicker, the visibility far more limited. Nothing appeared, and the sound receded quickly, too quickly to be a man. JJ turned to look at Jasper, turning his hand palm up in a question. Jasper just shrugged and shook his head.

It's his planet, and he doesn't know what that was?

Which wasn't too charitable a thought, he knew. He hadn't gone out into the wild areas on his own Nuevo Oaxaca, and he didn't even know what wildlife had been introduced there. So, if Jasper couldn't tell what deer, cow, or whatever had just run away, then that could be expected. It wasn't a danger, and that was all the mattered.

He knew he was just on edge. JJ hated the unknown. He hadn't been nervous before launching the attack on the three mercs the day before because he knew what to expect. Here, he couldn't see ten meters in front of him sometimes, and that made him nervous.

He fingered the rip in his utilities, or more exactly, the gouge in the polydeflexion of his breast plate. The merc's big .370 round had hit him with a glancing blow, and while it hadn't penetrated the body armor, it had left its calling card. If the round had hit at a more direct angle, Mrs. Portillo's favorite son might have been zeroed. JJ's ribs were sore, but that was nothing. When he got back, whenever that was, he was going to claim the breast plate as battle damage and get it mounted in a shadow box.

Another copse of thick brush blocked his way. He held up a closed fist, the time-honored signal for the others to stop. For a moment, he thought about forcing himself through, but he'd heard far off mechanical sounds, and he couldn't be sure how close any mercs might be. Instead, he pointed to his left, letting the others following know he was changing the route.

It was a good choice. Immediately after passing a large tree of some kind, something too large to be natural given the fact that the planet had only been terraformed for close to 60 years, the brush dwindled to just a few perched on a small drop-off. Two meters below the drop-off was a paved road. They'd finally reached Highway 44. If JJ had bulled his way through the brush, he'd have fallen smack dab on the road surface.

He immediately dropped to his belly as he scanned the road and the far side. A few moments later, Sergeant Go crept up beside him, followed by the lieutenant.

"See anything?" the sergeant whispered.

"Nada."

"OK, sir, this what we call a danger area. If we cross, we can be spotted, either by mercs or sensors," Sergeant Go told the lieutenant.

"But we have to cross, so what's the SOP?"

JJ still couldn't draw a good bead on the lieutenant. He'd seemed a little hesitant when the sergeant had reminded him about Clause 4 of the code, but here he accepted that they had to cross the road.

"Well, with only four of us, we can simply rush across together. That limits our exposure. Or we can cover each other and cross one at a time."

"And you recommend?"

Sergeant Go took a few moments to look down both directions of the road before answering, "One at a time."

"I'm used to having wingmen cover my six, so one at a time is the ground version of that, I guess."

Sergeant Go motioned Jasper forward to join them while JJ tried to pick his path. He could cross right where they were, but the other side of the road was covered in thick brush. He'd have to find a way through that. Down to the left, there looked to be a natural runoff going down the slope. There had to be a culvert there, and the far side directly opposite of that was free of vegetation. For a moment he was tempted to drop down right over the culvert, then crawl through. But if he'd controlled the area, he'd have sensors emplaced in it at a minimum, even booby traps if he had them. JJ was confident that the Marines were the most professional ground force in human space, but that didn't mean the mercs totally ignored the art of warfare.

"I'm going to send Lance Corporal Portillo first while we cover him. We heard the mercs as we came down this last hill, so they can hear us, too. You, two," he said, indicating the lieutenant and Jasper, "you've got rifles with loud reports. When Portillo crosses, I want your eyes peeled, but do not fire unless I tell you. My M90 is much quieter, maybe enough not to be noticed at a distance.

"So, Lance Corporal Portillo rushes across and takes a position. You, Mr. van Ruiker, you're next. Go to the same spot, then pass Portillo and take a position ten meters deep on the other side. Lieutenant, then you're up. Once you're set, I'll be following. Is that all clear?"

The two assured the sergeant that they understood.

"OK, Portillo, where're you heading?"

"Right over there," JJ said, pointing to the far side of the runoff. "I can cover all of you from there."

"Should we move down there to give us a straight shot?"

"I don't think so. There's no water now, but it's eaten away at the hill, and the footing looks loose. We can just jump to the road right from here, then sprint to the other side."

"OK, it's your call," the sergeant whispered into his ear. "Don't fuck up."

JJ crept to the edge of the drop-off. In the distance, there was the rumble of a large engine of some sort. He took a deep breath, swung his legs over the edge, and pushed off, landing on the road bed, bending his knees to take in the shock. The poleynes on either side of his knees were more flexible than the rest of his armor, and they served to give strength and stability as well as protection. Still, with almost 50 kg of battle rattle, he hit pretty hard, his breath whooshing out with the force of the impact.

He immediately jumped up and sprinted down the road and across, slowing down and gathering himself as he reached the other side. It looked like an easier jump down, so he twisted himself so he would land facing the road and ready for anyone who might have spotted him. Just as he started to jump, a head popped up in his way, a rather confused look on his face. JJ's knee collided with the merc's forehead, knocking him to the ground.

JJ was knocked off balance as well, and he landed awkwardly on the ground before falling on his face. With a roll, JJ brought his M90 to bear on the merc as the man scrambled back to the culvert, reaching inside it just as JJ sent a stream of darts into his chest.

The merc was in his skivvy shirt, and the darts tore his chest apart.

Voices shouted out from inside the culvert, and JJ got to his feet just as someone inside fired. JJ fumbled for a frag, depressed the arming slot three times, and with his back up against the raised roadbed, swung his arm around and flung the grenade into the mouth of the culvert.

Three presses of the thumb set the frag for two seconds. JJ heard the frag hit the deck, then a shout of panic reached him just before a loud whump filled the air, a shock wave barreling down to rush past him. JJ immediately stepped in front of the mouth and sent off another burst of darts before stopping. There was no need. What had been two men and what looked to be an old-fashioned tea samovar were nothing more than a bloody mess.

"Portillo!" the sergeant shouted from across the road. "What's going on?"

JJ clambered up the raised roadbed a few steps until his head was clear. "Three mercs. I zeroed them."

There was a snap behind him, and JJ whirled to see someone rushing out of the trees, a roll of toilet paper in his hand. Before JJ could react, the startled face turned and disappeared. JJ fired off a burst, but he was sure he'd missed.

"There's another guy here, too. He got away."

"Fuck no! Go get him!" Sergeant Go shouted as he jumped out and onto the road.

JJ wheeled and blindly ran, trying to close the distance. The merc hadn't fully exposed himself before running, and JJ wasn't sure if he'd been armed. Chasing as wildly as he was, all the merc had to do was stop and nail JJ as he rushed up.

The sound of someone crashing through the underbrush just ahead of him spurred him on. He fired a few times in the direction of the sound, hoping for a lucky hit.

"Feddies. . . platoon-sized. . .send help. . ." JJ caught from ahead.

Shit! He's reporting us!

The merc had been in trou and a skivvy shirt. JJ had 50 kg of battle rattle. There was no way he was going to keep up. He slapped the release on his left pauldron, and like a zipper, his armor peeled off, taking his harness and engineer kit with it. JJ had to kick free of the leg pieces, but within ten seconds, he was free of their weight, and he forced his legs to move.

He still couldn't see the merc, and it seemed like the man had increased his lead when the trees started to thin out. And then, maybe 30 meters ahead, JJ finally spotted the merc's back. On instinct, he pulled his trigger, starting low and to the left and sweeping the muzzle up and to the right. The M90 had negligible recoil, but while running and becoming out of breath, JJ wasn't sure he had a well-aimed shot in him. The merc looked like he was going to dart around a stand of trees as several of the darts struck his back, sending him falling forward on his face. The body bounced once, then bent at the waist to land on its side.

JJ ran up, combat changing his mag. He kept the muzzle on the merc while he reached out with his foot and nudged the man. The man was dead, blood oozing from his back.

JJ could barely make out an anxious voice coming out of the man's earbuds.

"Portillo!" Sergeant Go half-shouted, half-whispered from somewhere behind him.

"All clear!" he said as he started back.

The light breeze felt good on his chest, clad now only in his own underlayer shirt. He hadn't been out of his armor now for over three days, and he'd forgotten how uncomfortable it could be. With the muggy weather, he knew why the mercs had been out of their own hardshells. They paid the price for that momentary comfort, though. The Marines hypervelocity darts could penetrate the mercs' standard body armor, but those hardshells would have been enough protection against JJ's frag.

Sergeant Go was standing over JJ's discarded combat armor as he walked up.

"What the fuck, Portillo?"

"He was getting away. I had to go light."

"Did you at least get him?"

"Aye-yah," he said mimicking one of Jasper's pet words. "But he reported us. Sounded like he said we were an entire platoon."

"A platoon?" the sergeant said with a bemused expression.

"Aye-yah, Sergeant."

"I'll fucking 'aye-yah' you, Portillo," the sergeant said without rancor. "But unless you want to fight in your underlayers, we need to see what we can do about your armor. It'll be pretty fucking hard to patch it back together since you went and did an emergency molt."

Marine Corps polydeflexion plate armor was the best available, but it was rather unwieldy to put on and take off. When a Marine initiated an emergency molt, many of the connections were cut, and without an armorer, they could not be repaired. JJ knew he could jury-rig something, but it wouldn't be the same.

"Come on, pick this stuff up. If your merc reported us, we need to get far away before they get enough of a force to come battle this Marine platoon."

Between the two of them, they managed to pick up all the pieces of JJ's armor, harness, and engineer kit. It seemed much heavier than when on his body, but the sergeant was right. They had to gather up the other two and get the hell out of there.

Chapter 14

Jasper

"I don't think it's going to get back together," Jasper told JJ.

"Sure it is. Just force it in there."

"I am. But it won't snap in."

Jasper quit kneeling on JJ's back where he'd been trying to force the pieces of his armor to reconnect. The breastplate attached to the backplate, and the pauldrons, JJ had called them, fit loosely over them. The greaves hung loosely from the cuisse—the thigh protection—but nothing kept them up until JJ had used some line to tie them to his combat harness.

When covered by the camo cloth, the Marine armor simply made Sergeant Go look a little bulky. On JJ now, they looked like some Carnival revelers had tried to put together bits and pieces of odds and ends as a costume. Jasper didn't see how the lance corporal would be able to move well.

The armor plates themselves seemed surprisingly light to Jasper, and they had a degree of flexibility. But most of the flexibility seemed to come from the clever interlocking of each piece to the next. After his emergency molt, many of the fastenings were inoperable, so the pieces wouldn't snap back together. Jasper considered himself a decent back-yard engineer—a man almost had to be in order to be an independent farmer—but this armor, looking deceptively simple, was actually pretty high tech.

"What's this piece?" Jasper asked, holding a strip of polydeflexion about 15 centimeters wide.

"You got me," JJ said. "But it doesn't look important."

Jasper wasn't so sure about that. The close tolerances and obvious manufacturing skill used in making the armor left little doubt in his mind that each and every piece of it was important to the overall effectiveness.

"You two about done there?" Sergeant Go asked. "The lieutenant wants us to keep moving."

They'd only left the site of the battle 30 minutes ago, but it was obvious that JJ was ineffective with his arms full of his armor pieces. Mountie had called for a halt, then asked Jasper to try and help JJ get the armor back on. The big pieces were sort of in place, but many of the smaller pieces were a lost cause. Even if they knew where each piece fit in, the fastening points were toast.

"We can't figure out some of these parts," Jasper said, holding the strip.

"That connects the gorget to the breastplate at the front," the sergeant said, "but without a clip gun, you're not going to be able to connect the two."

"Do you have one of these clip guns?" Jasper asked.

"Only an armorer does," JJ said. "Too easy for us mere grunts to screw the armor up. It has to be handled gently, don't you know."

Jasper's mouth dropped open as he looked at the piece in his hand, then down at those on the ground that they couldn't attach.

Handle gently?

He shook his head and broke out into a laugh. It took a moment, but JJ joined him as he tugged up and down on the line holding up his leg armor.

Even Sergeant Go cracked a smile and said, "Yeah, Portillo, fucking gently!"

"Hey, why don't you just advertise to the entire merc army that we're here," Mountie said, rushing up to them with a scowl on his face. "What the hell's so funny?"

"Nothing, sir," Sergeant Go said as Jasper tried to stop laughing.

It really hadn't been that funny, but then again, maybe it was. More likely, though, Jasper knew he needed the relief from the excitement and stress of the fight. Still, Mountie was right. They shouldn't be making so much noise.

"That doesn't look right," Mountie said, pointing at JJ.

"I think it's good enough for Federation work, sir," JJ said as he rotated his arms and twisted his body. "Not 100%, but I can still move about, and I still get some protection."

He slammed his fist hard into his chest, where it hit with a solid-sounding thunk.

"See?"

Mountie didn't seem convinced, but he shrugged and said, "Well, then, I think we need to keep moving.

As if on cue, the whine of a large copter approached from the east. All four men froze in place. Jasper could hear the approach, getting closer and closer until he was sure they'd been spotted. The pitch of the whine suddenly started getting lower, and the copter passed beyond, going on its way.

"Do you think they saw us?" Jasper asked, fearing the answer.

"If they had their heat arrays on, they would've," Mountie said. "We would have stood out like roman candles."

"But they flew on," Jasper said.

He thought—hoped—they hadn't been spotted, but he wanted confirmation from one of the military guys.

"So, they either weren't searching—" Mountie started.

"—or they acquired us and are sending ground troops to scoop us up," Sergeant Go interrupted.

"Yes, there's that. So, all the more reason for us to get moving, right? Lance Corporal Portillo, you ready to resume point?" Mountie asked, turning to Jasper before JJ could answer.

"How much farther to the river, Jasper?"

"I don't rightly know, Mountie. Not too far, I'd guess."

"You don't know? I thought this was your home," Sergeant Go said, the slightest sound of exasperation tingeing his voice.

"Donkerbroek's my home. I've been down to Wieksloot often enough, and down to the capital once since I made planetfall. But I've never been up here."

"But it's only, what 15 klicks from your village?"

"Some of us have to work for a living, Sergeant," Jasper said, a bit of steel in his voice.

Paying off an indentured contract doesn't leave much free time for a vacation, he thought. *Not that you'd know about that.*

"OK, OK," Mountie said, physically stepping between the two. "If Jasper's never been here, he hasn't. We'll make the river when we do, and the sooner we step off, the sooner that will be, so Lance Corporal Portillo, if you will?"

Jasper gave the sergeant a long look before stepping off behind JJ. He gave the sergeant full props for his expertise, but he wasn't going to take any guff from the man. He'd never been much beyond Pirate's Cave, at least to the north. He knew where Red Rock Trail and the highway led, and he knew the general geography to the north, but he was hardly a navigation comp that could calculate positions and distances.

He let his mind wander as he marched. It shouldn't bother him so much, he knew, but it did. And he also knew he had to keep on the alert. But the more he tried to forget the sergeant's questions, the more they stayed in his mind. Finally, though, as the sun began to sink towards the horizon, he was able to let it go.

Right about then, he became aware of a faint, low rumble. It had to be the Beneden Merwede. He turned back to catch Mountie's eye, and he pointed forward. Mountie nodded.

Of course, he already realized it. He's been paying attention, not worrying about a slight that probably wasn't even there. Don't be so blooming sensitive, van Ruiker!

JJ, on point, slowed down. That made sense to Jasper. With so much of the planet undeveloped, rivers constituted not only a means of waterborne transportation, but roads were often built alongside them.

It still took them almost 30 minutes to reach a point where they had eyes on the river.

"Up or down, Jasper?" Mountie asked.

Jasper tried to look back to get his bearings, but the trees blocked the way.

We broke off Red Rock Trail on the left. There's the footbridge at Camberet, he considered as he tried to bring up the map in his mind. *The Blue Trail Highway crosses further to the west at Klipspringer Station.*

He knew they hadn't crossed the highway, but had they bypassed the Camberet footbridge? He wished he could get closer to the river to see if there was a road there. If there was, they had to head east. If not, then the crossing was still to the west of them.

"I think to the west," he said. "But I'm not positive. If there's a paved road down on this side of the river, then the footbridge is east of us."

"To the west we go, then. Sergeant Go, do you concur?"

"I'm not sure we should start off in that direction, then have to double back. The river itself can't be more than a klick away. Why don't you two hunker down here and let Portillo and me take a quick look to see if we can spot if there's an improved road down there or not."

Mountie looked up towards the sun, then checked the sleeve readout from his flight PA, checking the time. Jasper wasn't sure why. None of the three of them had switched from standard time, while Nieuwe Utrecht was on a 21-hour, 12-minute rotation. Sunset here went on local time, today about 1630. Jasper had no idea when that would be on standard time.

"I think we have about 50 minutes until sunset," Jasper offered.

Mountie seemed to consider that, then he said, "You two see if you can spot the road. I want you back here in 30 minutes, though, understand?"

"Roger that, sir," the sergeant said. "Come on, Portillo."

The two broke away, and within a minute were out of sight in the trees.

Jasper wanted to say something to Mountie about not knowing the area, but he didn't know how to begin. He didn't want to sound like he was making an excuse. The pilot spoke first, though.

"So, are we still going in the right direction? I mean, for your family?"

"I . . . I really don't know. Over there, those are the Grangers," he said, lifting his chin to point at the mountains in the distance, their tops still in the direct sunlight. "But exactly where the trail to get up to Spirit Lake is, I'm not sure."

"But we're all still going in the same direction, right?"

"Aye-yah, we are at that."

"OK, then, that's good enough for me," Mountie said, then asked, "But the river there, how would they have crossed it?"

Jasper's heart fell. He looked up in surprise, never having considered that. He'd assumed the group would split up after coming out of the hills, but there weren't many places to cross the river, which was too deep and fast to swim. Down by Azure Lake, it spread out and slowed down, but that had to be 200 klicks downstream.

"I don't know. We never discussed it. None of us thought we'd be in a position to even try and rendezvous with them."

If Mountie had anything to add, he was interrupted when Sergeant Go and JJ came back out of the woods.

"It's been only five minutes. Is the road below us?" Mountie asked.

"No, it's not," the sergeant said.

"So, we have go west," Jasper said, anxious to see if the women and children were in Camberet.

"No, to the east. We got a good look at the bridge. It's only two klicks. But it's got a dozen mercs on it, with guardposts on both sides. They're checking whoever is trying to cross."

"People are crossing?" Jasper asked, too loudly.

"Yeah. We saw a woman with two kids in tow. She got checked on the near side, then again on the far side. There's no way we can just walk across, and if we take out one post, that's a long way across with nowhere to hide to take out the second post," JJ said.

"The woman, what did she look like?" Jasper asked.

"The woman? I don't know. We were glassing the bridge, not checking out faces," Sergeant Go said. "Just a woman."

"But what Lance Corporal Portillo didn't say is that in the little village, there's two APTs."

"Two personnel transports? So, there're at least 24 mercs there," Mountie said more to himself than to the other three.

"Right, sir. Twelve apiece, not counting drivers. A little much for us to take on."

"Jasper, there isn't another bridge?"

"Well, aye-ah, but down on the Blue Trail Highway. If they've got mercs on this bridge, then for sure there're more on that one."

"So, we swim it," Mountie said with conviction.

The two Marines didn't blink, but Jasper said, "It's kind of swift in this valley. I'm not sure we can do it."

"Well, it's either that or we sit here on our asses until the fight is over. If the road ends over there by the footbridge, I'm guessing there won't be much in the way of patrols farther east. So, let's keep up here moving east until dark. In the morning, we can go down and find a place where we can cross. Are we onboard with that?"

"Roger that, sir," the two Marines said in unison.

"Jasper?" Mountie asked.

Jasper turned back towards Camberet. His wife and grandkids might be down there, waiting to make their way across. He wanted nothing more than to make his way down to the small village and see for himself. But he was under no impression that he could just merrily make his way across. If the women were trying to cross the river, he could best assist them by staying out of the way and crossing on his own.

Or with two Marines and a pilot.

"Roger, that, Mountie. I'm with you."

Chapter 15

Mountie

"This is the best we've seen," Sergeant Go said as the four stood on the rocky banks of the river.

"Best" was relative. The river beneath their feet wasn't bounding through rapids, but the flow was still strong and swift. Twenty-five meters of rushing water separated them from the north bank.

"Do you think it gets any better farther up?" Mountie asked Jasper.

"I don't really know. This is wilderness. There are still some terraforming stations out there, but that's about it until you get close to the coast."

They'd been marching along the river bank since dawn broke, almost ten hours before. They'd climbed and dropped more than they'd covered lateral ground, and Mountie figured they'd only made a couple klicks from where they'd first come down to meet the river. Mountie had been tempted to try and cross at several points they'd come across earlier, but none of them would be particularly easy. This spot wouldn't be easy, either, but it was better than anywhere else he'd considered so far.

"We've no guarantee we'll find an easier crossing, so this is it. Sergeant Go, you said you have crossing gear?"

"Yes, sir. Portillo, give me your hook."

The lance corporal dropped his pack and rooted around inside. He still looked like a bum with his haphazard armor, but it hadn't seemed to slow him down. He pulled out a dull metallic rectangle, about 20 centimeters long. Holding it out straight, he thumbed some sort of release Mountie couldn't see, and three backwards-facing prongs shot out from the tip.

Sergeant Go released some line from one of the pouches on his harness. The pouch wasn't very large, but the sergeant hand-over-handed out meter after meter of line. Mountie was surprised the pouch could hold that much.

He reached out and touched the grey cord. It had a much smaller diameter than he'd expected.

That's going to be tough to hold. It'll probably cut our hands.

For a river crossing, something with a larger diameter would be more appropriate, but Mountie could understand carrying a lighter line so more could be carried.

Both Marines had to be humping 50 kg while Mountie just had his SERE kit, the last of his rations, the dead merc's Gescard, and his Prokov. He'd offered to carry more, but both Marines had refused.

With a couple of sure twists of his hand, Sergeant Go attached the end of the line to the grappling hook.

"Now what?" Mountie asked.

"Now we throw it."

"You don't have something to shoot it across?" Mountie asked, surprised.

"Not with us, sir. If we had a tube of some sort, we could make a field expedient gun, I guess. But it's only 20 meters across, so we should be able to grunt it over."

Twenty-five meters, maybe, but OK.

Sergeant Go jumped onto a rock that extended into the current and looped the line several times around his hand, the bottoms of the loops touching the rock's surface. He let the hook drop a meter and started twirling the hook around and around, making a vertical loop. On the fifth rotation, he let go of the running end of the line just as the hook was swinging up, sending it arching over the river—only to be jerked short as the line reached full extension. It splashed into the water as Sergeant Go furiously pulled it in.

Go had a look that could kill, so Mountie made sure he didn't catch his eyes. The sergeant gave himself another four or five loops, and Mountie figured he now had enough slack to make it across the river to the far side. He started swinging the hook again, gaining a little more speed with each rotation. Just as the hook reached the bottom of the loop and was coming back up, Sergeant Go released.

Too high! You need to release sooner.

Mountie was right. The grappling hook shot across, but at a high angle, climbing at least 15 meters before it arched back down, falling into the water barely half-way across the river. Sergeant Go reeled the hook back in, his body tense with frustration. Slowly and deliberately, he looped the line again, making sure it hung free from his left hand, then starting twirling. Six, seven, eight rotations— Mountie wanted to yell out just to do it.

"You've got it, Sergeant!" JJ shouted out in encouragement just as Go released the hook, a split second earlier in the loop than on his previous throw.

It made a pretty arc as it flew across the water, and Mountie thought the throw was good—until it seemed to lose momentum and fall weakly into the river a good five meters from the far bank. Mountie could see that Sergeant Go was getting upset with himself.

"Mother-virgin-fuck!" the sergeant shouted as the hook hung up on something in the bottom.

He pulled up hard, as if a fisherman trying to set the hook, but the grappling hook was stuck fast. He yanked several more times.

"Wait a second, Sergeant. Don't pull!" Jasper said, hopping up on the rock. "Here, give it to me."

Sergeant Go glowered at the smaller man but handed over the line without a word. Jasper took it and hopped downstream on top of the rocks on the bank, keeping a steady pressure on the line. Once he made it a dozen or so meters past where the hook seemed stuck, it suddenly came free. Jasper quickly reeled it in, looping the line around his hand and elbow.

He started back, slipping once with a foot going into the water up to his left knee, but he maintained his footing with his right leg. A few moments later, he reached the sergeant and handed over the line and hook.

"You give it a try," Sergeant Go said, handing them over to Lance Corporal Portillo.

The junior Marine stood for a moment on the rock, staring at the other side before he lifted his right arm, and lasso-style, started twirling the hook and line in a horizontal circle. After six rotations, he let the hook fly. If anything, his throw was short of the sergeant's. He tried twice more, neither time getting close.

"Let me see that," Mountie said as Sergeant Go rolled his eyes.

"I think I can get it," Lance Corporal Portillo said, handing it over. "Just need to get a little more height on it."

Mountie took the loops of line in his left hand and hefted the hook in his right. It was surprisingly light. He gave it an experimental twirl with less than a meter of line. The sergeant had twirled it clockwise, with the downstroke behind him and releasing on the upstroke. Mountie wondered if going counterclockwise would make a difference.

He started twirling, downstroke in front of him and upstroke behind. He built up a little speed, which was difficult with the light hook, then released it at the apex of the loop. The arch was beautiful, and his breath caught, but it was as if the weight of the line itself was holding the hook back. It fell into the water still five meters short of the far shore.

Come on; this is ridiculous!

"JJ, can you give me a couple of zipties?" he heard Jasper ask behind him while he reeled in the hook.

Trying a different tack, he coiled the line on top of itself, placing the coil on the front of the rock at his feet, thinking that it might run freer.

He stood back, ready to try again when Jasper said, "Mountie, can I see the hook for a moment?"

Mountie turned to see Jasper standing behind him, his knife in hand. He shrugged, then handed the militiaman the hook. Jasper took it, hefted it once or twice and nodded before placing his beat-up work-knife alongside the main stem of the hook. With economical movements, he attached the knife with two of the zipties, pulling tight to make sure it was secure. He handed the hook back to Mountie.

"Here, try it now."

Mountie took the hook and jiggled it up and down at the end of the line. It felt much heavier.

Shit, it might work! Why the hell didn't I think of this?

He twirled the hook a few times, then stopped and checked it. Jasper's knife was still solidly attached.

"OK, let's give this bad boy a shot," he said.

He started twirling the hook in earnest, only realizing after five loops that he was going clockwise, the same as Sergeant Go had done. Deciding it didn't make much difference, he didn't stop. He put his arm and shoulder into it, building up the speed. As he released it and the hook arched up into the air, he immediately knew it was going to make across. The hook came back down and bounced on the far shore, a good three meters past the edge of the water.

"Ooh-rah, Lieutenant!" Portillo said.

Mountie started pulling it back, trying to catch on one of the rocks.

"Steady, sir!" Sergeant Go said. "Don't pull too hard!"

Only he did, and with a hop over the rock he was trying to snag, the hook landed in the water. He gave it a couple of small tugs, trying to catch something close to the edge, but to no avail.

Sergeant Go grabbed the line in front of Mountie and with huge, quick pulls, retrieved it. He checked the knife as soon as he pulled the hook from the water, but it was still firmly attached.

"Can I try, sir?" he asked.

Mountie wanted to try again himself, but it really didn't matter who got it across, and he could tell that the sergeant was anxious to override his earlier failure. He ceded the line to the sergeant and stepped back off the rock.

Sergeant Go quickly prepared the line, then started his throw, releasing the hook after only three loops. It didn't make a difference. The hook easily cleared the river. Getting it to snag on the other side was another issue—it wasn't until after the third subsequent throw that the hook caught between two boulders.

"Finally," the sergeant said. "OK, Portillo, get ready. I'm going to tie this end off now," the sergeant said as he hopped off of the rock and took the line to the nearest tree.

Lance Corporal Portillo sat down to take off his boots when Mountie said, "I'm going to be the swimmer."

"Sir?" the sergeant asked.

"The swimmer. That's going to be me."

"Uh, with all due respect, sir, Portillo, he's a strong swimmer, and he's pretty fit."

"Was he a CAA[7] swimmer?" Mountie asked as he pulled off his flight boots.

"CAA? No, he never went to no university," the sergeant said as Portillo laughed.

"Well, I did. Second place at the University Games in the 200 free. First in the 800 medley relay."

Mountie knew that the two Marines, while giving deference to his rank, still thought him less than their equal regarding fieldcraft, and that frankly grated at him. He was a Navy pilot, and how many people ever achieved that? It was probably elitist, but there were a hell of a lot more Marines than pilots in the service.

But while Sergeant Go knew more about grunt-type work, Mountie knew there was no way any of them were stronger swimmers than him, and this was his chance to step up. It was not only ego speaking, but he really was the best choice. The river might not be roiling rapids in this stretch, but she was still a powerful bitch who'd take any of them into her embrace if she could.

"No shit? I mean, sir? That's pretty freaking gorbo," Portillo said.

Mountie didn't know what "gorbo" meant, but the tone was clear. He'd impressed the young Marine.

He disconnected the front release of his flight suit, almost recoiling as the stench escaped.

Whoa! I really need the water, he thought. *Three days without a shower.*

Every Navy pilot flew with a skinsuit underneath whatever tactical flight or deep-space suit was needed for his particular aircraft. The skin suit had the connections to the various sensors as well as provided G-force protection. Mountie debated getting out of

---

[7] CAA: Collegiate Athletic Association

it as well and swimming naked, but it was a real pain in the ass to get it on and off. It shouldn't hamper him, so he kept it on. He disconnected the three line hubs and dropped the flight suit on top of his Gescard.

"You taking that?" Sergeant Go asked, pointing at the merc rifle.

"No, I don't think so. Too bulky."

"Then maybe you should take your Prokov, sir. We don't know if anyone is over there."

Good point, he acknowledged.

But his calf holster, which held both his Prokov and his Hwa Win combat knife, was made to attach to the slots on his flight suit, not his skin suit. He unhooked the holster from the empty flight suit and stood looking at it, wondering how to attach the thing.

Sergeant Go held out a hand for the holster, so Mountie gave it to him. The sergeant pulled two small straps from his engineer kit, slipped them through slots in the holster that Mountie had never even noticed, then handed it back.

It didn't take a bubblespace scientist to figure the thing out, and Mountie slipped it around his calf and tightened up the straps.

Next, he circled his waist with the pull line. He had to drag that across the river with him so he could help pull the others over one-by-one.

"Give me another piece of line, about a meter-and-a-half," he told the sergeant.

With that small piece in hand, he stepped into the water, going in to his waist—and almost recoiled in shock. It was *cold!* Suddenly, he was glad he wasn't in his starkers. The skinsuit had thermo-barriers, so it was giving him at least some protection.

Even this close to the shore, the river grabbed at him and tried to drag him downstream. He had to turn sideways to keep his feet.

He took the line the sergeant had given him and made a loop around both himself and the line crossing the river, keeping it loose. He didn't want to be constrained, and he needed freedom of motion.

"I want everyone to have one of these before he crosses. I'll have you on the pull line, but the safety loop is there in case there's a problem.

"Now, for my crossing, I'm going to keep one hand on the line, then do a modified side-stroke to get across. Once I'm on the other side, give me some more slack so I can secure that end over there. Then attach the pull line so I can get it over. Do we have enough line for all of this?"

"Roger that, sir. We'll use Portillo's line for that."

"I'll give you the OK, and whoever's next gets attached to the pull line, and in he goes. I want you to keep the pull-line taut, but not so tight that I can't haul it over."

Jasper listened closely to him, but the two Marines seemed to be barely paying attention. They'd probably done this many times before, but Mountie didn't see any harm in going over it as many times as he deemed necessary.

"Well, that's about it. I'm off."

He turned around and faced the river. The line dipped into the river at the middle of the span, bouncing up and down as it was caught and released by the flow. He took a breath, then half-leaned, half dove into the water on the upstream side of the safety line—and was immediately swung under it to the downstream side. He'd intended to swim with his right hand and hold on with his left hand, but this wasn't a pool. The current whipped him around to the downstream side of the rope, and he had to hold on with his right and swim with his left. Using the side-stroke, though, most of the power came from his legs, and with a few scissors kicks, he was on his way.

Five meters from the near bank, the current felt like it doubled in power, yanking him downstream as it tried to break him free of the safety line. Swimming became almost impossible as he had to grip the safety line too tightly to let his hand slide along it. Within a few moments, he gave up and brought up his right hand to grip the line as well. Then with a modified frog kick, he kicked and moved hand over hand out into the river.

"You've got it, Lieutenant!" Portillo yelled out.

As the rope dipped lower, the river was getting more powerful. Mountie's face kept going under at the bottom of each bounce, and he swallowed more of the water than he would have liked. He was getting pounded, but he kept at it, kicking for all he was worth and pulling on the rope. It was so thin, though, that it was cutting into his hands. He could see small blooms of red on them that disappeared each time his hands went under.

Somehow, he managed to make it past the middle of the river. He craned his neck to see ahead.

Less than ten meters!

And suddenly, the pounding and bouncing stopped.

Am I across? he wondered for a split second before he realized what had happened.

The far side hook had come free, and he was stuck in the flow of the river. Immediately, he grabbed the line with one hand and started breast-stroking to the far side. He had only seconds. Once any slack behind him was taken up, he would be swung back out into the current, and he'd slide down the end of the rope, either catching on the hook at the end, if it was still connected, or to slip right past the running end and be swept downstream.

He felt the rope behind him going taut, and he started to be pulled back, so he let go, and with both arms, started pounding the water, striving to reach the other side before he was caught in the middle. He was barely aware of the line zipping past him—until the grappling hook hit him hard in the side, a lancing pain flashing through him. He wanted to double up, but the image of the rapids just 300 meters downstream kept flashing through his mind as he doubled his effort, concentrating on getting the most out of each stroke, each kick.

A boil in the water almost flipped him, but he powered through, straining with each kick. His fingers hit a rock, and he panicked, sure he'd already hit the rapids, but after another stroke, the pounding ceased. He had reached an eddy downstream of a boulder half in and half out of the water. His knees hit the river bed, and he managed to stand up, only to double back over to one knee, hand clutching his side. He risked a peek; his side was bleeding, his skinsuit torn.

But he was across. He forced himself upright and turned.

All three of his companions were standing on the throwing rock, anxiously looking across.

"Are you OK?" Sergeant Go yelled, his voice muted by the power of the river.

He raised a tentative hand, thumbs up. Carefully, he climbed up around the boulder and onto the bank. He wanted to do nothing more than to lie down on his back for a few moments, but he knew that would freak out the others. Instead, he started walking back to where he'd intended to reach this bank. He'd been swept at least 150 meters downstream during his little swim. It took almost three minutes to clamber over the rocks and reach the spot opposite them. Once he arrived, he swung his left arm in circles. They'd just have to throw the hook over again.

The three had been watching him the entire time, and after he signaled them, they hurriedly recovered the hook. He leaned back against a large boulder, watching as they got the line ready. Within a minute or two, Sergeant Go was making his loops, and on his first throw, the hook sailed across to land right at his feet. Trying to isolate the pain in his side as well as the bumps and bruises that were beginning to make themselves felt, he reached down and picked it up. It was still in pretty good shape, but Jasper's blade had taken a beating. The edge had several nicks, and there was a dent in the cheek.

Jasper's knife was a working man's blade, nothing fancy, but practical. It was nothing like his Hwa Win, which had cost Mountie almost a month's pay. He glanced down to his calf, and it was only then that he noticed that the holster was gone, along with this Prokov and Hwa Win.

"Son-of-a-one-eyed-bitch!" he said, looking down the river, but the river taketh and the river keepeth.

Both were long gone.

He straightened up and dragged the rope to a tree ten meters back from the bank where he secured it. The safety line was in place. Back on the other side, the three had attached the pull line to a clip in the middle of the safety and gave him the signal. He pulled on the safety line, drawing over the pull line, all the time his side making itself known with jolts of pain. He unclipped the pull line and secured it to the same tree while the other three pulled back on the safety line, bringing it taut once again. It was a messy way to deal with ropes, having each line more than twice the length of the width of the river, but that was the only way to move something back and forth with each end of both lines secured on opposite banks.

Finally, it was time for the others. Jasper was hooked into the middle of the pull line first. He stepped into the water, and after a safety loop secured him to the safety line, Mountie pulled him across. Jasper helped a little, but the bulk of the horsepower came from Mountie's aching arms. It took three minutes before a sputtering Jasper stepped up on the bank.

Jasper gave a pointed look at Mountie's torn and bloody skinsuit, but Mountie waved him off. He wanted to get everyone over as quick as possible.

Next came the two packs with all their gear, one after the other. Mountie felt a lot more comfortable when he had his Gescard slung around his shoulders.

Lance Corporal Portillo followed, coming across without incident. The Marine was able to assist his crossing more than Jasper had, and he had a huge smile as he came out of the water, much to Mountie's disgust. He'd evidently thought it was fun!

Sergeant Go was a little more difficult. With no one needed to retrieve the pull line, he detached the far end of it and attached himself to the running end. The three on the near bank pulled in all the slack before the sergeant entered the water and half-swam, half-clutched at the safety line as the other three hauled his big body across. Unlike with Portillo, the sergeant had a hint of panic in his eyes when he finally made it.

There wasn't a way to detach the safety line on the far side, so Sergeant Go reached out and cut it, letting the near end sink into the water. The current caught it and started sweeping it downstream. Someone walking on the other side could see the end still attached to a tree, and they'd know someone had crossed there, but Mountie hoped that would happen long after they gone and been re-united with their units.

With that done, Mountie breathed a sigh of relief as he sunk down on the ground. He took his SERE kit, pulling out the NueSkin spray, which he liberally applied to his side. The cool, soothing properties of the spray immediately deadened the ache as it cleaned and stabilized the wound as Jasper and Portillo hovered over him, worry on their faces.

"No big deal. Just give me ten, and we'll be on our way."

Mountie knew he'd been correct in taking the crossing himself. If it had been Lance Corporal Portillo doing it, he was sure the Marine would have been lost. He'd made the right decision, and in doing so, maybe he'd shown the others what he was made of.

All told, though, he thought, *I think I'd much rather be in my Lizard.*

Chapter 16

Jasper

Jasper dug the last bits of the date-crumble out of the wrapper, then wadded that up and threw it into his mouth as well. JJ and the sergeant sure complained about their field rats, but he didn't think they were bad. The date-bar was rich, and the wrapper had that sweet crunchiness that had become popular over the last few years. Jasper loved his wife dearly, but neither of them could cook worth a darn, so they relied on fab food. Given that much of his crop probably made its way to food fabricators across the galaxy, that was probably appropriate.

The travel rats, as JJ called them, were small, but packed with calories. They might not bulk much, but they kept a Marine alive, and that worked for militiamen as well. JJ was almost out, but he was making sure he shared with Jasper as well.

The four of them had stopped for the evening, crawling deep within heavy brush in a marsh. No one would be able to sneak up on them unnoticed. Sergeant Go's PFG-cloth coated body armor was laden with all sorts of suppressors, but JJ's armor was in taters, and neither he nor Mountie had any type of suppressor capability in their clothing. The three of them could still be spotted with surveillance gear, but with the Navy and Marine air superiority, the Tenner air was limited.

Jasper would have rather put a few more klicks behind them, but by unspoken agreement, they knew Mountie needed to rest. He'd been beaten up pretty good at the river crossing, and he could use a bit more down-time to let his meds work.

When the grappling hook had come free, sweeping Mountie downstream, Jasper had been sure he was lost. But the guy had somehow beat the current to crawl out on the other side. It had been pretty amazing, something that hit home when he had crossed next. They didn't have pools in Donkerbroek, and the Rustig Stroom was just about big enough for wading. Jasper had flailed his way across, almost entirely pulled by Mountie. He'd been shocked and badly frightened by the pure power of the river.

He licked his fingers and looked up to see Mountie staring at him. Not knowing what else to do, he nodded.

"I haven't mentioned it yet, but that was pretty smart what you did with your knife and the grappling hook. What gave you that idea?" Mountie asked him.

"It was pretty obvious that the hook was too light to get over, so what else to do except add some weight?"

Jasper knew the Navy pilot meant well, but the inference was that Mountie was surprised that he, some hick farmer, was just as intelligent as the others. He may not have attended a university like Mountie, and he may not have been to engineer school like the two Marines, but during his life as an algae wrangler, both as an indentured and now as a freeman, he'd had to learn a lot of seat-of-the-pants engineering just to survive. The hook needed weight, he added it. Simple as that.

"Sorry about your blade," JJ said. "It took a beating there."

"No worries. I'll just hammer it out when I get home."

Not that I have a shop anymore.

He pushed that thought out of his mind. He didn't need to be dwelling on things like that now.

"You can do that?" JJ asked. "I fucked up my Spyderco last year, and I just had to get a new one."

"That's because it was aligned cero-steel, most likely. Once the molecule chains are disrupted, there's no fixing that. Not like mine," Jasper said, pulling out his knife and holding it up. "I made this out of a chunk of an old holding tank."

"You mean, like you made the whole thing? Why not just order a real one?"

"A real one? This doesn't look real?" Jasper asked, shaking the blade a few times, then rapping the cheek against the barrel of his rifle.

"No, I didn't mean that. But it's easy to just order one."

"Why? Margins are tight farming algae, and this took me maybe 40 minutes to make. Didn't cost me a credit, either."

"Hell, Mr. van Ruiker. Margins are tight?" Sergeant Go said. "I seen how you farmers grow algae and that stuff on 'How Things Work.' Every three days, you can harvest a new crop."

Jasper couldn't stop himself from rolling his eyes.

"Sure, we can. If we get decent sun. If the temperature remains steady and we don't have to expend energy raising or lowering the bath temp. If we manage the flow of fertilizers and additives to match ambients. If the nitros don't explode and take out half of your tubes."

"That can happen?" JJ asked.

"Well, not to me. But our fertilizers are nitrogen-based, and yes, if you don't upkeep your equipment, you can get a huge explosion. Happened last year to Kale Hastig. Let the nitros flow too freely, and boom, his tubes and Maarten's were destroyed. A freeman for all his life, he had to sell his contract to cover the expenses, but who wants to keep an indentured on the farms if he makes that kind of mistake."

He didn't mention that Kale had been drunk on his butt when he blew up his farm and a quarter of Maarten's.

"And even if we do everything right, what do we get for our efforts? Not much. We get paid the DR. The government decides on the Dedicated Rate without our input, but you can bet the big corporations give theirs.

"So, to answer your question, I made my own blade because I can, and I didn't have to pay anything for it other than 40 minutes of my time. As an algae wrangler, we learn to make do whenever possible."

"Hell, I can't make shit, Jasper," JJ said. "I can blow it up, for sure, but not make anything. You're a real gyver.

"Hey, Sergeant Go, maybe we should call him 'Gyver.'"

"What's a 'gyver?'" Jasper asked.

"You know, like you. Someone who can make things out of something else, like a blade out of a holding tank, or, what, a rocket out of a stylus."

"You can make a rocket out of a stylus?"

"I don't know. I was just pulling something out of my ass. Just anything out of nothing."

Jasper had been fascinated by the dynamics of his companion's nicknames. Lance Corporal Portillo was "JJ," Sergeant Go was "Go-man," and the lieutenant was "Mountie." Mountie called the two Marines by rank and last name. The sergeant used rank and name for Mountie, but JJ was usually just "Portillo." He called JJ and Mountie by their nicknames, but not Sergeant Go. Mountie had made mention of another pilot, "Skeets." Jasper didn't know what to make of all this, but he found it all fascinating.

And, surprisingly, he felt a bit of excitement when JJ said he should be called "Gyver." It was almost as if getting a nickname was some sort of rite of passage. He still didn't quite know what "Gyver" meant despite the explanation, and he wasn't sure if it was complimentary or not, but that wasn't as important as the fact that JJ thought he deserved a nickname.

JJ seemed to be pleased with his suggestion, but Sergeant Go merely harrumphed while Mountie never looked up from where he was cleaning his fingernails. The slight bit of excitement Jasper had felt quickly faded. He should have known better. He was a militiaman, not a professional soldier, and the other three didn't hold him in the same class as themselves.

Jasper didn't know what to say to that, but he was saved from having to make a response when a flicker of bright white light reflected off the top of the trees.

Lightening? Jasper wondered.

Something seemed unnatural about the light, and the low boom that reached them a few seconds later was nothing like thunder.

"Someone's getting into it," JJ said somberly.

More light flickered, followed by more rumblings and booms. A battle was going on off in the distance, a big one by the sounds of it. Men were fighting and dying over there, as they fought over his home-planet while the four of them sat huddled in a marsh.

Jasper forgot about nicknames, the perils of farming, and making knives as he sat with the others simply listening to the sounds of war.

Chapter 17

Mountie

The explosion knocked Mountie to the ground, his wounded side erupting in pain. He tried to scramble to his feet when he felt Sergeant Go's strong arms grab and lift him.

"Move it, sir," the sergeant said as he bolted at right angles to their previous direction of march.

Mountie took off, dodging through the trees. Another explosion sounded behind him, the pressure wave pressing against his back. Bits of wood and leaves rained down from the trees.

"They're using air bursts!" Sergeant Go shouted. "Stay under the trees as much as possible."

Bad choice on their part, the professional side of Mountie noted. *They need to be using something to penetrate the canopy to detonate around us.*

The four dodged around tree trunks as three more explosions sounded behind them, each one successively farther away as they ran. Mountie wasn't about to stop, though, not until they'd put far more distance between where the rounds had landed and them.

But what if they're waiting for us ahead?

The firing had stopped, but the worry about fleeing pell-mell through the forest was eating at him. After less than a minute, he called for a halt. He looked back, figuring they'd probably covered 200 meters.

"Was that intended for us?" Jasper asked.

"No, they just decided to fire randomly into the forest, and out of all these square kilometers of trees, we just happened to be there," Sergeant Go said, barely breathing hard.

Mountie ignored the sarcasm and asked, "How do you think they picked us up? Were we spotted?"

If the sergeant thought his question was foolish, his military discipline didn't let it show.

"I don't think so, sir. The forest is pretty dense here. We've still got secondary and tertiary growth going."

Mountie usually didn't care about vegetation while he was up in the air in his Lizard, but he knew enough about terraforming to know that old growth, even when genetically sped up, still took close to 100 years to create a mature forest. As Nieuwe Utrecht was only 50 or 60 years old, the undergrowth was dense, making visibility limited.

"I'm guessing we got too close to a sensor. They already know by now we're out here, and you can bet they're searching for us. They can't afford to let a platoon run loose in their rear."

"But we're not a platoon," Portillo said.

"Doesn't matter. They think we're a platoon, thanks to your runner.

"They tried to reach out with their arty, and they would have wanted to zero us, but they also wanted to let us know they are on to us. If we were a platoon on a mission, that might disrupt the mission and send us packing back to our lines."

"But they have a location on us, and probably the direction we were heading, right?" Mountie asked.

"Yes, sir. They were pretty close on target. Hell, if the round had penetrated the canopy . . ." he said, leaving that thought unfinished. "So yeah, they had a few scanner hits to give them our direction. And that means they probably have a welcoming party for us up ahead."

"And we are about seven or eight clicks to the Grangers," Mountie said, not really asking a question.

"I was hoping to be up in the mountains today and rendezvous sometime tomorrow. But we've got to change up. Let's keep going to the east like this for now before turning back north. It'll add a day to our march, but I think we have to do it."

"Aye-aye, sir," Sergeant Go said. "Portillo, keep heading east."

Mountie stole a glance at Jasper. He didn't know if this would put them farther from the route up to Spirit Lake or not, but if they ran into a Tenner ambush, they'd never make it to the Lake— or to Federation forces.

He was acutely aware of the fact that they were about out of food. Adding another day to their march meant that much longer without eating, but that couldn't be helped. His mission was to get Jasper to his family and the Marines and him back to their units, and if that took an extra day, so be it.

Chapter 17

Jasper

"What do you think are in them?" Mountie asked as the four lay on their bellies, trying to see through the trees.

"Look at the fourth one," Sergeant Go said. "See how low it's on the rear tracks? I'm guessing ammo or something. But we don't know for sure."

"You couldn't see?"

"No, sir. The tarps are drawn closed. But the trucks aren't empty; I'm positive of that."

"So, getting back to my earlier question, what do we do now? We've got mercs on our asses, we've got another five klicks until we reach the Grangers, and possibly some vital Tenner war equipment just sitting there, ripe for the taking."

"It's your call, sir, but you know my opinion. Clause 4, sir."

"Did you get a solid count of the men?"

"I saw four walking around or in the cabs. Probably just the drivers."

"What about A-drivers?"

"They're mercs, sir, not Federation. Lean and mean, like they say. We have to have A-drivers by regulations, but I'm betting they can't afford to spend the personnel. And they probably feel pretty comfortable so far from our forces."

"Only, our forces are sitting right here in their backyard, ready to explode on their asses," JJ added. "Four of us."

"Their bust," Sergeant Go said. "And they'll pay the price for that mistake. If we hit them, sir."

"How many rounds do you have left, Jasper?" Mountie asked.

"Seven," Jasper answered, seemingly surprised to be brought into the conversation.

"And your charges are full?" Mountie asked the two Marines.

"I'm at 92%. Portillo's at 43%, but I gave him an extra powerpack. We're good for a couple of thousand darts between us."

"You've got that many darts?" he asked, sounding surprised.

Sergeant Go patted his vest and said, "They fold up tiny in the mags, Lieutenant. They're only 8mm after they leave the barrel. We've got more than enough. We'll run out of power for the mag-rings before we run out of them."

Jasper could hear the longing in the sergeant's voice. He knew Go was aching for the mission, but it was up to the lieutenant. As for himself, he wasn't sure. If he knew for sure the trucks offered a valid target, he could see destroying them. He thought Sergeant Go, however, was trying to will them to be important to justify the mission. But risking themselves just to attack four merc drivers didn't in and of itself justify the risk, in his opinion, especially with who knows how many mercs trying to track them down.

He wanted to make that opinion known, to tell the others that in this case, discretion might really be the better part of valor, but he held his tongue.

What the heck do I know? They're the professionals, not me.

"Well, I guess we'd better kick some merc ass, then," Mountie said with conviction.

"Roger that, sir. And I've got an idea, if that's OK."

The other three pulled closer to the sergeant as the Marine outlined his plan.

Chapter

JJ

No one ever said Sergeant Go's got any finesse, JJ thought as he crawled into position. *He's like, just punch them in the mouth and take it from there.*

He wasn't critical of his sergeant. Sometimes, pussyfooting around just gave the enemy time to react.

Oh, now I'm some sort of Rottweiler Williamson, I guess, hero of the Corps. Better just leave the tactics to the Go-man.

JJ had been playing infantry for almost five days now, and during that time, he'd killed at least four mercs. He was pretty proud of that, but he knew it had been mostly a result of training and luck, not that he was some sort of tactical protégé. He'd been a grunt during his first tour, as was the case for almost all Marines, but for the last two years, he'd been an engineer, learning out to blow up things. He was a far cry from the recon team who'd escorted them to the bridge. If those snake-eaters hadn't survived the mission, JJ was under no false conviction that he'd automatically survive every engagement.

Except that a tiny part of his ego did believe that. He fingered the crease in his breastplate again. It should serve as a wake-up call, but instead, it seemed to buttress a feeling of invulnerability. Which was dangerous.

JJ was about to go into a fight with patched-together armor and with only one other Marine, a pilot and a militiaman. That didn't look good on paper. Still, he felt the rush of competitive juices, as if he was back on San Filipe getting ready for a punchball match. He was confident that the four of them would prevail.

He gave his M90 a quick check. The magazine was full, 300 darts ready to go. His power was at 43%. He switched the diagnostics to resistance: zero ohms. His hypervelocity rifle was primed.

The door of the second truck opened, and a merc stepped out, sucking on a stim. He wandered around behind his cargo bed, then after carefully looking forward to see if anyone was watching, he pulled a flask out from where it was hidden under his blouse and took a swig, hesitated, then took another. He wiped his mouth with his forearm, turned to look around the end of his truck to check if anyone had seen him, and then put the flask back inside his blouse.

I hope it was some good shit there, buddy, 'cause that's the last taste you're ever gonna get.

If we ever kick this thing off. What's taking them?

He checked the time. The assault was already almost ten minutes late. He understood the confusion back on the comms relay hill with Jasper being on local planetary time and the rest being on 24-hour time, but ten minutes was too much to be explained by the difference. Sergeant Go and the lieutenant had gone forward, crossed the road, and were supposed to be on the other side of the trucks now, ready to launch.

He turned to Jasper. The militiaman was lying prone behind a fallen tree trunk, ten meters away. He still had his old UKI, saying he was used to it. But with only seven rounds left, JJ wasn't sure he'd be much of a factor. No, it would be up to the sergeant, the lieutenant with his appropriated Gescard, and him to win this battle.

JJ tried to pierce his vision into the trees on the other side of the trucks to see if he could spot the other two. He couldn't, and that was a good thing, all told. If he could spot them, then so could any mercs looking their way. But not knowing what was happening was driving JJ batty. He'd never realized how wedded Marines were to their comms, himself included. In training, they'd gone into exercises with a comms blackout, but never for five days, as they'd now been off the circuits since the bridge.

When the first truck powered up, the hyped JJ almost fired his M90. In a moment, the second truck, the one right in front of JJ, powered up as well, rising a few centimeters as its road system activated.

For a moment, JJ thought they had been discovered, but there was no firing from the mercs. Either two of the half-tracs were getting ready to leave, or they had to power-up every once in a while to keep the electronics going.

JJ raised his head slightly until he could partially see into the cab. Someone's legs were visible, feet on the dash. JJ felt a rush of relief. That didn't look like a driver who was ready to leave, more like someone wanting to escape the muggy air and enjoy the cab's air-conditioning.

JJ had just started to lower himself when he caught motion on the other side of the trucks. It took only and instant to realize that Sergeant Go and the lieutenant were charging out of the brush.

No! They're not leaving! he wanted to shout.

It didn't take a bubble space scientist to know that the two must have heard the trucks power up, and they'd charged, abandoning the previous plan of measured fire from cover.

"Fire, Jasper," JJ shouted as he triggered a burst at the side window of truck number 2's cab.

Stars exploded in the glass as the legs jerked down and out of sight. For a moment, JJ thought he'd gotten another kill, but then he realized that the window had held. His darts generated tremendous speed, and despite their relative paucity in mass, they impacted with tremendous force. Evidently, though, the armored glass, or whatever the window was made of, could withstand them.

The truck lurched, the back tracks spinning wildly, which caused the rear end to slide around to the left. Whether that was by accident or through impressive skill by the driver, the end result was that the front of the truck was pointed out of the line, giving it a clear way to escape.

JJ reached into his harness and pulled out his lone Ferret. The tiny, hand-launched rocket was only 30 mm across, but it packed an intense pencil of super-heated plasma that could burn through most armor. JJ stood up as the truck lurched forward, the back tracks gaining traction. The front of the truck was facing him as he stepped forward, Ferret in his hand. He didn't need the flip sights at this range; he simply thumbed the release. The rocket popped out ten meters until the tiny pulsejet motor took over, getting in one pulse before the warhead hit the front grill of the truck. Through the windshield, JJ could see the look of horror on the face of the driver as he realized what had just happened.

There was a flash of light as the shaped charge deployed. The plasma ate through the engine, reverting metal and ceramics back to their component atoms. The truck shuddered, but to JJ's surprise, it didn't stop.

JJ could hear grinding noises above the sound of the battle, but the truck continued forward, coming right at JJ, the face of the driver turning from fear to one of glee as he tried to run him down. JJ fired another burst from his M90, but as before, the only effect was to create starbursts in the glass.

JJ ran forward and to the side, almost getting caught on the edge of the front fender. He wasn't sure quite what he was going to do, but his mind was racing as to his options. He was just about to jump up on the truck's running board beneath the driver's window when something pinged off the side window, zipping past his ear. He dropped down when bam, bam, bam, three more rounds impacted. He scrambled out of the way, spotting the lieutenant, his Gescard at the hip in the best Hollybolly tradition, hammering away. The fourth round hit the truck with a denser "thunk."

To JJ's surprise, the frame of the cab was warped, right at the window. The round hadn't penetrated the cab, but there was a tiny gap now between it and the glass.

"Cease fire, Lieutenant! I've got it!" he shouted, pulling out a shock instigator.

The E-22 Explosive Instigation Device worked like an old-fashioned blasting cap. C-10 was a very powerful, slow explosive, capable of moving vast amounts of soil, rock, or man-made-objects, but it was too stable to be detonated by electrical or chemical detonators. It needed a big boom to start the reaction, and that big boom was normally the E-22. It produced a powerful blast that set off the C-10. Best of all, was its size, packing a powerful punch in a small object.

JJ jumped back up on the running board, arming the instigator. The warp in the cab frame was very small, and for a moment he wondered if the device would even fit through. But he was committed now. There was no disarming it.

The man inside the cab looked confused, but when JJ reached to push the E-22 through the gap, he knew it couldn't be something good. He dove to block JJ just at the Marine started fitting it through. For a moment, the two were at a stalemate, the shock instigator half in and half out of the cab. The merc inside started to swing around to bring two arms to bear.

JJ was holding the E-22 with one hand, the M90 in the other. If the merc could knock the E-22 back out, JJ would only have a few moments to get clear. The little device wasn't designed as a weapon, but it could do a number on a person who was within a couple of meters of it when it went off.

Just as the merc started to reach forward with his other hand, JJ dropped his right hand just as he swung the butt of his M90 with all his might with his left arm, striking the protruding half of the instigator and sending it shooting into the truck cab.

The merc's face contorted into horror as he dove towards the E-22. That was a dumb move, although in the confined cab, it probably didn't make any difference. JJ jumped back and managed two steps before a muffled whump and a moderate shock wave hit him. He turned and jumped back onto the running board, M90 at the ready, as he peered into the smoky cab.

It wasn't a pretty sight.

JJ jumped back off, spinning to take in the rest of the fight. The lieutenant was changing magazines, his back up against the cargo bed of the first truck. JJ jumped back to the ground to rush over when two rounds impacted against the side of the truck, centimeters from his head. He turned his jump into a dive, rolling on the ground and trying to bring up his rifle.

On the first truck, from the opposite side of the cargo bed from the lieutenant, a merc was leaning out from beneath the bed cover. JJ tried to swing his M90 around, but the muzzle caught in the dirt, slowing him just enough so that he knew the merc would fire on him again before he could fire back.

He tried to roll to make him miss when the merc dropped his weapon and slumped forward, his head and torso hanging limp. Beyond the truck, just coming into JJ's focus, Jasper stood upright, his old UKI aimed at the dead merc.

"Holy shit, old man, thanks!" JJ said under his breath.

"Coming up on you, Lieutenant!" he shouted as he jumped up and ran to him.

"What's happening?" the lieutenant asked, his face flushed.

"A merc was in the cargo bed. He had me dead to rights until Jasper zeroed him."

"Here? In this cargo bed?" he asked, stepping back away from the truck.

"Yeah, I think we'd better clear it, sir."

"Where's Sergeant Go?"

"Sounds like over at Truck 4," JJ answered, pointing to where a large volume of fire was emanating.

"This driver's dead. He tried to get out of his cab, and the sergeant nailed him. Let's go help him, and then we can come back and check the inside."

JJ didn't like leaving until the truck was secured, but the lieutenant was already running.

"Keep this truck covered!" he yelled at Jasper as he took off after the pilot.

Truck 3 was on fire, and up ahead, Sergeant Go was firing into the cab of Truck 4—with the same amount of effect as JJ had on Truck 2.

"Target the cab with your Gescard!" JJ shouted to the lieutenant who a moment later, fired two rounds into the windshield.

Sergeant Go looked up as a victorious grin spread across his face, and he jumped on the running boards. He reached for the door handle with his left hand, his right on his M90. JJ wanted to yell out that the door was locked from the inside, when to his surprised, it opened.

That must have taken Sergeant Go by surprise as well, because he stumbled back, fighting to keep his balance. JJ saw the hand reach out from the cab, the unmistakable outline of a handgun its grasp. JJ tried to bring his M90 up, but before he could engage, the handgun spit out a flash of fire, sending Sergeant Go flailing backwards off the truck. By the time JJ's darts were impacting, the door had already closed.

JJ rushed forward in a rage, ready to run amok on the merc. He'd seen the burst of blood explode from the back of Sergeant Go's head before the body fell to the dirt. He knew his sergeant was dead, and his mind was solely focused on killing the man responsible.

He emptied his magazine at the windshield as he charged, and when the magazine was empty, he threw down his rifle and fumbled for his engineer kit. Jumping on the front bumper, he stopped to show the merc inside the toad he pulled out, grinning maniacally. He mimed arming it, then used his hands to indicate an explosion.

Pulling himself up higher, he leaned back so he could toss the device on the roof of the cab.

"I surrender! I surrender!" the merc shouted over an external loudspeaker.

JJ ignored the man.

"I said I surrender! The Harbin Accords!"

"I can't hear you," JJ said, leaning back down to look inside the cab. "Bad ears, you know."

"I surrender!"

JJ started to straighten up when the voice of command reached him, "Lance Corporal Portillo, halt! Stop!"

By instinct more than anything else, he froze.

"Get down. That man surrendered," Lieutenant Klocek said in a steady voice. "Climb down from there, son."

JJ turned to where the lieutenant was slowly walking up, then back to the toad in his hand. With a start, he dropped the unarmed device, bouncing it off the bumper of the truck to fall to the ground.

Holy shit! I was about to burn this guy.

JJ looked through the windshield into the cab at the merc, who had backed up as far as he could go, both hands held out in supplication. Anger came rushing back, and he wanted to break the windshield and pulverize the man's face, but discipline had taken ahold of him. The lieutenant had issued a command, and a Marine follows orders.

"It's OK, sir. I know he's surrendered."

JJ used the muzzle of his M90 to motion the guy to get out of the cab. He could see the guy was scared shitless, and he didn't want to get out. JJ reached in and pulled out his other toad, holding it up for the merc to see.

"JJ—" the lieutenant started.

"Just convincing him to get out. And if you can go cover the door, I'd appreciate it, sir."

The merc evidently understood JJ's implied threat, because he crossed himself, then scooted over to the door. He only hesitated a moment before he opened it. JJ jumped off the bumper and motioned for the man to get on his face.

The merc slowly got down, but kept his face turned to watch JJ's every moment. JJ resisted the urge to smash his head down with the butt of his rifle. Instead, he pulled out a set of zipties and secured the merc's hands.

"If you can cover him, sir, I need to check on the sergeant, then clear Truck 1 and retrieve Jasper.

He turned to where Sergeant Go lay on his back. Dull, dead eyes stared at the sky. The round had hit him in the mouth and had probably taken out most of the back of his head, given the amount of blood that was pooling under it. JJ didn't need to check his pulse.

He didn't say a word as he straightened out and marched to Truck 1 where Jasper was still standing guard.

Please, let there be someone in there!

He whipped open the back.

It was full of chairs, simple folding chairs that anyone might have. The legs and butt of the merc Jasper had killed were still in the cargo bed, draped over the rails. The bed smelled of shit, and the stain in the merc's trou pinpointed the reason.

"What happened?" Jasper asked as JJ waved him over.

"Sergeant Go's dead. We got the mother-fucker who did it, though, as a prisoner. And for what? This truck's cargo is chairs. Freaking chairs!"

"Sergeant Go? Dead?" Jasper asked, his expression one of horror.

"Yeah, ain't that the kicker," JJ said, not even sure what he meant by that. "Let's check the other trucks to see what vital war gear we captured."

Truck 2 had what looked to be bedding material. Truck 3 had food rations. JJ was steaming as he moved to the last truck. He marched wordlessly past the lieutenant who still had his Gescard trained on the prisoner and flung open the back.

It was wood. Not synthetic building materials that were manufactured to look like wood, but real, organic wood.

"Fuck!" JJ shouted to the skies.

He threw the flaps closed and strode around the back of the truck. Jasper was folding Sergeant Go's hands across his chest, but JJ barely noticed.

"Chairs, beds, and wood, that's the vital war materials we hit!" he screamed.

"You thought we had war materials," the merc asked, sounding surprised.

"You shut the fuck up!"

"JJ, Sergeant Go? What do you want, you know . . . ?" Jasper asked.

JJ looked up and was surprised to see tears forming in the older man's eyes. That brought him around to reality. He was angry, angry that the sergeant, *his* sergeant was dead, angry that it was all for nothing. It wouldn't even be worth using up his explosives to destroy the trucks. Focused anger could be useful, but more often than not, it could get someone killed. He had to control himself.

"Lieutenant, I'd like to bury him, if I can," he said, fighting to keep his voice calm.

"Of course. I'll help. Jasper, if you can cover our prisoner."

"All out of ammo, Mountie. Fired it all."

"I had you covering the first truck with no ammo?" JJ asked. "Why didn't you tell me?"

"Didn't look like you were going to listen. And I figured that if someone came out, I could bluff him."

JJ looked at the militiaman incredulously for a moment when his emotions collapsed and he broke out laughing. He brayed like a donkey before they turned more into sobs than anything else for a moment, then back to laughs.

"You're OK, Jasper, you're fucking OK," he said as he regained his composure. "Here, take my Prokov, and if the bastard so much as flinches, blast him. If that's OK, Lieutenant."

JJ stripped Sergeant Go of his gear, handing his M90 to Jasper and taking back his Prokov. He flipped the safety on and off in demonstration, but that was it. At this range, the M90 was pretty foolproof. JJ consolidated the sergeant's engineer kit with his and contemplated taking his armor to replace his own mess of armor. But the sergeant had 30 kilos on him, and there was no way it would fit.

Attached to the side of the truck was a shovel, so he took that and quickly dug a shallow hole. The lieutenant offered to help, but he wanted to do it himself. When it was a meter deep, he and Lieutenant Klocek pulled the sergeant's body into it, and JJ covered him with the loose dirt. It was not intended to be a permanent resting place for him, but rather a temporary shelter until the fight on the planet was over or a truce called and he could be recovered.

"Hey, merc! You got coordinates on this spot?"

"Yes. On the dash console," he said, his voice tense.

JJ climbed into the cab, located the nav console, and recorded the coordinates. He could have flashed his combat PA to get them, but he didn't know if that would be enough for the mercs doing surveillance to get a bead on them.

Suddenly, exhaustion hit him, and hit him hard. Along with the others, he'd been pushing himself, but he knew this was more emotional than anything else. Regardless, he needed to sit down. He collapsed against the left front wheel of the truck and took a long swig of water. He knew he should eat, too, but he doubted he could keep anything down.

Neither the lieutenant nor Jasper had camelbacks—the lieutenant had a thigh pouch, and Jasper had an old canteen and a Cleanstraw. Jasper had pulled down a can of water from the trucks side to replenish their limited carrying capacity. JJ wondered if he should have pulled Sergeant Go's camelback, but it was intertwined in the armor, and trying to extract it would probably create more problems than it fixed. It might be worth a try, though. He looked over to the shallow grave where the sergeant rested, wondering if he should attempt to recover it.

What a waste, he thought as his anger rekindled. *He was twice the Marine of anyone else. Killed to line some corporate CEO's pocket.*

The more he thought about it, the angrier JJ became. It was one thing to fight for your home or to protect others. Fighting for financial gain seemed perverted to him. He couldn't understand how anyone could do that, yet right there, just five meters away, was someone who had made that very choice.

JJ sat staring at the merc for a few moments before he stood up, strode over to the man, and kicked his feet.

"How the hell can you live with yourself?" he shouted, scorn dripping from his words.

The merc tried to scramble back, but with his hands secured behind him, he wasn't making much headway. He looked up at JJ, eyes wide-open in fear.

"Hey, it's war. I was just doing my job!" he protested.

"That's just it. '*Job.*' You're fighting to get paid, pure and simple!"

The merc stopped trying to scoot away, his brows furrowed as he took JJ's words in.

"I . . . I don't understand," he said, looking to Mountie as if seeking help.

"It's simple. You're a fucking merc, a mercenary. You take money to fight."

"I what? I take money? But you get paid, too," he said.

"I'm fighting for the Marines. For the Federation. I get paid, but I'm fighting for the right."

The merc shook his head, then said, "And I'm not?"

"Of course, you're not. You're taking money from the corporations to fight the Federation."

"I . . . I don't know where to start, Lance Corporal . . ."

"Lance Corporal Portillo, United Federation Marines. And that was Sergeant Gary Go you killed."

"And you killed how many of my team?" the merc answered with a flash of disdain. "That's what happens in war. It's shitty, but that's what it is.

"But to your point, Lance Corporal Portillo, I don't know if you really believe the hogwash that the Federation vomits up, but it's you Feddies that are in the wrong here."

"Bullshit! Lieutenant, are you hearing this?" JJ asked, turning to Mountie.

Mountie shrugged.

"How the hell can you say we're in the wrong?"

"Because you levy taxes on the new worlds without giving anything back? How about that?"

"Taxes, we all pay taxes. And if you're talking about the Far Reaches, well, the Navy found those worlds, and how else do we pay to terraform them?"

The merc sat up straighter, then leaned forward.

"The Federation doesn't pay for that. It's the corporations who foot the bill, them and pioneer groups."

That didn't seem right to JJ. He looked to Mountie, but the lieutenant wasn't objecting to the merc's statement.

"Your precious Federation graciously accepts a trillion-credit charter fee for each planet—yes, I said *trillion*—then levies a 22% administration fee, based on GPP, for 20 years in exchange for the privilege of simply existing."

"It costs a lot to run the Federation. You think all of that is free?" JJ asked, unwilling to concede the point.

"No, your Navy is not free. But what does the Navy do for us?"

"It protects you!"

"From what?"

"How about pirates?"

The merc huffed and said, "Pirates? Do they really cost us that much?"

"Pretty close," Mountie said, finally breaking his silence.

The merc rolled his eyes.

"OK, pirates can be a problem for some of the corporations, but not everyone. Not for Fastblend."

"Where?"

"Fastblend. My home. We've been chartered for 11 years now, and you Feddies bleed us dry."

"Isn't that a PEG planet?" Mountie asked.

"PEG is on the planet, but we don't belong to them. We're pioneers from Avery's World."

"And did Avery's World pay for the terraforming?" Mountie asked.

"Well, no. We asked PEG to help out."

"And they did this out of the goodness of their hearts?"

"No, of course not," the merc conceded.

"How much?" Mountie asked.

"35% of GPP for 45 years," the merc said, much subdued.

"Ha! More than the Federation! And for longer!" JJ crowed.

"But that was our choice, and they did the terraforming. You Feddies just stepped in to demand your cut after doing nothing."

"And that justifies you invading a Federation planet?" JJ asked.

"You're freezing accounts, you've landed Marines and FCDC troops on our planets, so we had to open up another front to relieve the pressure," the merc said, sounding to JJ like he was spouting an existing party line.

"Fuck your sanctimonious bullshit. You have to destroy villages to 'relieve pressure?'

"Jasper, what's the name of your village again?"

"Donkerboek."

"Yeah, Donkerbroek," JJ said, stumbling a little over the name. "Gone, destroyed. All the women and children disappeared."

"I didn't destroy any village," the merc said, fear appearing back in his eyes. "I didn't kill any women and children."

"So, who did? The Star Fairies?"

"I don't know. But the Willamette Brigade, we don't do anything like that. We follow the Harbin Accords—just like you're supposed to."

"How can you follow something you haven't even signed? You're rebels!"

"Doesn't matter, we follow it. We don't kill non-combatants."

JJ had seen what was left of Jasper's village. Someone sure had flattened it, and it sure as hell wasn't the Marines. That left only one other force.

"Uh, Mountie. I may not be a professional soldier, but I'm thinking that we might want to move on. Maybe this merc's friends are going to come around to see what just happened," Jasper said.

"Hoowah! You're right," Mountie said. "We need to move out."

"What about him, sir?" JJ asked, pointing at the merc who went completely still.

JJ knew the rules of the Harbin Accords, and he knew you couldn't execute a uniformed prisoner. But he was angry, angrier than he thought possible, and if the lieutenant ordered him to do so, he'd put a .30 cal slug from his Prokov right through the traitor's forehead.

Mountie hesitated as he thought it over, then stood up and walked to where Jasper had placed the merc's gear. He rifled through the pouches, took out the magazines, and pocketed them. He picked up the merc's Gescard and held it out to the other two. JJ shook his head, but Jasper reached out and took it, slinging it on his back, but keeping Sergeant Go's M90 at the ready.

"We leave him. Ziptie his legs and put his canteen beside him with the nipple extended. Someone will find him, even if it takes a few days."

The merc seemed about to say something; then discretion probably took over and he remained silent.

JJ didn't know how he felt about the lieutenant's decision. This was the man who had killed his sergeant. Killing him wouldn't bring the sergeant back, but it would fill at least part of the human need for revenge. On the other hand, he wasn't sure if he could kill a man in cold blood like that. And with the lieutenant's decision, JJ was not going to be a war criminal.

JJ got out another ziptie and bound the merc's feet. He pulled out the nipple of the man's canteen, then placed it next to him, but just out of reach. Call it petty, but he'd make the man squirm a little if he wanted to drink.

The lieutenant scribbled something on a piece of contact plastisheet with his fingertip, then dropped in on the merc's lap.

"What's that, sir?" JJ asked, puzzled.

"A receipt. I've got one energy bar left, so I've just sent Jasper to take some of the rations from the second truck."

JJ looked at the lieutenant in amazement.

He's leaving a freaking receipt?

"Food and water are Cat 1 supplies," the lieutenant said when he saw JJ's expression.

The Harbin Accords didn't just cover treatment of prisoners. It was intended to be as extensive a set of "rules of war" as possible. JJ had forgotten from bootcamp training that Cat 1 supplies couldn't be confiscated from prisoners. As a peacetime Marine, there had never been a need to remember that. It still seemed stupid, rules or not. The truck looked full of food rats, and there was only one prisoner, someone who they would be abandoning.

Still, regs were regs, and JJ thought officers could be rather anal about them sometimes.

"Roger, that, sir. Got it."

JJ checked the merc one more time, pulling on the zipties. He avoided looking at the mound that marked Sergeant Go's grave.

"OK, let's move out," the lieutenant said when Jasper returned, arms loaded with half-a-dozen ration packs.

He pointed to the west. They'd been heading north when they'd spotted the trucks, but if the merc was going to be left alive, a bit of misdirection was in order.

"I didn't kill any women or children," the merc said in a low voice as JJ moved to take point. "I swear I didn't."

JJ didn't know whether to believe the man or not. In the long run, it probably mattered, but in the short term, the three of them had to get to friendly forces. With his thumb on his M90's safety, he stepped off into the woods.

Chapter 18

Jasper

The smell reached out to the three as they wended their way through the trees. JJ was still on point, and his body was tense as he carefully pushed forward. Jasper followed, the smell of smoke and explosives tearing him back to Koltan's Hill four days ago. He was almost overwhelmed as the sounds, heat, and smells of that fight washed over him. He faltered and had to put a hand up on a tree trunk to keep from falling.

"You OK, Jasper?" Mountie whispered from behind him.

Get it together, old man, he told himself.

"Aye-yah, I'm fine," he said, taking a deep breath and trying to clear his mind.

JJ suddenly stopped, holding up a fist, the signal to freeze. Jasper put his thumb on the safety of Sergeant Go's M90, outwardly ready for anything, but his thoughts darting around his skull like a songbird in a cage. He didn't know what was ahead of them, but his imagination was running wild. Surely it couldn't be that bad.

In a way, he was right. It wasn't *that* bad—it was worse.

JJ turned to look past Jasper and whispered to Mountie, "We've got a house up there, or what used to be a house."

"Anyone alive?" Mountie asked.

"I see a body, but nothing else. Local, not merc."

"We've got to check for survivors," Mountie said. "Move forward, but high alert."

JJ nodded, and step after slow step, advanced. Jasper followed, and as he passed a copse of laurel, got his first view of the small settlement. There had been four buildings in the farm, three of which were now piles of debris, tendrils of smoke rising from hotspots. The layout made it clear—this was a typical independent farm, straight from the Wal-Lotte catalog. Not all agriculture on Nieuwe Utrecht was tubes and hydroponic shelves. There were more than a few dirt farmers growing a wide variety of crops for both local consumption and export. The "farm-in-a-box," between its price and the attractive financing options, was one of the cheapest ways for a free citizen to start a farm. With the local government giving 20-hectare freehold claims to anyone who would establish a farm, thousands of immigrants to the planet had done just that.

And the man who'd done that was lying face-first between the barn and chemical shed—which was the only one of the four buildings left undamaged. His attempt at making a place for himself on the planet had been cut short. As Jasper followed JJ out of the embracing cover of the trees and into the compound, he couldn't help staring at the man. He knew he should be watching for mercs, but his eyes were locked on the body. JJ knelt, touched the man's neck, and shook his head.

The man looked young, maybe 25 years old or so. He had on work boots and tan yodzhis, another Wall-Lotte staple. His shirt was a simply black denim, but with white and red embroidered flowers covering the back.

Jasper almost threw up when he realized they were not white and red flowers; the red was from the young man's blood. Several rents showed where rounds had passed completely through his chest and out his back.

Still grasped in his right hand was a long-handled shovel. Jasper could picture the man, shovel raised, trying to protect his farm, and being cut down for his impertinence.

"You should have just let them go," Jasper whispered. "Your buildings, your crops, they weren't worth your life."

Out past the small farmhouse, the bulk of the farmers 20 hectares was planted with what looked to be various vegetables, only now breaking through the soil. The farmer would never see those come to full growth and yield their bounty.

"Lieutenant, come here!" JJ shouted from where he'd walked around the demolished farmhouse.

Jasper hurried over, and when he saw what JJ was standing over, recoiled back.

Because of his young age, Jasper had assumed that the farmer was single. Most young immigrants were, and they only married when they had enough credit to support a family. This young man was an exception.

Four bodies were laid out in a row beside the house, all face down. One was an adult woman, her checked dress torn and bloody. One arm was over the back of an infant. The top of the baby's head was a bloody mess. Next to the baby were the small figures of two children. The first was a boy, possibly five years old. He had on a miniature version of his dad's yodzhis, the tan color stained with soot and blood. His black denim shirt might have had embroidery as well, but Jasper couldn't see for sure. The last body was a burnt corpse, withered, blackened arms reaching up as if beseeching for a savior. Jasper couldn't tell if it was male or female.

Jasper immediately fell to his knees and vomited up the Tenner rations he'd eaten two hours ago. His throat burned with gastric juices as he heaved, his body spasming. Images of his granddaughter, Amee, reaching out to him for help while a merc shot her in the head invaded his thoughts.

"Fucking mercs! No, they don't kill women and children!" JJ almost spat out.

Jasper felt a hand on his shoulder. Mountie said nothing, but his mere presence was a help. Jasper drive-heaved twice more, then wiping his lips and taking a deep breath, stood back up. Mountie handed him his canteen, and Jasper gratefully took a swig, swished the water in his mouth, and spit it out before taking another swig and swallowing.

"Take your time," Mountie said. "It's pretty rough."

"Was it the mercs?" Jasper asked him.

"I don't know. Probably, I mean. This is still their AO."

"Could we, I mean the Federation, have we ever done that?" he asked, pointing toward the bodies but refusing to look.

Mountie's eyes clouded over as he said, "I'm a pilot, and the Navy's got big ships that have bombarded planets before. It's one of the burdens, to know civilians suffer in war. They always have."

"But like that? I mean, they were executed. One was burned," Jasper almost pleaded.

"It could have happened. Probably has happened somewhere. But if I ever find someone who's done that, I'm not waiting for a court martial or trial. I'll blow their fucking brains out."

Jasper didn't want to look again, but something beyond his control twisted his head until he could see the four bodies. No wonder the farmer had stood his ground. He had far more than a few buildings and some equipment to protect. He had his life there in those four sad bodies—just as Jasper had his family to protect. He looked up to the Grangers, hoping that his wife and grandkids had made it through, hoping he could find them.

"We've got company!" JJ shouted, rushing past them. "Get back into the trees!"

Down the road, Jasper caught movement. Some kind of armored vehicle was emerging from around a bend out beyond the farmed fields and was heading their way. Mountie pulled Jasper around as he took off in a sprint.

Jasper took one more look over his shoulder as he bolted for cover. He couldn't do anything for this poor family, but he hoped he could still do something for Keela and the grandkids. He was tired of playing soldier-boy. He needed to find and protect his own family.

Chapter 18

Mountie

The Marine Viper's vulcan spewed out 30mm kinetics, chewing up the road and destroying at least three vehicles before it inverted and flew upside-down over the trees, immediately disappearing from sight.

"Get some," Mountie said as JJ high-fived Jasper.

The Viper was not nearly the bird his own Lizard was, and the Lizard was low-man on the Navy fleet's totem pole, but it still packed a powerful punch. It was not invulnerable, though. Mountie didn't spoil the mood of the others by mentioning that the SOP for Vipers was to hit in two-plane formations. He also knew that the Marine battalion had four Vipers attached to it, so if only one had hit the merc column, that didn't bode well for the fates of the other three.

It had taken much of the shorter Nieuwe Utrecht day for the three of them to make their way north of the destroyed farmhouse to the foot of the Granger Range. For most of the day, movement had been decent as they walked silently, the image of the dead kids etched into Mountie's mind. They'd reached Baseline Road after another hour, but merc traffic was much heavier on it than they'd expected. Something was up, and the mercs were all over the place. Mountie knew that there were probably Tenners still searching for them, and now, with what looked to be at least a regiment getting ready for an operation, Mountie felt trapped.

Like the other two, he'd reveled in the Viper attack, but he wanted to get past the mercs and through the range to Federation forces. If there was a big merc push coming, he needed to be in the air supporting the Marines. The carrier had an unassigned Basilisk, and if he could catch a ride to the ship, he could power that Lizard up and get back into the fight.

"What do you think those trucks had in them?" Portillo asked from where they lay glassing the burning trucks.

As if on cue, one of the trucks erupted in a huge fireball, knocking down the mercs near it and sending others scrambling for cover. A few moments, later, the shock wave crossed the intervening klick and brushed past the three men.

"I'm guessing ammunition?" Jasper said, stating the obvious.

"And I'm guessing you're right," Lance Corporal Portillo said.

"I wonder why they just sat there, though," Jasper said.

Mountie had wondered the same thing. The three of them had come up to a small creek that meandered through low marshy ground just before the Viper had launched its run. When first spotted, Mountie had thought that the trucks and half-tracs were just making a halt, but now, he'd have thought they would have scattered. When the ammo truck blew, it had even set two more trucks on fire. Mountie watched mercs rushing to extinguish while the other vehicles remained in place.

"Let's sit here for a few moments and watch," Mountie said as something niggled at the back of his brain. "We can't really cross the road now anyway."

They might be a klick from the gathering of trucks, but between the creek lowland and the clearing around the road, they could be spotted from quite a ways off should they try to bolt across it.

Mountie was glad he had Sergeant Go's binos. His SERE kit had a small loupe he could have used like an old-time wet-water pirate, but Go's compact Zeiss Conquest 4s were amazing, bringing everything into sharp focus. The fires on the other two trucks were quickly put out, and as the mercs regrouped, they began to act as coolies, hauling the cargo out of sight up the far slope. Some of the boxes were heavy, with two mercs hauling each one. The Zeiss binos were excellent, but Mountie couldn't make out the writing on the boxes.

"Here comes four more," Portillo said.

Mountie spun around to see four trucks coming down the road. There had to be 100 meters between each one, and Mountie wondered why. One-hundred meters was far more than normal, but on an improved road like Baseline, a Lizard or even Viper didn't care if it was 100 or 300. The trucks rumbled past on the other side of the creek, just 150 meters from the three men.

"It's ammunition," Jasper said suddenly.

"What do you mean?" Portillo asked.

"They're storing ammo. Look at how heavy the trucks are loaded, and look at the mercs carrying it. You guys said that something big is up, right? They're going to make a big push, right?"

"Yeah," Portillo said. "They're going to try and hit us with something big."

"But we're hitting them with air, right? We just saw them lose a truck full of some sort of ammo. So, they have to protect it until they make their move. There're lots of caves in the Grangers. I'm guessing they're staging their ammo in one of the caves so they don't lose it all before they attack."

Hell, he's right! How could I have missed that!

"How big are these caves?" he asked.

"Some are small, some are big enough to store whatever you want."

"What about right there?"

"Don't know. Like I told you, I haven't been here before. But if they are unloading there, I'd bet they've found some good caves."

Mountie considered that for a moment.

"Where do you think the trail is for Spirit Lake?" he asked.

"Spirit Lake?" Portillo asked. "What's that?"

"I think over there," Jasper said, pointing to the next peak to the east. "I think that's Mount Rand, and so the trail would be just on the near side of it."

"What trail?" Portillo asked.

Mountie ignored him. Initially, he'd planned on keeping Jasper with them until they reached Baseline Road, then letting him go on his way. With all the increased activity, though, he was sure that the major avenues through the Grangers would be blocked. Jasper had told him that the trail to Spirit Lake ran completely through the range to the plateau beyond, and given the size of the trail and the poisonous air around the lake itself, it was doubtful that the mercs either knew of it, or if they did, they considered it passable. But if they climbed up and around the lake itself, they could make the trek, with or without Jasper's family. Mountie hoped they were there waiting, but given what they'd gone through themselves to cross the valley, he wasn't holding out much hope that a bunch of women and children could have managed it.

Mountie snuck a sideways glance at Jasper, who was back to watching the unloading of the trucks through his old SERE loupe. He knew his job was to get back to where he could fly again, and he knew that Jasper was driven to find his family. But Sergeant Go had stressed Clause 4. Sure, Mountie was a pilot, and that was how he was trained. But more than that, he was a sailor, a member of the Federation military. His real mission was to advance the Federation cause and protect it from adversary. If the mercs were, in fact, storing their ammo in a cave somewhere, then his mission should be to destroy that, be that from a Lizard or any other way at his disposal.

"Lance Corporal Portillo, do you have anything in your engineer bag of tricks left that could blow some ammo?"

"Huh? I mean, you want to blow it up?"

No, that's why I asked you! he thought, but instead said, "What do you have that could do it?"

"I'm not sure, sir. Let me look."

Mountie watched as Portillo rolled to his side, pulling his kit in front of him.

"I've got my toads, but they'll just burn, not detonate anything," he muttered to himself, his eyes scrunched together in concentration. "Ten, no eleven detonators and five E-22's, but those have to be attached. I guess if I could get access, that would work . . ."

Over Portillo's head, Jasper looked at Mountie, raising his eyes in a question. Mountie knew the older man was anxious to get up the trail to Spirit Lake, but he held out a hand and shushed him. Jasper didn't look happy, but he didn't say anything.

It took Portillo five minutes, but finally, he looked up at Mountie and said, "Sir, I've got detonators and a few charges like some C10 that could set off most munitions, and with enough of an initial detonation, we could blow a shitload of whatever they have."

Mountie felt a jolt of excitement and opened his mouth to reply when Portillo interrupted him with, "But the problem is, they gotta be either inserted into the explosives or placed right next to the munitions, and even right beside, say, a 175 shell, there's a good chance nothing will happen.

"Now, I've got a lot that can set off their detonators, either their engineer gear or the fuze caps of their shells, but no one stores those near the munitions. Even the mercs can't be that stupid. Powerpacks, detonators, and munitions are always stored separately. If you're thinking of them over there, I'm betting they put each into a different cave. The powerpacks would take much space, the detonators more, but it's the munitions that'll take the biggest cave."

"So, you don't have anything that, you know, you can shoot in a cave opening and bring the place down?"

"Not with me, sir. We were on a bridge mission, not a bunker. A MAPAW would work, if it actually reached the munitions and hit them, but I don't have one."

The Man-Packed Assault Weapon was basically an all-purpose direct-fire artillery piece carried by grunts, and if Portillo said it could work, so be it. But since none of them were packing a MAPAW, he might as well wish for his Lizard and a Snipe. The missile was armed with a thermobaric warhead, a *big* thermobaric warhead.

He didn't have a Snipe, but he knew someone who did. If he could just get word back to the airfield, they could get a Lizard in the air. Heck, if they wanted to risk a destroyer, they could bring one into high orbit and drop a Cowboy on the site. A ton of bomb penetrated pretty far with a lot of force—the warhead that detonated was sometimes more of an aftershock. His own comms were shot, but Portillo still had his. They just hadn't powered up knowing that doing so would bring down a world of hurt on their heads.

But something had to be done. Mountie was not the hero-type. He'd gone into battle fully expecting to come back home. Even when coming in winchester on the hill, he hadn't thought that he could get shot down. That happened to other people, not him.

Blowing the mercs' ammo could make a huge impact. There was no way all of their ammo was being stored in some cave, but there were enough trucks to show that a good percentage was, and if that was gone, not only could it save lives, but it could turn the tide of the battle.

Before he could talk himself out of it, he held out a hand and said, "Portillo, give me your comms."

"Sir?"

"Your comms. Give them to me."

"But sir, if you power up, they'll have us."

"I've got to get word back to the squadron. We've got Snipes with thermobarics that can set all of the mercs' munitions off. This is too important.

"Listen, I want you two to head east. You've got to take Jasper to a trailhead he knows about. Listen to him. It will get you over the range and into what's Federation-held territory. At least I hope it still is."

"What, you're just going to sit there until the Tenners drop a missile on your head?" Jasper asked, sounding angry.

"No, I'm not going to 'sit there,'" Mountie replied. "I'm going to send the message, then run like hell. But I want you out of the way, first. They'll still probably come running, so you'll have more of them on your asses soon enough."

"You might not have enough time to come running, sir. A Nine-line is going to take some time to get transmitted."

Don't I know it.

"I'll be quick, don't worry. So now, I want you two to make your way east. See that half-fallen tree down there?" he asked pointing to where a tree leaned out over the creek about 300 meters upstream.

"I'll be watching. Once I see you, I'll go ahead and send the Nine-line. If you see me wave my hand, run. If you see me get up and run, run. I'll catch up to you somehow. Understand?"

"I'm guessing there's no way I can talk you out of this?" Jasper asked.

Mountie almost snapped that the mission was far more important than the risk of more mercs chasing them, but the concern in Jasper's eyes stopped those words stillborn. It was obvious that the man was concerned for him, not that he himself would be in any greater danger.

"No, I wish you could, but it has to be done," he said instead.

"Well, that's that," Portillo said.

Jasper started to slide back deeper into the trees, but he stopped, then reached out to hug the surprised pilot.

"Run fast, Mountie," he whispered in his ear.

Portillo watched, then held out a hand, saying, "Balls, sir. Big balls." Then as Mountie took the hand, added, "Pretty impressive for a sailor."

"Fuck you . . . *JJ*," Mountie said, squeezing the Marine's hand.

JJ's eyes lit up as he replied, "Get some . . . *Mountie*, sir," before he turned and scrambled back.

Mountie almost laughed out loud. They'd been together for four days, and it took this shit to break the ice. Then the import of what he'd decided hit him. He wasn't sure he could get a Nine-line out before the mercs responded. And even if they didn't, he'd be far more valuable as a forward air controller than fleeing wildly through the forest. He didn't want to face it, but in the back of his mind, he knew he needed to stay.

He settled down, binos to his eyes, switching from the merc offload to the leaning tree. It seemed to take forever, and he was beginning to wonder if they'd misunderstood him when he realized there was an extra lump at the base of the tree that wasn't there before. He increased the zoom, until he could barely make out Portillo's—JJ's—outline. His armor might be all messed up, but even the pattern on the PFG cloth made him difficult to see.

Mountie gave JJ a slight wave, then turned over to his back, JJ's PCD[8] in hand. He switched the selector to open circuit, no frequency hopping. Anyone on a standard Federation frequency would be able to pick up the transmission. He powered up the PCD, took a deep breath, and depressed the transmit button.

"All Federation forces, this is Lieutenant Caster . . ."

---

[8] PCD: Personal Communications Device

The PCD indicated a steady green ready. There were none of the red indicators the showed any signals reaching the circuits.

He depressed the transmit again and said, "All Federation . . ." then stopped.

The green indicator showed that the PCD had power, and it was ready to transmit. A red one would mean that the PCD was actually getting something out into the comms circuits.

What the hell?

He switched to the diagnostics, and immediately the readout went crazy. The PCD was being blanketed by heavy jamming. He couldn't communicate. He looked up, half-expecting to see incoming, but then he realized that if he couldn't reach the net, then the mercs had nothing to see. He couldn't reach Federation forces, but that meant the Tenners still couldn't see him, either.

Mountie was washed over with a wave that was part relief, part anger. He wasn't about to eat a merc arty battery, but the mission was stillborn. He tried the comms twice more before giving up. Sliding forward, he held out a hand and waved the other two back. A hand rose out of the shapeless lump that was JJ, thumb up. A moment later, the shape melted back away from the tree.

Ten minutes later, Jasper and JJ crept up beside him.

"What happened?" JJ asked.

"Jammed. No comms."

"Shit. So now what, sir?"

"I don't know. Maybe if we can push forward fast enough, we can get out of the jamming and try again. Jasper, how much time to get through the trail?"

"I think about seven hours in daylight. It'll be hard to make that time at night, though."

"From the tempo, I think whatever they had planned is going to kick off before then," Mountie said. "I don't know. I don't see an option but to just push on. That sucks, though. Right here, we could have done something."

"Wait," Jasper said.

He seemed to be warring with himself, which didn't make any sense. He should be happy that they were going to be back on the move to the lake without drawing any more attention to themselves.

"You mentioned thermobarics. If you had, say, a source of a Cat 4 substance, like ammonium nitrate, could that work?" he asked.

"Well, sure," JJ said. "But it would take a couple of hundred kilos, minimum, and it would still have to be fairly close to set off any munitions."

"And with HPP?"

"Hydrogen Penta-Peroxide? Add that to the mix, and you're down to 50 kilos. Why?"

Jasper took a deep breath as if considering what he was going to say next. "And with an accelerating oxidizer? Like a Patterson Arms V60?"

"Shit, Jasper, like, uh, like Mountie says, you might as well wish for a Snipe. A V60 is a military-grade accelerant."

"But if you had it. All of that?"

"If you had all of that, and if you could contain it somehow until needed, I'd guess that ten kilos of ammonium nitrate—refined ammonium nitrate—would do the trick. Depending on the munitions, it would still have to be within five or ten meters, but it could work."

"Why do you want to know, Jasper?" Mountie asked, wondering just where the militiaman was going with this.

"Because I think I know where we can get them."

Chapter 19

JJ

Stepping back into the burned-out farm was hard, and JJ felt the anger rise within him. The merc they'd let go was glib, and he tried to make excuses for being a traitor, but here was hard proof that the Tenner movement was evil. This poor farmer was killed and his family executed, and for what? What tactical purpose did that serve?

He stopped before he reached the women and children, turned to Jasper, and said, "Now what?"

"Over there," Jasper said, pointing to the one building left standing.

JJ was in a foul mood as he marched up to the door, which was secured with a large mechanical lock. He gave it a few tugs. It was very low tech, but it was massive. It wouldn't give in to a couple of butt-strokes from his M90. JJ thought this was all a wild goose-chase, and he wanted to get it over with, so he pulled out a toad to burn through the lock.

"No!" Jasper shouted, reaching to grab JJ's hand. "If I'm right, you could blow us up where we stand."

"Bullshit," JJ said.

"Trust me."

Jasper had proven to be a pretty good guy, and JJ knew that some fertilizers could be made into explosives, but what else could be on a farm? He wasn't buying Jasper's assertion that the place would have any military-grade accelerant.

He shook his head, then turned and gave the lock a tentative rap with this rifle butt. It bounced but nothing more.

"So how are we going to open it?" he asked.

Jasper was using the merc's Gescard as his prime weapon with Sergeant Go's M90 slung on his back. He dropped the magazine, checked the chamber, and walked right up to the door. The Gescard was a heavier weapon than the M90, and much sturdier, but JJ didn't think that would make much of a difference. The lock was just too massive.

Jasper nodded, then lifted the Gescard, butt high, and brought it crashing down . . . on the hinge on the side of the door, not the lock itself. It bent, and with the second stroke, it broke right off.

Shit! And I'm supposed to be the engineer?

He started to step in to finish the job but then thought better of it. He was going to let Jasper whale away with his Gescard. The M90 was a fine weapon, but if he knocked the mag rings out of whack, it became just a large paperweight.

While Jasper went to work on the second hinge, JJ turned back to look at Mountie, who had a bemused expression on his face. JJ felt the heat of his face reddening.

It took Jasper about a minute to knock off the three hinges and for the door to hang free. JJ reached under Jasper, and with the two of them yanking, they pulled the door back and away. Jasper looked inside, spotting several barrels with NH_4NO_3-C^2 on the side. The NH_4NO_3 for the ammonium nitrate, the C^2 the commercially accepted sign for "molecularly concentrated" where the military simply used the term "refined." There was enough in there to blow a good-sized building away—if it could be gotten to the target. There wasn't any way the mercs would just let them merrily roll barrels into the caves.

Various chemicals cluttered five shelves that ran along one of the walls of the shed. There were more varieties on the shelves than a Monsanto-Bayer chemist would have. JJ scanned the shelves before spotting some blue vacpacs.

"Here's your hydrogen penta-peroxide," he said, pulling out a pack. "That'll help, but not enough. We can maybe make a few grenades, but a few grenades won't set off any munitions."

He turned to see Jasper rooting around the back of the shed.

"It's not enough, Jasper. It was a good shot, but we've got to get out of here," he said, acutely aware of the road that ran by the farm.

He looked to Mountie, who was standing in the door, and lifted both hands, palm up, while shrugging his shoulders. Mountie raised one finger and mouthed, "Wait."

"I got it!" Jasper finally shouted.

He waved JJ over and pointed to the low black box he'd just uncovered.

"Is that a cocoon box?" JJasked moving close to see.

"Sure is," Jasper said, grinning ear-to-ear.

"OK, that's something."

Cocoon boxes were containers with small dampening fields. No electronic pulses could get through to whatever was inside the box, nor extreme changes in temperatures or pressure shocks. They were used to protect volatile substances. He didn't understand why a farmer would have one of them, but its very presence was promising.

"Is it locked?" he asked.

Cocoon boxes never had modern locks, only mechanical. Jasper smiled as he twisted the handle, and with a whump of released air, the door slid open.

"As I figured," Jasper said, reaching in and pulling out an olive-drab seal-pack. He handed it to JJ, who immediately saw the circle-P of Patterson Arms. Under that, his eyes locked onto the V60.

"Holy shit. This is the real deal," he said, carrying the pack outside into the direct sunlight.

Mountie took it from him, turning the thing over and hefting it.

"How . . . why . . . I mean, what is it doing here?" JJ asked.

"Saving credits. A little pinch of V60 makes the ammonium nitrate go a lot further on the crops."

"But it's dangerous, hellaciously dangerous!"

"If a few credits can make the difference between going red or black, and red means your family isn't going to eat, you go with dangerous."

"How do you get it?" Mountie asked.

"Really? You think this isn't available on the black market?" Jasper said as if talking to a child. "A large shipment came in last year, along with the recipe of how to use it with our fertilizers. It was all over the local undernet, so no big secret."

"I guess I've lived a sheltered life," Mountie answered, handing the pack back to JJ.

JJ had grown up on Nuevo Oaxaca, and he knew a thing or two about the black market, but it still boggled his mind to think that a farmer was sitting on enough V60 to stock a regiment.

"So, do you think you can use this?" Jasper asked.

"Theoretically, yes. But we have to have a way to make it. I don't see a machine shop and lab sitting around here for us to use."

"What do you need?"

"Well, a casing, for starters. We can't just mix this in a bucket and throw it at someone. We've got to contain the pressure long enough for the reaction to take place. We need a detonator, which I've got, but it has to be fixed in position."

"OK, let's do it," Jasper insisted.

"I just told you I don't see a machine shop or lab around here, Jasper," JJ said, looking to Mountie as if confused as to why Jasper didn't seem to understand.

"We don't have labs and most of us don't have machine shops, yet we get things done. Let's see what's around here that we can use."

"This place? It's destroyed," JJ said, pushing back the images of the dead children that tried to force their way into his thoughts.

"You think you can find something here?" Mountie asked Jasper, his voice tinged with doubt.

"We won't know until we try," Jasper said, then to JJ, "What kind of casing do you need? What size?"

"I'm not sure. Say, about like this," he said, holding his hands about 50 centimeters apart.

"Then let's see what we can come up with. Hold on a moment," Jasper said, leaving the shed.

"Where're you going?" JJ asked, following him out.

Jasper didn't answer but headed towards the fields, making a wide detour to miss where the children's bodies lay. He raised a hand to his eyes, scanning the field. Spotting something, he took off across the emerging crops, JJ and Mountie in tow.

Up ahead, at the side of the field, was a red tractor, the big white "W" of "Walker Agricultural Machines" on the side. JJ had seen the huge corporate harvesters on the holos, immense beasts that could harvest hectares of crops in hours, taking in full plants and shitting out neatly packaged products ready for shipment. In the shade of the trees at the edge of the field, this Walker must have been from the bare minimum school of farming. Barely two meters long, it didn't even have a seat for the operator.

Jasper made a beeline to the Walker, hurrying, but taking care to step over each row of crops, avoiding the plants themselves.

Kind of moot now, Jasper, JJ thought with the farmer who owned these fields laying dead behind them. *He probably doesn't even realize he's doing it.*

Still, JJ followed suit, half-hopping over each row trying not to trample on anything. Jasper probably had more practice doing that because he was already pouring over the Walker by the time JJ and Mountie arrived.

"Look for the controls," Jasper said. "I'd like to take this back to the chemshed."

"Just push it."

Jasper gave JJ a condescending look before saying, "This is a PT Manzo 2, no controls."

"Then how do you work the thing?" Mountie asked.

"It's got a decent AI, so it's self-serving. But to instruct it, you need the remote. It's not here, so he . . . he probably had it on him or had it in the barn.

"Do you need it?" JJ asked, figuring it would be up to him to search the now-bloating body of the farmer.

"No. This is what I wanted to show you," Jasper said, pulling up a panel and revealing a 60-centimeter-long cylinder. "Will this do?"

"I don't know. What's in it? Methane?"

"Glucose. Methane's specific density's not high enough to be that efficient, and unless you've got livestock, harder to come by out here. No, this is an A4 cylinder, big enough for 72 kilos of glucose, and that will keep the Walker running for a long time."

"I've never seen a glucose engine," Mountie said, his voice piqued with interest. "We don't use them."

"That's because you have all sorts of fuel and energy sources you need, and you don't need a FASS to keep the output high."

"FASS?"

"Oh, a flexible asymmetrical solid-state supercapacitor. Tricky buggers to keep up, and expensive. I can't see how they would be practical for military work, but out here in the sticks, glucose is one of the easiest fuels we can produce."

"How do you produce it?" JJ asked, interested despite his initial skepticism.

"Over there," Jasper said, pointing to the far side of the field. Those are genmodded sugar beets, but some people use cane, or melons. Dates, too, but not around here. Back in the barn, there're probably the remains of the still used to make it.

"But will this work as a casing?" he asked JJ.

"Maybe. Do you know its volume?" JJ answered, stepping up to thump on the cylinder with his forefinger nail.

"It's an A4, so just over 42-thousand cubic centimeters."

JJ tried to run the numbers though his head. Without the V60, no. With the V60, maybe.

He said 72 kilos of glucose, but that seems like a lot. What's the density of that? And with the ammonium nitrate, can I fit 10 kilos . . .

After a few moments, he looked up at Jasper, then Mountie, and said, "I don't know for sure, but maybe. It'll be close."

"There's the spare underneath. Can we do it with two?" Jasper asked.

"That's not the issue. This is one of those cases where two-plus-two doesn't equal four. We need to get the 10 kg in one container to create a big enough shock wave."

He looked up at Mountie and asked, "Well, sir? Do we try?"

"Nothing to lose, so of course, we try."

Jasper released two clamps and started to pick up the cylinder, but JJ pushed him out of the way and picked it up.

That's why he wanted to drive the tractor closer! This thing weighs a ton!

It really wasn't terribly heavy, but without a handle, the round cylinder was difficult to grasp. JJ managed to carry it out of the field, but not without crushing flat more than a few of the crops.

"So how do we open this?" he asked.

"We have to vent it, first. It's under a lot of pressure."

Jasper brought the small screen on the side of the fuel tank to life, then punched in some commands. JJ couldn't hear anything, but a sickly-sweet aroma filled the air, and he could see the pressure numbers fall. When they equalized, Jasper flipped a recessed lever in the top of the cylinder, tilted the bottom up, and started pouring out a thick, syrupy liquid.

"It's OK to dump it on here on the grass?" Mountie asked.

"It's been processed and manipulated to increase the power output, but basically, it's still just plant sugars," he said, sticking a finger in the flow and then bringing it up to his mouth where he took a lick. "I wouldn't do this too much—it's no longer pure. But just a taste won't hurt you."

He tipped the cylinder to JJ, but he refused, seeing no benefit in taking any sort of chances. The Marines used fuel cells, biodiesel, magcells, and a host of other power sources, but none of them were safe to eat.

"Mountie, can you look in the chemshed and get a blue glass container of dichloromethane? It should be about a liter-sized, with a roaring lion on the front," he asked as he tipped the cylinder higher.

The flow of the glucose fuel slowed and finally stopped. Jasper looked inside, then reached in, twisted, and pulled out a small black rectangle.

"The FASS," he told JJ as he wiped it on his trousers and slipped it into a pocket. You won't need it."

Mountie came back, gingerly holding a blue glass bottle that he handed to Jasper.

"Step back," Jasper said as he carefully poured some of the solvent into it, holding his head back out of the way of any fumes. He twirled the tank around, then tipped it over away from the other two. As soon as it was empty, he dragged the cylinder back a couple of meters, away from the smoking mess on the ground.

"OK, JJ, here you go. How's this?"

JJ cautiously approached, his eyes glancing back to the hissing mess that Jasper had poured out.

"Is it safe?"

"Just don't stick your nose in and take a sniff right now. But in a few moments, it will all have evaporated."

JJ touched the outside of the cylinder, expecting it to feel hot. To his surprise, it wasn't. Tipping it to look at the open top, he could see that the walls of the cylinder were much thicker than he had assumed them to be.

Shit!

"What's the max pressure these can hold?"

"I'm not sure. Typically, they're pressurized to 0.2 kilobars, but with a safety cushion? I don't know. I've never heard of one bursting. That's good, right?"

"No, not at all," JJ said. "We can detonate the ammonium nitrate, and I'm sure it'll burst the tank, but probably in one spot," he said, putting a fist on one side of the tank, then whipping it away as he opened it, fingers splayed.

"A directional charge," Mountie said, nodding.

"That'll turn the cylinder into a rocket, shooting it who knows where. We need the container essentially to fall apart, all at once, so the blast wave propagates outwards in a nice, even sphere.

"Sorry, Jasper. It was a good idea, but this probably won't work."

Jasper took back the cylinder, turning it over, his brows furrowed in thought.

Finally, he looked up at JJ and asked, "What if we score it? Run several lines from top to bottom?"

He ran a finger along the cylinder, top to bottom, to trace what he meant.

"Well, yeah, that might work. But we're not going to be able to do much with our knives, now, will we? That's plastisteel, and as you said, there's no machine shop here."

A smile broke out on Jasper's face as he said, "Wait one."

He hurried over to the burnt barn as JJ looked to Mountie and said, "What's he doing now?"

"No idea, but let's see what he can come up with."

Jasper rooted around in the burnt ruin, kicking at debris and bending down to look at whatever he'd uncovered. It took him a couple of minutes before he shouted, then held up a disk of some sort in triumph.

He ran back to them, saying, "I've got it."

"OK, a circular blade, cerro-tungsten. That'll score the cylinder, but I don't see a saw to spin it."

"Oh, ye of little faith," he said, a broad smile on his face. "Follow me—with that," he added, pointing to the cylinder.

With a sigh, JJ picked it up. It was much, much lighter now, but he felt lost, not knowing what was going on. Every time he brought up a problem Jasper seemed to have some sort of answer. And if JJ wasn't mistaken, the militiaman was *enjoying* the moment.

Jasper ran back to the Walker, beating the other two, and pulled out the spare fuel cylinder, horsing it into the cradle. As JJ and Mountie approached, he held out a hand to stop them, then opened the engine compartment and pulled out a small lifting arm, the kind used to lift bundles.

JJ stood there for 20 minutes as Jasper, *humming* for God's sake, disconnected the drive belt, took out a pully housing, and with much hammering and pounding, jammed it into the end of the lifting arm.

"Hell, he's making a saw," Mountie said in awe.

He's right! JJ said, stepping forward to help.

Between the two of them, they managed to set up an ugly, but possibly working contraption.

"I thought you said we needed a remote," JJ said as the thought hit him.

"To drive it, aye-yah. But not to turn it on," Jasper told him as he started to attach the blade.

"Uh, let's see if it works, first, before we put that thing on," JJ said.

"Hah! Right on that. Well, then, here it goes!"

He pushed a red button, and the Walker immediately came to life. The belt drove the pully."

"It works!" JJ shouted just before the pully started to screech in protest. Jasper lunged for the stop button when with a snap, the pully broke off and flew away, almost hitting Mountie.

"Sorry about that!" Jasper shouted as he chased down the offending piece.

The two huddled over the pully and the crane arm, discussing what went wrong. After another ten minutes, the pully was mounted once again, and this time, when the engine was turned on, it ran smoothly.

"You ready?" JJ asked Jasper.

"Let's do it."

JJ felt adrenaline pumping through his body as Jasper pushed the start button. At the end of the lifting arm, the round saw blade started spinning.

"Ooh-fucking-rah!" he shouted, high-fiving Jasper.

Part of him tried to calm him down, to remind him that they were still behind enemy lines in pretty dire straits. But it had felt good to have his mind occupied for half-an-hour, focusing on simple engineering instead of walking point.

He rushed back to pick up the cylinder and brought it back under the spinning blade. Holding it up to the blade, he pressed it home, only to have it skitter off the blade and to the side. A cero-tungsten blade should have no problem with any normal plastisteel, and for a moment, JJ wondered if this was some sort of exotic material. But then he realized that the problem was that he wasn't holding it still. With a vise, it would be child's play.

Calling Mountie forward, and with a little experimentation, they managed to find a way to cut into the cylinder, scoring it a few millimeters deep. They made five lengthwise furrows, each one with about 15 score lines. It was ugly as sin with wavering lines, but it should work. With arms trembling—more from mental than physical exhaustion—JJ finally deemed it enough.

The three returned to the chemshed, the sweet smell of the glucose still heavy in the air—which was welcomed as it hid most of the underlying scent of decaying bodies.

JJ insisted on mixing the chemicals himself, with both Mountie and Jasper 20 meters away. The ammonium nitrate and HPP were harmless without a detonator, but he was worried about the V60. It wasn't kept in a cocoon box for nothing. JJ stripped naked to do the mix. He knew it was gross overkill, but he didn't want any possible emission that could set the V60 off.

To his surprise, he was able to stuff over 13 kilograms into the cylinder. If it detonated correctly, it should be able to set off any standard munitions within five or ten meters, and some of the more volatile at even greater distances.

Now he had a cylinder full of explosives, but the top was open. Luckily, it was a standard size opening, and JJ's E22's had sleeves that could be used to attach it to several munitions.

"Nice look," Mountie said as JJ came back to get dressed.

JJ considered giving him the finger, but nicknames aside, he was still a lieutenant. He finished dressing and went back to the cylinder. He pulled out an E22 and threaded into a CC ring. Satisfied that it was tight, he started to screw the entire detonator housing into the neck of the cylinder.

What the . . .?

The housing slipped right in. He pulled, and it slipped right out. Looking inside, he could see it wasn't grooved for screw connections.

"Jasper, what's this shit?" he called out.

Both Jasper and Mountie rushed forward.

"I can't screw this!" he said, frustration taking over.

"No, you need a tongue-in-slot fitting," Jasper said.

"Who the hell uses tongue-in-slot?" JJ asked, his voice rising.

"Walker Agricultural Machines does, for one."

"Well, the Marine Corps doesn't!"

"Calm down, JJ," Mountie said. "There's got to be some way to secure it, at least enough so we can use the bomb."

"No, we can't just 'secure it.' If the detonator blows before the cylinder breaks apart, it'll be the rocket I told you about. We need it to be stronger than the casing itself."

He'd been so pleased with himself, somehow making a viable device out of nothing, and now, to see it fail because Walker Fucking Agricultural Machines had their own proprietary connection, well, that was freaking ridiculous!

"Can't you attached it to the outside, then close off the opening with the top of it?" Mountie asked.

"No. The detonator can't penetrate the cylinder walls. It has to be attached in the opening."

"How strong does it have to be?" Jasper asked. "The connection."

"Fucking stronger than the rest of the casing. It cannot give out first," JJ shouted.

Jasper flinched, and JJ felt a twinge of guilt, but he couldn't calm down. All the frustrations of the last five days had pushed him to his breaking point. Sergeant Go would probably solve the problem, but he was dead, killed by a freaking truck driver, and now it was up to him. Only, he was at his wit's end.

Jasper spun around and ran off, and for a moment, JJ thought he'd driven the militiaman away. But Jasper ran into the chemshed.

"Get ahold of yourself, JJ. I can't have you losing it," Mountie said.

Mountie hadn't yelled, nor was there any obvious condemnation in his voice, but the tone of command was evident. It was the proverbial slap across the face.

He's right. Pull it together!

"Sorry, sir. I'm OK."

Jasper darted out of the shed, one hand held high with a tube of some sort in it. He ran back and handed the tube to JJ.

"Will this do?"

JJ looked at the label. It was "Buffalo Lock," a brand with which he was unfamiliar. But then the "molecular bonding" caught his attention. He turned it over, and in the product blurb, he read the magic word, "metals." Molecular bonding did not merely slap two surfaces together. The active agents "sunk" into each surface, passing through the molecular space before locking in. They didn't penetrate far, but the connections were extremely strong.

Different molecular bonding products worked on different materials. One for plastics might not work for ceramics. But this Buffalo Lock, this beautiful Buffalo Lock, was made for metallics. It would work!

JJ put an arm around the anxious Jasper's neck and pulled him in where he gave him a big kiss on the forehead.

"I was right. You're a gyver, the best fucking gyver I've met. Hell, yeah, this'll work!"

He released Jasper, who stumbled back, but with a smile on his face. Reading the instructions, he wiped down the detonator sleeve and inside the cylinder neck. Turning the nozzle to the right, he squeezed out a paste and applied it liberally to the sleeve. He was tempted to apply it to the neck as well, but he thought it prudent not to introduce any of it to the explosive mixture in the cylinder.

On second thought, with both hands occupied, he asked Jasper to reach into his engineer kit and pull out a pad pack. These had many uses, most for which they were not designed, from reheating a food-pack to being emergency toilet paper, but their main use was as padding when emplacing charges in structures. He walked Jasper through opening the pack, then stuffing three of them down the neck of the cylinder, creating a barrier between the mix and the detonator—and the Buffalo Lock.

With that ready, he thumbed over the nozzle lever and squeezed out the activator. He coated the paste, rubbing it in deep. He had limited time, but he couldn't afford a gap in the connection, so he checked twice that every square centimeter of the sleeve was covered with both the connecting paste and the activator. With a sure hand, he pushed the detonator home. An unbroken ring of Buffalo Lock gushed up and out. JJ didn't let go, holding the detonator firm for three minutes, twice the time required.

Slowly, he pulled back on the detonator. To his relief, it held firm. It had worked.

"Gentlemen," he said, laying the cylinder flat. "It seems we have ourselves here a thermobaric bomb. What say we go out now and blow up something?"

Chapter 20

Jasper

"So, any bright ideas?" Mountie asked as the three were back at their position with eyes on the target.

The sun had gone down before they'd made it back, and the lieutenant had said he'd hoped that would make it easy to slip in and set their bomb. But even without decent binos, Jasper could see that there were more mercs, if anything, working at a fevered pitch. He got the strong impression that they were rushing to finish the task before whatever was planned went down. For all he knew, a major Tenner operation could be just hours away.

He'd been pretty overjoyed when they'd managed to make the bomb. Evidently, though, none of them had actually thought through the mechanics of delivering it. The mercs running back and forth up there weren't going to let them march right up and leave it.

He glanced over at Mountie, wondering what the lieutenant was going to do. Jasper still felt guilty for allowing Mountie to go forward on his aborted suicide mission to call for air. It hadn't been his decision, but to watch the man calmly go to his death had been an awakening. He'd been so damned determined to get to Spirit Lake that nothing else had mattered. Then Mountie had shown him what sacrifice looked like. When he hadn't been able to send out his message, Jasper had been overjoyed. But he also realized he had to capitalize on that. Keela could wait—if she were even at the lake. Jasper had no proof that she was.

So, when he realized that they could make a home-made bomb, he'd hesitated only a moment before volunteering the information. And then to see it become a reality had filled him with satisfaction.

But it was all coming to naught unless they could figure out a way to get it inside the cave.

"What if we jump one of the mercs, take his uniform, and then just walk in?" JJ said.

"Harbin Accords, JJ. We can't put on an enemy's uniform," Mountie told him.

"Shit, sir. It's not like it'll matter, right?"

Jasper realized that JJ was saying someone would go into a cave, but not come back out. Both of his companions seemed willing to die to get this mission accomplished. He realized on an intellectual level that by doing so, many Marine lives would probably be saved. And Jasper understood the concept. Hell, he'd do it to save his family. But for unknown strangers? He wasn't sure he had that kind of courage.

He pulled up the loupe and glassed the area. Mercs in their fighting gear were emptying a truck with long, rectangular boxes and hauling them up the hill. He idly wondered if they were artillery rounds or anti-armor missiles, not that it made that much of a difference.

"What if we found some civilian clothes? Would that work?" JJ asked.

Jasper's heart fell. The closest set of civilian clothes were on the dead farmer. He didn't want to go back and strip the body.

"No. Same thing. We need to be in a uniform, and even with yours, it might work at a distance, but as soon as you got closer, they'd know you for a Marine."

Jasper had to agree. The Marine combat uniform was bulkier than the merc uniforms. If JJ casually walked up to them, the mercs might not notice at first, but they'd catch on before he got close. No, that was a dead line of thought. And it wasn't as if they had a closet of uniforms to select one that looked more like the mercs'. As far as he knew, none of the Federation uniforms were similar.

All are different, but from what? he wondered not quite sure of where his thoughts were taking him.

He looked back at the mercs. Almost all were in their combat uniforms. In the darkness, his loupe couldn't discern colors, but he had to think that they were the same. Something tickled at the back of his mind, crying for attention. Then he remembered. Four mercs in what looked like overalls had hauled a squat square case up the hill shortly before. He glassed for a few moments and was rewarded when two of them came back down to stand by a small utility truck that looked like it had been confiscated from a farm.

"Hey, who are the two guys in overalls by the civilian truck, to the far left?" he asked.

Mountie shifted his binos, then said, "I don't know. Some contractors, I guess."

"The Tenners use contractors?"

"Of course. The mercenaries cost too much with the hazard pay, so they hire contractors for maintenance and such. I can't tell from here, but if those are orange overalls, I'd say they're aviation techs. We've used them ourselves sometimes on training exercises."

Jasper knew the answer was there somewhere, but he couldn't make it gel. His mind scrambled, trying to put together the pieces.

Then it hit him with almost a physical force. He almost blurted it out before he grasped the ramifications. Looking at Mountie, he almost decided to keep quiet, but he knew he couldn't. The decision should be Mountie's, not his.

"I think there might be a way," he said.

"How?" JJ asked.

"The Tenners have pilots, right?"

"Sure. Of course," Mountie answered.

"And what do they wear? I mean as a uniform?"

"Like our Service Dress? I don't know. I guess they have something ginned up."

"No, I mean out here, in combat."

"Oh. Well, they don't have any orbital planes in their fleets, at least here. So, they'd be in flight suits. Why?"

"Like yours, right?"

"Well, yes."

He hesitated again. He could still back out, but once he said it, things would be out of his hands.

"It's like this. When I saw you, back on the hill, I didn't know who you were. I've seen enough war flicks, but you know, with a pilot, it's usually the deep space pilots, or you're in a cockpit. I had to ask if you were Federation or a merc."

"Yeah. . ." he said, sounding like he was beginning to see where Jasper was going with that.

"So, what if a Federation pilot, in his Federation flight suit, marched up there and demanded entrance, you know, to check out some bombs or something. Especially in the dark, would they notice that?"

"That's crazy, Jasper," JJ said. "They'd just let an enemy walk into a sensitive area like that? No freaking way!"

Jasper felt a wave of relief. It had been a stupid suggestion, and now it could be forgotten.

"Erik Roelfzema," Mountie said quietly.

"Who?" JJ asked as Jasper's heart fell.

Jasper realized why he'd thought of his idea.

"Earth, World War II. A Dutch pilot in the RAF, a resistance fighter, and a spy. He was given orders to gain access into a shore installation before the invasion of the European mainland, so he donned a full British dress uniform, and he walked right past the installation's German guards."

There had been a remake of the old film movie *Soldaat van Oranje*, "Soldier of Orange," that had made the rounds of various Dutch diaspora communities around the Federation about 12 years prior. It hadn't gained much traction among the general viewing public, but Jasper was not surprised that Mountie had seen it.

"So, what does that do for us?"

"What Jasper means is that if I walked right up there as if I belonged, I might be able to pass through all the mercs and get into the cave."

"Bullshit, sir. With all due respect, I mean. I don't buy it first, and even if they somehow didn't notice the big Federation patch on your shoulder, you're just going to carry a bomb right past them?"

"Probably not. But do you have a better idea?"

"No, sir. But give us some time. We can think of something."

"I don't think we have time, JJ. We need to do something quick, and so far, Jasper's the only one of us to come up with anything with even a remote possibility of working."

JJ glared at Jasper as if he'd done something wrong.

Jasper half-agreed with that and refused to meet the Marine's eyes.

Mountie had agreed upon a suicide mission before, only to be granted a reprieve. Now he was facing the same thing. It was too much to ask of a man.

But as he noted before, the decision wasn't his to make.

"We're doing it," Mountie said with finality.

"But—" JJ started.

"No buts. That's an order."

Jasper swallowed hard. He was sure his bright idea had just sentenced his friend to death.

Chapter 21

Mountie

Four hours later, Mountie crouched at the side of the road, building up his nerve. His flight suit was still damp after a semi-successful attempt to get the worst of the last four days' grime off of it. Jasper had taken the Federation patch off the shoulder after they concluded that doing so would still keep him within the accords. He felt naked, but still a little less conspicuous than with the big white and red patch shouting out "United Federation."

He knew his operation had three possible outcomes. First, he'd get in, set the bomb, and get out, all in one piece. Second, he'd get in, set the bomb, then die in the explosion. Third, he'd get captured by the mercs and held for ransom after the war ended. He was praying for number one, but he hadn't decided if number two or three was worse.

He also knew that sitting here crouched beside the road would quickly attract some unwanted attention. He had to get up and move forward. The only problem with that was that his legs didn't seem to want to follow his commands.

Come on, Castor! Just do it.

With a huge force of will, he stood up, and with the bomb in JJ's engineer pack and on his back and his Gescard slung, not at the ready, started walking towards the pile of trash alongside the main staging area. He'd taken only a dozen steps when he heard a rumble behind him, and a few moments later, the blackout lights of a vehicle lit up his back. He kept walking, expecting to hear shots and shouting, but a few moments later, the truck whispered past, the smell of burnt fries enveloping him. He let out a sigh of relief.

A couple of minutes later, he reached the edge of the trash. The mercs were screwing up. They obviously wanted secrecy, yet they'd dumped hundreds of boxes and shipping cartons in the trees. They should have removed them with each outgoing truck. As it was, they were a signpost to any Federation surveillance that something was going on in the area.

Mountie kicked the first box he came to, but it came apart, split up the back. Without using his binos' light-gathering capabilities, he couldn't see that well in the shadows, but he stumbled across three more cases before he found one that might work. He quickly kneeled, unslung the pack, and slipped the bomb out.

The case might as well have been made for the homemade explosive. It fit perfectly, the memory bottom forming around and cradling it. He gave the case a shake, and the bomb remained secure in place. He glanced up to see if anyone was looking towards him, then carefully set the detonator for 20 minutes. As he saw the countdown begin, he closed the display. To a casual observer, the bomb was inert.

He and JJ had debated on the amount of time to set. He needed enough time to get it into the cave, but not long enough for someone to stumble over it and turn it off. If something delayed him, he could reset the timer, but that might be difficult to explain with a bunch of mercs around him. Closing the case, he stood up, lifting it by the handles, and struggled out from around the trash heap.

Mountie made it almost 100 meters, stopping once, before someone called out, "Who's that?"

"You, get over here. I need two bodies," Mountie said in his best command voice.

"Who are you?" the voice repeated, a shadow stepping forward, weapon at the ready.

"I'm someone who's going to have your ass unless you follow orders and help me. I don't have time to screw around here."

The shadow lowered the weapon and stood a little straighter, then called back. "Spec, I've got someone coming in. He says he needs help."

"Who the hell is he?" a voice from further back in the trees asked.

"I don't know. He looks like a pilot."

"And a pilot who's getting mighty pissed off!" Mountie shouted.

He heard a subdued "Shit!" then a louder "Banks and Ming, go help the officer!"

The shadow in front of him didn't move, and Mountie stood there, trying to control the slight trembling of his hands. He stood there, wondering if he should simply bull ahead when two mercs came rushing forward.

"Sorry, sir. What can we do?" one of them said.

"You can pick this thing up, is what you can do. First, you guys drop me off who-knows-where, then I have to break my back lugging it here."

"Yes, sir!" they shouted in unison.

"Uh, where do you want us to carry it?"

"Well, how about back to the flight line? I came all the way here just so we can return it. Come on, think!"

"Uh, right sir. To the depot." Then, "Which one?"

Mountie had already figured the ordnance would be stored in separate places, so he had an answer already planned for that.

"How the hell do I know? With the munitions, of course."

"Yes, sir," he said. "To Blue," he added to the merc on the front of the case.

The two mercs started moving into the bulk of the trucks, making their way to the back of the unloading area. Other mercs were moving back and forth, carrying boxes and coming back for more. No one gave Mountie a second glance as he followed his two porters.

As the three cleared the trucks and started to climb, Mountie couldn't help himself and gave a quick look back. Out there in the darkness, JJ and Jasper would have their eyes on him. He resisted giving a thumbs up.

It was going smoothly—too smoothly. So of course, before they'd even managed to climb 20 meters, two guards stood on the path. Three mercs had just been checked and were moving up to an opening in the side of the hill, another 30 meters up. Mountie tried to swallow, but his mouth was suddenly dry.

The two mercs lowered the case and stopped beside the guards.

"Inventory?" one of the guards asked.

"Sir?" his head porter asked, turning to him.

"I don't have one," Mountie said, trying to sound bored. "Just let me deliver this and get on my way."

"Sorry, uh, sir," the guard said, peering at Mountie. "We need an inventory chip before we accept anything."

Mountie had never considered that, although he should have. The Federation forces loved to refer to the Tenner forces as mercenaries, but many had probably served in the Federation Navy, Marines, or FCDC, so they would have adopted the same morass of regulations.

"Who the hell are you?" he shouted, immediately knowing he might have just overplayed it. He adjusted, "I mean, what's your name and rank?"

He saw a flash of something in the merc's face as his two porters stepped back and the second guard took a stride to the side where he'd have a clear shot at him.

"Ordnance Specialist Four Ibrahim . . . sir"

"Look, Specialist. This is your fault. Not you personally, but the idiots who picked up our ordnance. You were supposed to pick up 27 Victor 33's."

Mountie knew that the Tenner forces had the V-33 in their arsenal, and they roughly looked like their homemade fuel-cylinder bomb, but that wouldn't stand any kind of scrutiny, and if this spec standing in front of him were an aviation ordnance tech, he'd know if the V-33's were even on the planet.

"Yes, sir?"

"Well, you picked up 26 of them, leaving this one on the tarmac. The command . . . adant," he said, quickly changing from the Federation "commander" to the Tenner "commandant" for a unit commanding officer, "understands what's going on now, and he doesn't want anyone's ass, so he sent me to ferry this thing here."

The guard looked at him, not saying a word. Mountie could almost see the thoughts flashing behind his eyes as he considered his options.

"I think I need to get the captain here," he finally said.

"Look, it's up to you, Specialist Ibrahim. We can wait for your captain to come and clear this up. It's no skin off my nose. I've got to get back, for reasons I know you understand. So, I'll just leave the missing V-33 for you to deal with. You can explain to your captain why you keyed in 27 Victors, but you only have 26 on hand."

"I just got one duty 15 minutes ago, sir. I didn't make any mistake."

Bingo! He's beginning to buy it.

"I didn't mean you. But who was here earlier?"

"Spec Gladstone, sir."

"OK, Gladstone's going to have to answer, along with whoever picked up the load. My commandant didn't want anyone to fry for this, but if they fucked up, then so be it."

Mountie was aware of more mercs coming up the path, waiting to pass with their loads.

"So, up to you. We leave it here and I'm done, or we take it on in to marry up with the rest of the load. I'll let your captain deal with the fallout, and you know what that means."

Mountie didn't really know what that meant, but he thought the implied threat was better than anything specific. He'd let the merc fill in the blanks. And now it was up to him. If he had to, he'd leave the bomb right there. In another ten minutes, it would blow, but not do much damage. He wondered if he should take it back down to the loading zone so it could at least take out a truck or two.

He could tell the spec was wavering.

"We missed one?" he asked.

"It's right there in front of you. But look, I'm holding up the queue, and I've got to get back to the flight line. I'm passing this on to you, and you do what you deem fit. I'm done with all of this."

He turned as if to leave, and the guard quickly said, "No . . . sir! Can you, uh, go ahead and take it in with the rest. Spec 6 Wallenda is up there, and he can marry you up with the rest of the Victors. I don't think I need to bother the captain with this."

Mountie looked back down the hill as if he was contemplating it, but mostly he didn't want anyone to see his expression.

He gathered himself, then said, "I'm running short of time, but OK, Specialist." To his two merc porters, he said, "Let's go."

"Thank you, sir," the spec whispered as Mountie walked past him.

The mouth of the cave was lit with a low-level red light. Several mercs were milling about the entrance. The red light didn't provide great illumination, but it was more than outside, and Mountie felt that someone would recognize him as a Federation pilot at any moment. He brushed past them, telling his two mercs to hurry.

The cave had obviously had some recent excavation work, a widening and straightening of the corridor and a flattening of the floor. A decking machine had laid a path of poly planks to give more secure footing. Starting after only five meters, cubbyholes had been cut into the walls, and these were full of ordnance.

"Sir?" the senior of his two mercs said. "I think that was the spec 6 the other spec told you about."

"Was he?" Mountie said, stopping to watch the retreating back of a merc. "Well, no reason to bother him now, is there? He looks like he's got a lot on his hands."

"But—"

Mountie didn't give him time to say anything, pushing deeper into the cave, following the tracked lights on the deck. A few moments later, he entered the first opening. At the far side, a small commercial excavator chewed at the walls, expanding it. From the looks of the markings, what had once been a small cavern had been excavated to cover at least 300 square meters. Stacks of munitions were like little hills, each separate from the others. Mountie had expected much more, to be honest, but still, it was a significant cache.

"Just put it there," he told the two mercs.

"But we need to find the others."

"I don't need to keep you all night. You get back to your unit. I'll track down someone, and I'll have them place it with the rest."

"You sure, sir? We can stay until you're done."

"I'm sure. You two take off."

"Well, OK. Evening, sir," the merc said before leaving him, his silent partner in tow.

Mountie started counting. He was very aware of the timer in the case, ticking off the seconds, but he couldn't very well rush past the two mercs on their way out. He considered kneeling and extending the time, but there were too many mercs running back and forth.

"Excuse me, who are you?" a voice asked.

"Are you Specialist Wallenda?" he asked after swallowing back down the bile that had surged up his throat.

"No, I'm not. He's up there somewhere," the merc said, pointing back up the entrance. "Why?"

"There's a problem with the inventory that needs to get un-fucked. Thanks," he said, spinning to walk purposefully back to the entrance.

He waited for the shout, ready to sprint. He waited for the explosion as the bomb went off, and he *wanted* to sprint. But all he could do was march forward and hope for the best.

Chapter 22

JJ

"I'm moving over so I can get a better look," JJ said as they watched Mountie approach the trash heap.

"Mountie told us to stay here," Jasper said.

"Like that matters now. When . . . if anything happens to him, I'm in charge," he said. "You can come with me or not."

JJ knew he was being unfair to Jasper, but he'd been shocked—and somewhat hurt—when Mountie had told him about Jasper's family, ordering him to take Jasper up to this Spirit Lake place. It wasn't about the militiaman's family, but the fact he'd been kept in the dark, and Mountie's assertion that he'd kept the knowledge from Sergeant Go and him for security in case they'd been captured did nothing to appease him. He wouldn't have given up anyone's family, much less Jasper's.

He stood up, backed into the trees, and started moving west. JJ was relieved to hear Jasper following. He was probably pissed, but he'd understood that they needed to stay together.

JJ also knew he was disobeying orders, but Marines were taught to take the initiative. He knew Mountie had issued the orders to keep them out of harm's way, but if something did go down, they were just too far away to be of much help. JJ's M90 could easily reach that far, but even with the night vision capability of the scope, he knew he couldn't provide effective fire. Jasper, with the Gescard, would be lucky to even get the rounds in the area.

By moving forward, they could not only provide support, but they could have better eyes on target, maybe seeing up to where the cave actually was located. He slipped through the trees, senses on high alert, for a few minutes before he turned and crept up to the treeline at the edge of the creek's wetlands. He was now less than 700 meters to where a handful of trucks were unloading, and the bright red lights of what had to be one of the caves almost blinded him. He lowered the binos for a moment, and the glare disappeared to a very faint red glow. Raising them again, it only took a few moments for him to spot Mountie rummaging through the trash heap.

"Hell, they've got to see him," he muttered, noting how much in the open the lieutenant was.

"They're going to see him sooner or later," Jasper said. "That's part of the plan."

"I'd rather it be later."

They both watched Mountie in silence. Jasper had Sergeant Go's binos, so he now had full low-light level capability. Time stretched on while JJ became evermore nervous.

"Finally!" he said when Mountie seemed to select a case.

It still took a few more minutes before he'd packed the bomb and stood up.

"Twenty minutes," Jasper said.

No shit, JJ thought, but he kept silent.

Mountie started lugging the case forward, and for a while, it seemed as if none of the mercs knew he was there, which boggled JJ's mind.

"Piss-poor security," he said under his breath.

It wasn't until Mountie was almost to the nearest truck that a merc stepped forward to stop him. JJ put his crosshairs on the merc, ready to fire if he threatened Mountie. It was probably 700 meters, and in the dark, but if he fired enough darts, he was pretty sure he could drop the bastard.

"He's yelling at him!" Jasper said in amazement.

JJ had been focusing on the shot, not the merc's attitude, but he'd seen enough ass-chewings to realize Jasper was right. The merc hadn't come to a position of attention, but he had the posture of someone both afraid of an officer and not knowing what to do.

"Get some, Mountie," he said, smiling despite the gravity of the situation.

It took a few moments, but two more mercs rushed forward, picked up the case, and led Mountie towards the truck.

"Son-of-a-bitch, Jasper. You were right!"

It had been Jasper's idea for Mountie to try and order some mercs to help him, saying that they would both be camouflage for him as well as keep others from looking too closely for fear of being drafted to help out.

Shit, the old man knows grunts better than I do, he admitted to himself.

Both of them followed the three men until they passed through the trucks, then picked them up again as they climbed the hill beyond them and approached the cave mouth. Except that Mountie was stopped. Even with the binos on full zoom, JJ couldn't see what was happening other than there was some sort of conversation going on.

"Ten minutes," Jasper said.

Just put it down and walk away, Mountie. Get out of there.

JJ thought the gig was up, but was surprised when after a few more moments, the two mercs dutifully picked up the case and followed Mountie up the hill. All three went into the cave opening and disappeared from sight.

"How much time?" JJ asked, wishing he'd started a countdown as well.

"Seven minutes, fifteen seconds."

"That's enough time, right?" JJ asked. "Or he can reset it like I showed him."

Before Mountie had set off, JJ had tried to convince him to let him go instead. But the key to this was the flight suit, and Mountie was a good half-meter taller than him. There was that pilot swagger about him that seemed natural as well, a swagger that would do him well, a swagger that JJ lacked, or at least a style of swagger he lacked. JJ's bluster was a typical grunt's fist-fight-in-the-bar bluster, not the I'm-so-cool demeanor of pilots.

It wasn't as if resetting the detonator was difficult. The guy could fly a Lizard—he wasn't going to be stumped on resetting a clock.

"How much time now?"

"Six-twenty-two."

Less than a minute gone by? Oh, God!

The two lay in silence, binos trained on the cave opening. Mercs were going in and out without any sign of alarm. JJ waited, and when he was sure ten minutes had to have expired, he asked Jasper for another time check.

"Three and eleven."

"Mother of us all," he said, his heart threatening to jump out of his chest.

He tried to calm himself down. This was worse than anything he'd done so far on this god-forsaken planet. He knew it was because he had no control over anything. He was just a spectator.

The 20 minutes had crawled by with glacial slowness, but Jasper's "One minute" took him by surprise. Still, no sign of Mountie.

"I bet he reset the detonator," Jasper said.

JJ suddenly had doubts.

What if I fucked up? What if it won't work?

And then Jasper said, too loudly, "There he is!"

JJ had become so wrapped up with the thought that he might not have made the bomb correctly that he'd missed the lieutenant, but sure enough, there was Mountie, emerging from the opening. He immediately took a few steps off to the side and bent over, as if re-sealing his boots.

"Forty seconds," Jasper said an instant before a gout of fire erupted from the opening, reaching out over the trucks parked 100 meters below. It looked as if the entire mountain shook, and dust rose from a couple of hundred square meters of land. A moment later, a shock wave and boom reached them, pressing both of them into the earth.

"You said 40 seconds," JJ shouted, as leaves torn off the trees floated down them.

"I must have started it late!"

"Where's Mountie?" JJ asked, getting to his knees to get a better view.

There was chaos on both the hill leading to the cave as well as among the trucks. Mercs were only just getting to their feet—those that could, at least. A half-a-dozen bodies that JJ could see where still down and motionless.

"There he is," JJ said as he caught sight of a flight-suited man, stumbling down the side of the hill, rifle ready.

He'd only been meters from the opening, but off to the side and out of the direct blast. He looked unsure of his footing, but JJ was just happy to see him moving.

People were running back and forth. From the top of one of the trucks, a stream of water reached out, not quite reaching the cave opening. They both could hear yells reach across the road and wetlands to them.

Mountie made it down to the trucks, where JJ lost sight of him. When the lieutenant appeared on the near side, he almost shouted out his encouragement.

"He's going to make it!" he told Jasper, his previous anger evaporated into nothingness. "Let's get back over to meet him."

He stood up to put the binos back into their case when with his naked eyes, he saw the dark figure of Mountie stop, and an instant later, the unmistakable flashes of firing. He whipped the glasses back, with the light amplified, saw Mountie fire another burst at a merc, who fell beside a prone body. Mountie broke into a run.

"Fucking shit-sucking mother-humping hell!" he said. "Come-on!"

He broke into a sprint, running wildly through the trees to where the wetlands narrowed as the creek almost came up alongside the road. Without hesitation, he broke into the open and splashed across the shallow water, reaching the other side and struggling through the grass and muck to reach the edge of the road. He flopped to his stomach, M90 trained down the road as Jasper struggled through the muck to reach him. Fifty meters down the road, Mountie was charging. A flurry of shots reached out to him, and he ducked back into the cover of the trees. That slowed him down but kept him out of the line of fire for a moment.

JJ shifted his aim as three mercs ran pell-mell after Mountie, intent on their prey.

Losing situational awareness was a cardinal sin in combat, and JJ was about to demonstrate why. The three mercs were almost shoulder to shoulder, barely 100 meters away when JJ sprayed them with a full clip of 150 darts, dropping them all. Whether they were zeroed or not, JJ didn't care. They were off the lieutenant's ass, and that was all the mattered.

JJ turned to haul the foundering Jasper up the bank and out into the road.

"Come on, Mountie. Kick it into high gear," he shouted as he gave Jasper a push to get him going.

He waited a few moments until Mountie tentatively came back out on the road, looking back.

"I took care of them, sir," JJ shouted. "And we really need to diddiho now."

Mountie spun and took off towards JJ. When he reached him, JJ took off, matching the taller man's speed.

"I think they're kind of pissed at me," Mountie said as they closed the gap with Jasper.

"Yeah, that they are. And they're going to want to see who just shot the crap out of five of them."

"Well, JJ, I'd suggest we put a little distance between them and us before we plot our next move."

"Roger that, sir," JJ said as they reached Jasper.

Together, the three of them ran off into the night.

Chapter 23

Jasper

"Is this the trail?" Mountie asked.

"It has to be," Jasper answered as he walked out onto it, stomping his foot to feel the footing.

They'd almost missed the trailhead in the dark. In all the flicks, Marines had small monocles that lit the night as day, but evidently, those weren't issued to engineers or pilots. The two sets of binos and the loupe were all well and good, but they couldn't continually be held up as they moved. JJ, on point, would scan the area with his binos, move forward, then scan the next area. It was while he was doing this that Mountie, with his naked eyes, noticed the rock marker back on the side of the road. They'd been moving within the treeline and had actually stepped over the trail, which was lost in the evergreen needle litter.

Jasper felt a rush of emotion as he used the loupe to survey the path. He couldn't tell if anyone had passed by—the loupe flattened out what he was seeing. But with Mount Rand just ahead and off to the north, this probably was it.

"Do you have that thing that can tell if someone passed by here?" he asked JJ.

"You mean a sniffer? We're not recon. We don't go out to try and find the bad guys. And they're not even that effective all the time."

Another Hollybolly myth smashed, he thought, wondering just how accurate the flicks were.

In his heart, though, he was sure this was the trail. It was deceptively wide, enough for a Goat or ORV to haul people or supplies up the mountain. There couldn't be that many trails this size this far from any settlements.

"Well, then, let's head on up. If it stops, we can always backtrack and continue on."

Mountie seemed amazingly calm for someone who'd just entered the belly of the beast and come out whole. Jasper was amazed at his demeanor and extremely grateful that somehow, they'd all made it this far.

Not all of us, he reminded himself, remembering Sergeant Go.

This close to the road, the fir trees were thick. After only 100 meters, the trail started to climb, and the trees began to thin out some. As they emerged from the heavy cover, Jasper could see the purple dawn that heralded another day. He fervently hoped that by nightfall, he'd be back with Keela and the grandkids.

A sound of a truck turbine whined from behind them, and all three wheeled around, weapons at the ready. This hadn't been the first time they'd seen and heard signs of mercs, mercs who were undoubtedly searching for them. To Jasper's relief, the turbines kept east, bypassing the trail. They waited a few more moments until they were sure they were clear before turning and resuming their movement.

Jasper had expected a steep climb, but to his surprise, it was rather gentle. The mountains on each side rose steeply, but on the road, the rise was gradual, and without a stream alongside as might be expected. The firs gave way to a white-barked tree that Jasper didn't recognize, probably some genmodded form of Aspen. The science of terraforming was well beyond him. As a farmer, he wanted the latest and greatest in algae, but what they put in the wilderness had little impact on his life. Still, now that he was walking up the trail, his curiosity was piqued. Why firs by the road, but now the white-barked trees? Up ahead, it looked like more evergreens.

"Jasper, look," JJ said, interrupting his thoughts.

Jasper looked to where the Marine was pointing. There, on the side of the trail, was a Goody Bar wrapper, crumbled and discarded. He picked it up and gave it a sniff, not that that gave him some hidden insight. Someone had come up the trail, but who and when? Still, it gave him hope.

The trail rose in a series of ascending dips, and at each rise, he expected to see the lake below them. He'd seen enough images of the deep blue lake, situated in a bowl. The near side, where they were marching now, was wide and gentle. On the far side of the lake, the mountains rose like sentinels, and the trail they were now on became a series of switchbacks that climbed a couple of hundred meters before flattening out to the pass that crossed the range to the Van der Horst Plateau. Whatever geological forces shaped the area long pre-dated humans, and all of the introduced vegetation could not hide the planet's personality.

As they reached the next rise, Jasper moved forward to stand with JJ. Below them, slightly dipping down, was a shallow depression, about 200 meters across. It was scattered with clumps of dry grasses and a few scraggly and diseased trees.

"The planet wins," JJ remarked, pointing the muzzle of his M90 at the trees.

That commonly spoken truism was a vast understatement given the tremendous transformation of what had been an almost atmospheric-less hunk of rock and ice only 120-some years before, but still, despite the best efforts of man, the planet seemed to be fighting back. Spirit Lake might be the planet's ultimate statement that it had not given up.

"How much farther?" Mountie asked as he stepped alongside them.

"Can't be too far. Those mountains are on the other side of the lake, and how far away are they? Ten klicks?" Jasper responded.

"Let's push on, then. There's too much activity behind us, and they're going to expand their search. I'd rather be long gone before then," Mountie said.

"But if they're really kicking off something big, can they afford that?" JJ asked.

"Can they afford not to. We just punched them in the face, and they can't have Federation troops running wild in their rear. They have to come after us. Hell, we might have delayed an offensive push by them."

"That's good, right?" Jasper asked.

"Maybe. We just don't know if—" he started before JJ lunged forward and fired a stream of darts into the air.

"What the—" he started as JJ ran forward, dropping his magazine and inserting another in a few efficient motions before firing again.

Jasper looked high to see what he was firing at until a flash, much lower caught his attention. Sparks flew as a small object came into focus, zig-zagging as it fluttered to the ground to bounce 40 meters away. He instinctively chased JJ as the Marine sprinted to whatever he just shot.

Jasper arrived just as JJ was picking up the small, light object, which was flashing from the blue of the sky color to the sandy tan of the dirt and back again.

"Mother-fuck!" JJ said, pointing to a small green light on the underside of the object. "It's transmitting."

He dropped it to the ground and stomped on it, once, twice, three times until it was reduced to a pile of scrap.

"How long has it been on us?" Mountie asked.

"Don't know, sir. I just caught a glimpse when it moved in front of those mountains. The sky-camo gave it away."

Mountie picked up the scraps and examined them before dropping the heap back on the ground.

It was obvious what the tiny drone was, even if Jasper had never seen one before, but holding out forlorn hope, he asked, "What was that?"

"That, my friend, is our asses," JJ said, kicking the dead drone once more for good measure. "They know where we are, and they're going to come after us."

Chapter 24

Mountie

"Why don't they fire on us?" Jasper asked as the three slowed to a walk for a moment to catch their breaths. "They know exactly where we are now."

At least two drones were flitting overhead, darting in and out of their sight.

"They can't," JJ said. "Their arty is to the west, and these cliffs keep us in defilade."

"But don't they have missiles that can bend around? Or aircraft that can fly right at us?"

"Too expensive for just the three of us. For a missile, I mean. And unless things have changed, we've got air superiority with the Navy in orbit. They need to save their air for the big push."

"They're waiting to see where we're going," Mountie said.

He'd expected the mercs to hit them by now. He could hear them back down on the road near the trailhead, and he caught glimpses of activity. JJ had been right about the defilade, but they'd only just now reached that. When first spotted, they'd been vulnerable to Tenner arty. He'd wondered about why they'd been left to flee when it finally hit him.

They wanted to see why three Federation troops were moving up to a lake. If it was to marry up with a larger unit, they wanted to know. If there were a route through the mountain range, then they would really want to know. In trying to reach Jasper's family, in trying to use the route to marry back up with the Marines and the squadron, they'd led the mercs right to a path across the range.

The Federation forces, with the Navy ships and satellites, probably knew about the trail. The mercs were privy to the same sources, and on frontier worlds like this, records were sometimes spotty. But if they found a way through with a sizable force before the more limited-in-number Federation forces could react, they could gain a foothold in the key plateau. A thrust from two fronts could overwhelm the Marines.

"What do you mean?" Jasper asked.

"Why are the three of us running into what they think is a box canyon with a lake at the end? Are we rejoining our unit? Or is there a way to the highlands that they don't know about?"

"Damn! I never thought about that," JJ said. "So, what do we do now? Go east again?"

"Too late now. They know we're here. They'll be guessing there's something else here, too. And they used them," he said, pointing up to where the drones were flying, "To find out just what that is."

"My family?" Jasper asked, not verbalizing his concern.

"Can you find them quickly?"

"If they're here," Jasper said, with Mountie catching the hitch in his voice, "they'll be around the research platform. It's up on the west side of the lake somewhere. I've been trying to spot it, but nothing yet."

"Then I suggest we keep pushing. We'll pick up your family, then make it up the upper trail to the plateau. If we can outrun the jamming up there, we can get word back that there're mercs on the way."

"But the drones, they'll see the women and children," Jasper protested.

"And do what?"

"They burned Donkerbroek. They killed that family! What do you think?"

And the drones have feeds that are recorded. Someone killed that family, yes. But no one is going to attack civilians when it's all being recorded. They should be safe."

"'Should?'"

"Sorry, Jasper, that's the best I can do for now."

"We've got civilian camps up there, for refugees," JJ said. "All laid out with red crosses. They'll be safe there.

Jasper didn't look convinced, but Mountie couldn't waste any more time. They had to keep moving. He broke back into a ground-eating trot.

He had been elated about blowing the ammunition dump, sure it had improved the Federation's position. But if the end result was that they'd led the mercs to another route of advance, then it could have been a grave if not fatal mistake.

Chapter 25

Jasper

As the three jogged up the trail, Jasper forced all thought about the gathering mercs behind them out of his mind. He caught several glimpses of the research platform, but try as he might, he didn't see any signs of people.

What if no one's there, he wondered. *Have I been fooling myself?*

They crested the last rise, and the impossibly blue waters of Spirit Lake filled their view, a blue jewel set in a rocky mount, surrounded by green trees.

"Woah!" JJ said. "I've never seen anything like that."

Jasper had to admit that it made a pretty sight. He'd seen the holos and pics, but they didn't do justice to the raw beauty.

"There're bodies down there," Mountie said.

Jaspers' heart jumped into his throat, and he whipped out the loupe and focused down near the shore where two lumps were motionless on the ground. He dreaded what he would see.

"Mercs," Mountie said. "Two of them. Look like scouts."

Jasper thought he was going to faint. He could see that the two bodies were in uniform, and not the now-familiar Marine combat utilities. From all accounts, the two had died a pretty horrible death, coughing out their existence down on the shore. Jasper had to tear his eyes away, sick to his stomach that his wife might have even risked coming to the area.

"I guess they never heard what you told us," JJ remarked matter-of-factly. "You'd think the lack of vegetation all around the lake might have given them a clue."

"I take it that if we keep where the trees are growing, we're OK?" Mountie asked.

"Aye-yah, just stay on the road. Depending on the weather, that can move the gas up and down, but if we're on the road, we're OK—at least I think so."

"You think so?" JJ asked. "I'd like to be a little more sure than that. I don't want to end up like those two idiots down there."

"OK, OK. I'm sure. Look, the road curves around, then you can see on the other side where it starts to climb."

"I think I'll let you lead us," JJ said. "You can be the canary, and I'll cover our rear."

Jasper blew the "canary" comment off. With the mercs in the rear, it made sense that the Marine take up that position. Without another word, he broke into a trot towards the lake.

Despite his assurances to the other two, the closer they got to the lake, the more he tried to breath shallowly, the more he tried to smell the air. He wasn't a young man, and he wasn't used to running, so restricting his breathing was beginning to tell on him. He had to start gulping the air just to stay on his feet.

As the trail bent off to the left and leveling out, he felt another surge of relief. And up ahead by 500 meters or so, he could see the observation platform. He unconsciously sped up, ignoring his exhaustion.

"Keela!" he shouted as he got within 100 meters and broke into a full-out run.

There wasn't anybody in sight. The platform was empty.

"Keela!" he yelled, rushing up and looking over the restraining wall and down the hill to the lake.

Feet pounded behind as Mountie and JJ joined him.

"Are they here?" Mountie asked.

Jasper pushed past him to look up the side of the mountain, shouting out again, "Keela!" his voice now touched with despair.

"Mr. van Ruiker?" a tentative voice called out.

"What? Who's there?"

"It's me, Tyler. Tyler Portois."

Handel Portois' 12-year-old son tentatively crept out from behind a thick bush of some sort, saw Jasper, then ran to him, grabbing onto his legs and squeezing tight.

"Tyler, listen to me. Tyler!" he said, pushing the now sobbing boy far enough away to see his face. "Tyler, is my wife here? My grandkids?"

"I've been so scared! Me and Mark, we've been trying to take care of them, but we couldn't!"

"Tyler! My wife?"

"Yes, sir. She's back there," the boy said, wiping his nose with his forearm and pointing up a tiny path.

Jasper almost dropped the boy, pushing past him to bolt up the path, jumping over a set of logs that had been set into the hillside to serve as steps. He hit the switchback, climbed a few more steps to see the low roof of an open-air shelter. Figures were lying on the floor, most stirring to sit up as Jasper rushed in.

"Keela!"

"Jasper?" a familiar voice called out in bewilderment, a voice dear to his heart.

"Keela!" he shouted, stepping past bodies, ignoring the rise of voices as others became aware of him.

Keela was sitting up, her hair a bird's nest, her eyes puffy. Jasper had never seen such a beautiful sight in his entire life. He bowled into her, knocking her on her back as he hugged her for all he was worth. He wanted to devour her, to never let her go.

Until two small bodies jumped on him, shouting "Opa!"

Laughing, then crying, he leaned back and pulled Amee and Pieter into his grasp. "Where's Wevers?" he shouted before his oldest grandchild rushed forward, joining the family hug.

"How did you get here? I mean, I thought . . ." Keela said, breaking down completely as sobs wracked her body. "I thought you were dead!" she wailed.

"I'm not, I'm here now," he said, patting her back.

"Christiaan?" she asked.

Jasper couldn't say the words. He just shook his head.

Hovering over them, Radiant gave a gasp and fainted. Wevers rushed to his mother's side.

"What about my man, Jasper?" Hette Portois asked, wringing her hands.

"I'm sorry, Hette. He didn't make it."

She stood up straight, her chin quivering as she said, "I thought as much" as her eight-year-old buried her face in her hips and cried.

"What about Schuyler?" Sandy asked.

"I never saw his body. I think a few of us got away after the fight, but I can't be sure."

"So, he could still be alive?"

"I don't know. Maybe."

"And Ito? He said he was going to be with you," Tjares asked, her face blank.

"No, honey, Ito's dead. I'm so sorry."

She listened for a moment, nodded, and turned away. Jasper looked out over the anxious faces, suddenly feeling guilty for being alive. How had he made it when the rest had died?

JJ and Mountie had arrived, but were hanging back. JJ took a look around, then stepped back and climbed on a large rock, facing back down towards the highway, while Jasper saw Mountie was silently counting heads, and for the first time since arriving, he looked around.

"Where are the rest?" he asked. "Where's Carrie?"

"This is it. Twenty-two of us. We lost two of the children in the river," she said, quietly, nodding at Reisa Plantoning, who was lying almost comatose in the back of the shelter, oblivious to his arrival. "Reisa's little ones. For the rest, we don't know. We split up into six groups, and only the two you see made it this far."

"Uh, Mountie, they're coming," JJ said, jumping off the rock.

"Jasper, we need to get everyone going, now."

"Keela, can you get everyone up?" he asked.

"Why? What's happening?" she asked, her voice rising.

"Keela, I need you now. The mercs are on their way up from the road. We need to get you, all of you, up the trail and out of range."

"But . . ." she started before Jasper could see a sense of resolve wash over her. "Of course. Tjares, Gigi, get everyone up now." Then louder so everyone could hear, "We're going on another hike. Won't that be fun?"

A couple of the youngest started crying.

"I don't want another hike," four-year-old Willy ter Horst said.

The older kids seemed to understand, and Willy's eight-year-old brother, Haspin, stepped up to her and took her hand, saying, "Sure you do! It'll be fun, and we can play the song game!"

Jasper let go of Keela's hand for the first time since he hugged her and made his way past people getting up and packing what little they had in backpacks and shopping bags. He jumped up on the same rock and looked south. Even without his loupe, he could see a line of vehicles coming out of the dense fir trees near the highway.

"Are they going to attack?" he asked Mountie.

"I doubt it. Not with area weapons, at least. But I could be wrong. We don't know how the war is going."

"What about up there?" Jasper asked, pointing to where the trail climbed the mountain. "Do we know if that's still in Federation hands?"

"No, we don't," Mountie admitted. Anything I know is more than five days old. We had the squadron at Philips Landing, about 60 klicks from Oration Pass. The Marine battalion was centered at Gronigen, with a Nieuwe Utrecht militia division spread across the main avenue of approach to the industrial center."

"That's who we heard two nights ago, right? The fighting?"

"Probably Tenners probing the militia."

"Hell of a probe, Mountie. But what if they broke through? Are we taking the women and children right into their positions up there?" Jasper asked.

"We could be. But I doubt it. What I can tell you is I see a few tanks and wave blasters down there heading our way. I'd rather not be trapped here as they make their way up."

"Jasper, we're ready," Keela said, coming up to them.

"Keela, this is Mountie, Lieutenant Klocek. Mountie, this is my wife, Keela."

"Pleased to meet you, Lieutenant," Keela said, hold out her hand.

"I've heard so much about you."

Despite the situation, Jasper had to note that societal niceties were ingrained and had to be observed.

"And that's Lance Corporal Portillo, 'JJ.'"

"Ma'am, if you could start getting everyone moving? And Jasper, why don't you take the point and leave JJ back here with me," Mountie said.

"Aye-yah," Jasper said. "I can do that."

"Come on, people, up the road. Take the little ones by the hands," Keela said, taking over.

It took too long as the line of vehicles below them grew, but finally, everyone was moving. Two adults supported Reisa, who was barely able to stumble along. At the front, with little Amee's hand in his, he tried to hurry the group along. He kept pushing the pace, but then slowing down to let the rest catch up. With eight adult women, three almost-teens, ten children, and one baby, this was still an amorphous group without a single focus.

"Move faster, please," he pleaded and was rewarded with a few quick steps before they fell back to their original maddeningly slow pace. He was amazed that Keela had made it this far from Donkerbroek.

"Half-way here!" JJ shouted from the very rear, a good 40 meters behind Jasper. "I count ten vehicles, including two Pecker-3's."

The "Pecker-3" was the PCR-3, a midsize tank known for its efficiency and maneuverability. It couldn't stand up one-on-one with a Marine Lumsden, but they didn't have any of the big Marine tanks up there with them.

The research platform was thankfully close to where the trail started climbing. Still, it took almost 20 minutes for Jasper to reach that spot. With vehicles, the mercs should have been at the lake already, but Jasper couldn't see them. It looked like the mercs thought there was a way through, and were waiting for the group to show them the way. Jasper didn't want to play into their hands, but he wasn't sure what options they had.

The trail started rising steeply, and the group slowed down. More of the little ones were complaining. Jasper picked up Amee and put her on his hip, then took Pieter's hand in his and almost dragged him up. They reached the first switchback, then doubled back the opposite way. Below him, just 15 meters now, Mountie and

Jasper were just entering the first step. Mountie was holding one of the children while JJ walked backwards, weapon at the ready.

As he reached the next switchback, he looked to where the trail reached above the lake, and he sucked in a deep breath. Three vehicles—the two tanks and another that Jasper didn't recognize—were spread out side-by-side on the crest. At least a dozen mercs seemed to be gathered around them. Jasper guessed them to be almost two klicks away as the crow flies, and he felt extremely vulnerable climbing up the cliff.

A flicker of something interfered with his sightline to the mercs, and he realized the drones were still buzzing around, recording their every move. Looking up, he tried to spot where the trail breached the summit and into the pass and they could get out of the line-of-sight of those tanks. Just to his right and well above him, a small plume of water reached out of the cliff, turning into a mist. A rainbow shined in the plume, almost mocking him with its normalcy.

"Hurry up, children," Keela was saying just below him.

She had a huge smile plastered on her face, but she couldn't fool him. She was puffing, pushing her body far more than she should have. He wanted to tell her to rest, but he was more afraid of what might happen if she did.

I'm not doing so well myself, he admitted. *I'm too old to be doing this.*

No one was doing well, except for a few of the kids. Tyler Portois, Mark Caesar, and Greta Tanner were running up and down the trail, shouting encouragement. Their young legs didn't seem fazed.

And it hit him.

"Tyler, can you come up here for a moment?" he said to the young man, who was just below him on the last switchback.

He scrambled directly up the slope, ignoring the easier road.

"Yes, sir?" he asked breathing evenly.

"Who's a better runner, you, Mark, or Greta?"

"I am!" he said, slapping his chest.

"OK, who's next?"

"That would be Greta. She's pretty fast."

"OK, I want you to go get Greta and her mom, then bring them up here to me."

Tyler nodded then rushed back down to gather them up.

"Tjares, can you keep them moving?" he asked as she reached him.

She nodded and kept walking. Jasper took out one of his last pieces of plastisheet and scribbled down a note. A few moments later, Mark, Greta, and Marijke Tanner reached him, Marijke breathing heavily. Greta's mother was in her early 30's, and Jasper realized he was faring better than she was.

"What do you want, Jasper."

"I've got a job for someone young. It might be scary, but it's really important. Do you think you can run ahead and get up on the plains alone? Can you do that?"

Both kids immediately said yes, but Marijke's eyes widened with fear, and she started to protest. Jasper moved his head to face the mercs in the distance, tightening his eyes, then looking back at Greta's mother. She turned her head, saw the mercs as well, and with a resigned slump, turned back and gave Jasper the slightest of nods.

"OK, this is what I want you to do. Run as fast as you can. Up there, the road will level out, but it will still be very far to the plateau. There's also a little village up there. I don't remember the name, but it's there. If you stay on the road, you'll see it. I want you to run all the way there. If you see the mercenaries there, hide and wait for us to come. If you see Marines—can you recognize Marines?"

"Yes, sir. Like that guy there," Greta said, pointing at JJ.

"Good! If you see them, I want you to give them this note. And if there's no one there, I want you to try and call 911 and read them what I wrote here," he said, handing Greta the note, then reaching into his pocket and pulling out Amee's Lil' Bunny.

"Opa, that's mine!" Amee said, reaching for it.

"I know, sweetheart, but we need to borrow it for a little longer, OK?"

"But it's mine!"

"We'll give it back, Amee," Tyler said.

"Promise?"

"Cross our hearts."

That seemed to mollify Amee, so Jasper asked, "Can you read this for me first, what I want you to say?"

"Sure. Uh, 'To the senior Federation military commander. Lieutenant Caster Klocek, Federation Navy, Lance Corporal Javier Portillo, Federation Marines, and Private Jasper van Ruiker, Nieuwe Utrecht Militia, are accompanying 22 women and children from Donkerbroek on the trail from Spirit Lake. A large number of Tenner tanks and vehicles are in pursuit. They will be able to make it through the pass and into the high plains. Request you send forces to rescue the civilians and stop the mercenaries from invading.'

"How was that?" Tyler asked, looking up from the plastisheet.

"Very good. So, you understand what you have to do?"

"Yes, sir," they both said in unison.

Keela reached them and looked at Jasper, her eyes brimming with questions.

"OK, then. Do you have water?"

Greta held up two bulbs, Tyler, one.

"Then you two take off. Be careful."

"Wait!" Marijke said.

She reeled Greta into an enveloping hug, then released her, saying, "Run fast!"

"Thank you," Jasper said as the two youngsters broke out into a run.

"Safer up there than with us," she muttered as she started climbing again.

Jasper stood there for a moment, wondering if he'd just made a big mistake. If the tiny settlement up there still stood, it might have power, and if it had power, Amee's Lil' Bunny could communicate. And if they called 911, the circuit AI's would get them to someone who could tell the military.

But they were both 12, and this was a war. He could have just sent them to their deaths, and the thought made him start to shake as that fact hit him, and hit him hard.

"What was that?" Keela asked.

"I just sent them ahead to try and call for help, but I hope I just didn't kill them."

"Some of us have already died, and they could be safer up there. You did what you had to do, so forget it and keep these people moving, old man."

"Aye-yah, old women. I'll do that."

By now, the group was spread out over three switchbacks, not counting the two kids who were already up two more and not slowing down. Jasper started to shout, browbeat, beg, and encourage everyone to keep going. He felt like a fly on the wall, waiting for the swatter to come crush him flat. But he couldn't stop.

JJ had slung his weapon, and now he was carrying Reisa by himself, huffing and puffing but making good time. All the capable adults were either carrying or leading other children.

A cool mist hit Jasper at the next turn, and he looked up. The wind had changed direction, and the plume of water had come back to them. It was only a few more levels up, and it was only then that he noticed that the water was being discharged from a small pipe that jutted out a meter or so from the side of the mountain.

He let the coolness wash over his face, then looked back towards the mercs. Back down on by the lake, something was going on. Figures were running down to the shore itself. He pulled his loupe and looked down. Three more figures were sprawled on the ground, near the two dead merc scouts.

"Look at our friends," he told JJ, who had almost caught up to him and was just one level down.

Carrying Reisa, JJ had to turn slowly, but when he did, he let out a laugh and said, "Look at those dumb moth—" he started, before looking at the children beside him, "those dumb guys. They sent a collection team to pick up the casualties, and they sucked in the poison, too."

"Maybe they'll be too busy to pay us much attention until we've reached the top," Jasper said, but not believing it.

One of the tank's gun had steadily elevated as the group climbed, an ominous sign.

Jasper's legs were aching, and he wanted to stop, but all of them had to be hurting, and even the smallest child was gamely pushing on. It was just a little farther.

"Come on! Almost there," he shouted out, almost as much for himself as to encourage the others.

And suddenly, as he mentally prepared himself for the next switchback, it wasn't there. The trail disappeared into the gorge. Mountain walls still reached up 400, 500 more meters, but the trail had reached the next phase. As Jasper crested the lip, he could see a narrow canyon, the bed slowly rising until it looked like it opened up wider and finally out into the Van de Horst Plateau. A small stream trickled back and forth across the trail. At his feet, the stream flowed into a small culvert, then a pipe took it around the side of the opening and along the mountainside for 15 meters where it discharged the water out into the open air.

Jasper told Amee to stand by the side, then retreated to the open part of the trail, overlooking the lake and lowlands below.

"Come on! You're almost at the top!"

There was a flash of light below, and Jasper looked up just as an explosion rocked him, and 50 meters to his right, rocks and dust reached out from the mountainside. A chorus of screams drowned out the sounds of rocks slamming as they bounced down the slope.

"Run!" Jasper yelled, grabbing young arms and pulling children up.

JJ ran past, Reisa slung across his shoulders.

"Come on, Mark! Take your sister," he shouted as he passed the young boy, who was staring at the impact point.

He heard the whistle of the next shell just before it hit, sending another cascade of rock down the mountainside. The dust cloud expanded, and small bits of debris peppered the stragglers.

"They're just trying to scare us," Mountie said, his voice sure and calm.

Doing a good job at that!

Jasper looked over his shoulder as he dragged Fanny's two little ones up the last few meters to the top. The tank that had fired had lowered its gun, but with a puff of black smoke, it lurched to a start, moving down the trail.

Over the lip and into the gorge, the most of the villagers were huddled together, teary eyes looking up at him. After the two impacts, the pass was eerily quiet, with only snuffling and a few quiet sobs punctuating the tinkle of the brook.

"That's everybody," Mountie said, coming alongside Jasper and letting little Lori Atweiller down.

"Why were they trying to shoot us?" Hette asked, her arms around two of the children.

"They weren't," Mountie said. "They were trying to scare us, to make us stop."

"But now they're coming up," she said, raising a cry from the others as they heard.

"Yes, it looks like they are. But it'll be a tight squeeze for the tanks, so it will take them awhile. But that means you have to keep going. Look, up ahead. You've got maybe a klick, uh, a kilometer, ahead, maybe two, and you'll be out of the pass. You'll be into the plateau, and the Federation's up there."

"Our children are tired. They can't go on," she insisted.

"They have to go on, Miss. And we need the adults to help Jasper get them up there. OK?"

What? Help me? Jasper wondered if he'd heard right.

"So, everyone, take a drink of water, OK? You need to start in a minute."

He motioned for Jasper.

"You need to take them and get them up onto the plateau. As soon as you can, get off the road and put as much distance as you can from it. I don't think they'll follow."

"Me? And what are you going to do? You and JJ?"

"We're going to try and buy you more time," Mountie said as JJ nodded. "This is a good place to hold. The mercs have to come up the trail, and they'll be vulnerable."

"Horatius at the Bridge," Jasper said.

"Yeah," Mountie said, sounding surprised that Jasper knew his history. "Horatius."

"Except that Horatius never faced armor. And you don't have any anti-armor left."

"We don't need to defeat them. Just delay them and give you enough time to get everyone out of the pass."

"But—"

"But nothing. This isn't your fight. It never was. You were always going to get your family and make them safe. Leave this to us."

"Hell, we signed up for this, and that's why we make the big credits," JJ said with a laugh.

Jasper stood there, looking at the two men, and Mountie said, "You need to get going."

Without a word, Jasper spun and walked to Keela, who was squeezing the last of her water bulb in Amee's mouth.

"The mercs are coming, and they need to be delayed. You need to get all these children out of the pass."

She looked over at his two companions for a moment, then said, "OK, you take Amee and start out. I'll bring up the rear. We can do—"

Jasper saw when realization hit her.

"You said, *I* need to get the children. You're not coming, are you?"

"I swore an oath last week with Maarten. But more than that, they need my help. And you, all of you need us to stop them."

"But they were only scaring us! The lieutenant said that!"

"Aye-yah, he said that. But can we be sure?" he said, ruffling Amee's hair. "Can we afford that? Where are the rest of you?

"Look, I survived the fight on Koltan's Hill. I never should have. I think maybe God had a plan for me, and this is it."

"You need to move, now, Jasper," Mountie called out.

"But—"

"No buts, my love. I need to do this. And you heard him. It's time."

She stared at him, eyes wide. Then she broke, and she lunged at him, enveloping him in a crushing embrace.

"I love you," she said, leaving it at that.

He relished the embrace, trying to memorize her feel, her smell. But only for a moment. He gently pushed her away.

She squeezed his biceps one last time, then wiping the tears from her cheek, turned and shouted out, "Time to move! Sandy! Take two of the little ones and start walking. Hette, you and I are taking the rear. Now, everyone, now!"

Jasper didn't watch, couldn't watch. He returned to Mountie and JJ, who waited silently.

"You're wrong, Mountie. This is my planet, and those are my people. If it's anyone's fight, it's mine, not yours."

"Told you," JJ said to Mountie as he stepped forward to smack Jasper's arm. "So, *Gyver,* you ready to kick some ass?"

"Gyver? What, you're finally giving me a nickname? And that's it?" he asked.

"You're one of us. And don't knock the nic. It could have been worse."

Gyver looked over his shoulder one last time. The villagers, *his villagers*, were already moving out. Keela had her back to him as she helped Mark and Hette lift Reisa.

"Aye-yah, JJ. I'm ready."

Chapter 26

JJ

"Can you block this?" Mountie asked him, pointing to the ground.

"If I had a full kit, maybe. As it is, I don't think so," JJ said, fingering the rock walls on either side of the opening to the pass.

He knew the mountains in the area were primarily metamorphic with a similar composition to gneiss, but to him, they looked and felt more like granite. If he had to bet, he'd guess the rock would react like granite as well, being hard and strong. With the right equipment, he might be able to shear off pieces, but as far as bringing enough down to block the pass, he doubted it.

"Hey, Mountie! I see more vehicles coming," Jasper shouted from his position where the trail cut into the pass.

Mountie and JJ rushed forward to see. The view was spectacular, if he could ignore the threat arrayed against them. A haze stretched out for kilometers, but he had to be able to observe 20 klicks or more of the highway and most of the five klicks of the trail to the lake. And coming out of the trees, he could clearly see a line of vehicles.

JJ pulled out his binos for a better view. He counted 20 before the last one emerged from the firs along the road. Eight were Pecker-3s, three were APTs, and the rest a hodgepodge of whatever the mercs could put together. Along with the two tanks below them, that made a total of ten. Comparatively speaking, the Pecker-3 was not the most capable tank in the galaxy, but ten of them could create havoc maneuvering in the Marines' rear.

JJ took a step forward to look down the mountainside. At the second switchback, one of the two tanks already here was slowly making the turn. A bigger tank might not have been able to squeeze by, but the Pecker-3 was small enough to be able to use the trail.

"I give him 20, 25 minutes at that rate to reach us," Mountie said. "So, we need to come up with something before then. Why don't you see what you can do?"

JJ checked his kit for the 100th time to see if something had miraculously appeared that he'd missed the other 99 times. Nothing doing. He had the same five detonators, two breaching charges, a C10 pack, three E22s, two toads, and 15 meters of line charge as he'd had each previous time he'd checked. The line charges might make a nice boom that could startle someone, but they'd do nothing against the native rock. The toads could burn through maybe a meter or two of rock, and the breaching charges might be able to crack off a chunk. Only the C10 charge had the ability to move rock, but to be effective, it had to be drilled in.

"There's no way I can move enough rock to block the pass. I can knock off a chunk or two, but that's it."

"Can you drop a rock on top of that tank?" Jasper asked.

"If I timed it right, maybe. It won't do much, though."

"But would it slow them down?"

"Ha! If I got rang like that from above, I'd sure be cautious," JJ answered.

"So, let's try that," Mountie said.

"I wasn't serious about that. I can't aim a rock."

"But Jasper's right. It might make them slow down. They don't know what we can do up here, so let's give them something to let their imaginations run wild."

JJ looked at Mountie for a moment before just saying, "Aye-aye, sir." What he was asking was unreasonable. He could blow up a piece of rock, maybe even send it down the hill. But to actually hit a moving vehicle was asking too much. Still, maybe the threat of tumbling rocks might slow them down, and the day was just too beautiful not to try and extend their time in it.

There was a crack from the second tank below, the one still on the ridge overlooking the lake. All three ducked back down, and a moment later, the round whizzed over their heads to explode against the mountain walls some 400 meters down the pass. JJ didn't point out that the Pecker-3's 60mm round didn't have much effect on the mountainside, just sending dust and small pieces of rock flying off.

"Now if they had proximity fuzes, we'd be in trouble," Mountie remarked. "Uh, JJ, they don't have the fuzes, right?"

"I don't see why they wouldn't. That's real low tech. Been around for five, six-hundred years at least. Not too expensive, either."

Mountie grimaced, then said, "Well, either they didn't stock up on them, or they just want us to keep our heads down."

JJ didn't want to think of things that were out of their control. Keeping back from line-of-sight, he selected a detonator and, after a moment's contemplation, a breaching charge. The C10 had more power, but it exploded much slower, and without being drilled into the rock, he thought the force of the blast would just be directed outwards.

He crept up to look down the mountainside to his right. Above them, part of the slope was almost vertical for over 100 meters. From their position down to the bottom where the road started making switchbacks, it was still pretty steep, maybe a 35-degree incline and slightly steeper in spots. At the base of the sheer cliff walls, rocks from above had hit—some stayed there, others had kept on going down the hill. At least one looked to have taken some trees as it smashed almost all the way to the lake sometime in the near past.

Ten meters away, almost at their level, a large rock, about two meters high and a good meter-and-a-half thick was partially buried in the scree. At least that was what he could see. It could be part of the underlying rock jutting up, but from the formation patterns, JJ thought it had fallen from above. If it was not connected, it might be possible to give it a push.

If he wanted to push it, then the breaching charge wasn't the best choice. Discarding that, he connected an E22 to the C10. JJ didn't want to pulverize the rock, just push it over, and the C10 exploded slow enough to do that.

"I'm going to see about knocking over that bad boy," JJ said.

Mountie edged forward to take a look, and said, "That rock out there? What, are you going to toss your explosives at it?"

"No, I've got to place it."

JJ understood the lieutenant's concern. Besides being exposed to fire from below, he'd half to be half-mountain goat just to keep his feet. The scree at this level was loose, and if he slipped, the trail below should catch him, but then he'd have to run back up while the mercs used him for target practice."

"Your call. But maybe we can cover you," Mountie said.

"With what? That Pecker down there's all buttoned up."

Neither Mountie nor Jasper had a rejoinder, so JJ checked the connection on the E22, and before he could think of any of the thousand reasons that this was a stupid idea, jumped up and scrambled across the open area, feet slipping, but managing to cross to the rock.

Just as he reached it, the ground around him burst into small explosions as an automatic gun of some sort sprayed the area.

"Holy shit!" he shouted as he dove behind the rock, jamming himself in the small space and pulling his legs in.

A few chips of rock stung his face, but for the most part, the rounds were impacting all over. There was a shitload of them, to be sure, but without a tight grouping.

"You OK, JJ?" Jasper called out.

"I'm alive," he answered, looking over to see two worried faces.

He gave them a thumbs up just as a stream of tracer rounds reached up from below, some impacting on the edge of the road, some continuing on to the sky, sending them both scrambling back.

"That's the Pecker on the trail below!" JJ called out. "I think the one that fired on me was the one by the lake."

JJ didn't know what the mercs were using to take him under fire. If his comms weren't being jammed, he could query his AI on what machineguns a Pecker usually carried, but it looked to be either a .50 cal or 12.8mm at the least, maybe even a 15mm. The tank down by the lake was at least two klicks away, but even then, he thought the grouping was too loose. He had a feeling that the mercs were more concerned with budgets, and they'd cut corners when they could, to include substandard arms.

Maybe they're too cheap for proximity fuzes, too?

He wasn't going to get anything done huddled behind the rock. As if reminding him of that, another burst of fire splattered around him, a few rounds hitting the rock and making it vibrate against his back. Taking care not to expose himself, he scrunched around until he was facing the rock. He wanted to tip the thing over, so he activated the gecko pad and placed the charge about three-quarters of the way up. Clicking in the E22 detonator, he removed the control, and as at the bridge five days before, set it to dead man's switch-mode. The status lights flashed green.

He eyed the distance back to the pass. It was only ten meters, only five steps. Not far at all for most purposes, but way too far, as far as he was concerned. A few more questing rounds impacted above and to his side. The tank's machine gun may have crap for accuracy, but it could spit out a shitload, and all it would take was for one to hit him. It would probably cut him in two. And then there was the tank below him. If it could acquire him, the range was so close that the gunner couldn't miss.

On solid ground, he could cover that in two seconds. It would take the gunner on the far tank a second to acquire him and fire, maybe two-and-a-half seconds for the rounds to reach him. He should be able to make it.

Should.

Gripping the detonator switch, he gathered his legs under him, then bolted for safety. Two steps in, his right foot slipped, and he went to his knees, left hand grabbing to keep him up, right keeping the switch closed. He managed to bring his right foot back, and he lunged forward just at the rounds started impacting.

Jasper and Mountie both stood up and grabbed him just as his left foot slipped, dragging him onto the trail and down below the lip. More rounds chattered, banging off the rock walls, sending chips down on top of them.

"That got my heart pounding," JJ said. "Good times!"

Jasper laughed while Mountie just shook his head.

"You should have seen yourself," Jasper was saying. "Slipping and sliding like that. I thought you were going to the bottom, but you just kept on pushing it."

"I was there, I know," JJ said, feeling relief wash over him.

"Did you get the charge placed?" Mountie asked, interrupting them.

JJ held up his right hand, still grasping the dead man's switch. "Right here, ready to go."

"So now, the question is when to blow it," Mountie said, moving forward again.

Dust was still drifting down on them from the wall impacts, but the guns themselves were silent. The drone of the Pecker-3's green-diesels were getting louder below them. JJ peeked over the lip of the trail, ready to pull back at any sign of firing. Three switches below them, the tank was making steady progress. If they did nothing, it would reach them in four or five minutes.

JJ handed Mountie one of this two toads. The small grenades were meant to burn through obstacles of fortifications, but he didn't see any reason they couldn't burn through the top of a tank as well.

"If this doesn't work, when it gets to the last switchback below us, try these."

"Make sure this works, then."

Right, sir. As if I wasn't going to try.

Sometimes, officers just had to state the obvious.

JJ had three attempts to hit the tank with his rock. In a few moments, the tank would pass beneath the rock, but crossing two loops of the trail, JJ thought if the rock even detached, it could get hung up on a trail or get knocked to the side. If he waited for the last loop, the rock might not have generated enough momentum to do much damage.

Second one it is, then.

"What do you think?" Mountie asked.

"When it reaches there," he answered, pointing. "By that scraggly bush leaning away from the trail."

It seemed as if Mountie was going to say something, but if he was, he bit it back and said, "OK, it's your call."

The Pecker-3 whipped around the third switchback with barely a pause. The driver must be getting used to it and gaining more confidence. Hubris could be deadly, and JJ hoped the driver would miss the second-to-last turn. If he started to fall, the tank probably wouldn't stop until he hit the bottom.

But, no such luck. He took the next turn easily. JJ started to get to his knees to get a better view, but Mountie pulled him back down.

"You don't need to give them a target. You can keep down and still time this."

He was right, JJ knew. He was letting his thrill-of-the-hunt get in the way of solid tactics.

"Here it comes," Jasper said, Mr. Obvious.

JJ had tuned him out, though. He was focusing on the tank, coming forward at maybe 15 KPH. It wasn't fast, but JJ didn't have any experience even remotely related to this.

The tank reached the small bush that was his target, and JJ released the switch. There was a low boom, and a heat and shockwave rushed over the three prone men, making them flinch. JJ had his eyes on the rock, however, and he almost shouted in excitement as the rock tipped over and fell, or rather slid down the first slope instead of bouncing its way down. It reached the first switchback, and for a moment, JJ thought it was going to stop there. Somehow, though, the bottom caught, and the overall momentum picked the uphill side and flipped in over, crushing the downhill edge of the trail bed. The rock barely paused as it continued down—and JJ knew he'd failed. He'd detonated the charge too late.

Except for a horrendous brain fart from the driver.

JJ didn't know if the driver could see the rock coming down. He didn't know if the explosion itself had startled him. But for whatever reason, he stopped dead in the trail. A moment later, several tons of local rock bounced once and landed smack dab on the top of the tank, pushing it to the side of the trail and over the edge. Both tank and rock continued downhill, the tank rolling, the rock bouncing. At the next level of the trail, the tank landed on its top and stuck while the rock, gaining steam, kept on going, bounding its way to the bottom in a cloud of dust, and smashing into some trees above the lake itself.

"Holy shit!" JJ muttered.

Jasper pounded him on the back while Mountie just said, "I . . . I didn't think you could really do it. I'm sorry for doubting."

JJ didn't mention that the outcome had taken him completely by surprise. He hadn't even wanted to try it, yet, the results could speak for themselves.

As the dust started to clear, JJ could see the bottom escape hatch, now exposed to the sky, started to open. He whipped up his M90 and fired a burst at the hatch, which quickly closed.

"Down!" Mountie shouted as the tank on the far ridge opened up, joined by a few of the other vehicles.

As before, they only had to pull back less than a meter, and the tank's guns couldn't touch them. They made a lot of noise, though, and the three hugged the ground as rounds whizzed past just above their heads.

"Think that will stop them?" Jasper asked.

"Nah, but it's sure going to slow them down some."

"But that tank, it's blocking the road up."

"They can get one of the other tanks up there and just push it off the road. But they've got to be wondering if we've got anything else up our sleeves."

A drone swooped in low, and JJ fired off a burst, not hitting it but driving it away.

"No, if I were them, I'd be sending up the infantry to dig us out," he continued.

"We can fight them, right?"

"Sure," Mountie said. "And we can drop some. But there's a hell of a lot more of them than us.

"I think JJ's right. I don't see any signs of mortars, thank God. And I think they're under some huge time constraints. So, they're going to have to go with what they have, and that looks to be infantry."

He carefully edged back up, looked, and then said, "And that's that. They're dismounting their troops now."

"What, you figure two hours? They've got to come up to our right, off the road."

The mountainside to the west bent back away from the lake. Merc troops could climb that in defilade to the three of them. The same reasons why the mercs couldn't bring much to bear on the three of them from down there also worked to the mercs' advantage when it came to the three of them taking the mercs under fire.

"Do you think we can get around them somehow and hit them while they're climbing?" Mountie asked, seemingly just thinking out loud.

All three turned on their backs to look up the steep slopes to the top of the mountain.

"I doubt it, sir. I think it would take us longer to get up there than it will take them to get here."

"Yeah, I think you're right. So, if we want to stop them, it'll have to be right here."

"Horatius at the Bridge," Jasper said.

"That's the second time you guys have said this Horatio guy's name," JJ said.

"Horatius, not Horatio. Horatius Cocles," Mountie said. "During the Clusium War before Rome was an empire. The Etruscans were attacking Rome, and most of the Roman soldiers were running for their lives. Horatius decided that enough was enough, and on the Pons Sublicius, the first bridge over the Tiber, he took a stand and held off the advancing army. Because the bridge was narrow, they couldn't get enough soldiers at him to bring him down, and he piled the bodies in front of him."

"One guy held off an army?" JJ said, not believing it.

"Well, that's the legend, at least. Who knows how true it is? Maybe he held them off long enough for the Roman army to reform and attack. Still, it's pretty ballsy."

"Most accounts have it that there were three of them. Horatius, Spurius Lartius, and Titus Aquilinus, all standing shoulder to shoulder," Jasper added.

"Really? Three of them? I hadn't realized that," Mountie said. "Not bad knowledge of history—for a militiaman."

Jasper laughed and said, "Not all farmers as just dumb hicks, you know."

JJ took in the history lesson, then said, "The Romans, they were some bad asses, right? I've seen the flicks."

"Aye-yah, JJ."

"Well, no one is as bad as the Marines. There were three of them back there, and there are three of us here. So, let's make our own legend, OK?"

"Ooh-rah!" Mountie shouted, joined a moment later by Jasper. "It's legend time!"

Chapter 27

Mountie

JJ fired another burst from his M90 at the mercs climbing the mountain. It caused the mercs to dive for cover, but not much else. The light hypervelocity darts were deadly within 800 meters, and being mag-propelled, could be fired in the vacuum of space, but their mass could easily be blown off target at long distances. If they had one of the old M44s that used to be the Corps' prime combat weapon, they could actually do some damage to the mercs instead of just harassing them.

The Gescards that he and Jasper still carried weren't much better. It was a bullpup assault weapon, suited for throwing out lots of slugs, but with only a max effective range of 500 meters.

Mountie was wracking his brain for some sort of plan. He was an officer, and that is what officers were supposed to do, right? But all he could come up with was basically what Horatius had done. Just slug it out with the enemy.

Maybe something will come up.

But he knew he was running out of time. Already, at least a platoon of mercs had reached their level on the mountainside, and more were climbing to join them. All they had to do was to come across now to hit them. The mercs could get to within 150 meters or so before both groups were within sight of each other, and with all the vehicles lined up below them, Mountie knew they would simply pour fire at the three of them, giving the infantry cover to close that 150 meters. Mountie had the sinking feeling that this was going to come down to a very close-range fight, and one they couldn't win.

He looked back along the trail. It had been three hours since the women and children had left. He wondered if they had made it, and not for the first time, he thought about just picking up and getting out of there. But this had grown to more than just Jasper's family and friends. With the armored column down there waiting to get through the pass, they had to delay them until word got back to the ground commander and a response could be mobilized to meet them. It might sound like hyperbole, but the fate of the war on the planet could very well be decided right here.

"Ha! I think I got one!" JJ crowed.

"No, he's getting back up," Jasper responded. "Look, he's running."

Mountie listened to the two. All of their lives could probably be measured in tens of minutes, but here they were, voices as calm as if they were playing the latest IR game.

He was scared; there was no getting around it. Scared of dying, scared of failure. But if he was going to die, he couldn't have asked for two better companions. He hadn't known either of them five days before, but an amazing bond had grown.

"Hey, you two," he said, waiting for them to turn to him. "Thanks."

"Thanks?" JJ asked.

But Jasper nodded and said, "You, too. Thanks."

Mountie had given Jasper the chance to get away, to live, but the older man had decided to stay. It might have been foolish. It might have been wasteful. But it was appreciated.

Another drone flitted by, and Mountie instinctively fired a burst at it, as he'd been doing all day. To his surprise, there was a pinging sound, and the drone sputtered, spiraling in to crash first against the rock wall, then to bounce down the side to land on the road. JJ scooted farther back, then got up in a crouch and ran to it.

The drone hopped and jerked like a living animal, but JJ grabbed it, and holding it like a live lobster, carried it back to the other two.

"It's still broadcasting, right?" he asked.

Mountie saw the tiny green indicator light on top and said, "Yes."

"OK, OK, here, Gyver, hold it."

He handed it to Jasper, then undid his waist cinch.

"Point the lens at me," he said, bending over and exposing his bare ass at it. "Like what you see, assholes!"

"I see your asshole, JJ. Not theirs," Jasper said as both men broke into laughter.

"Wait, I'm going to shit on it! Let some drilot see a brown avalanche."

"No!" Mountie shouted as a laugh finally erupted from him as well. "If this is my last hour, I don't want to go out smelling your shit!"

"Oh, man! But it would be so good," JJ said as he pulled up his trousers.

He took the drone back from Jasper.

"Hey, Mr. Drilot," he said to the remote drone-pilot. "The lieutenant saved you from my ass, but your time's up."

He dropped the little drone and stomped on it.

The whine of green-diesel engines interrupted them, and all three dropped back down and crawled forward. Down below, two tanks and two half-tracs were moving forward along the basin up to the start of the switchbacks. All four had their machine guns pointed high.

"They coming up here?" JJ asked.

"Not until the infantry clears the pass of us, I'd have to guess," Mountie answered.

But the four vehicles didn't stop. They chugged right past the first turn and started up. The three Federation men simply watched. It was not as if they could do anything. But after the third switchback, the four vehicles came to a halt.

"Pretty stupid," JJ noted. "They should have stayed back. Now the angle to us is too steep. They won't be able to bring any fire to bear on us."

"The ones over there will," Mountie said, pointing to the rest of the vehicles staged by the lake-view crest.

"Can't hit much from there," JJ muttered.

"But they can throw a lot of fire."

Mountie watched the four vehicles below, wondering if they were there to try and rescue the crew of the upside-down Pecker-3. Twice, at least one person had tried to open the escape hatch, but a few well-placed darts and convinced them to stay buttoned-up.

"Hey, how far do you think it is to them," Mountie asked.

"From here?" Jasper said. "Maybe 50, 60 meters down."

"How far horizontally?"

"I don't know. A little more."

Mountie pulled out the toad JJ had given him earlier and bounced it up and down in his hand.

"Why? What're you gonna do?" JJ asked.

"I think I can bounce one down to them. How do you set the timer on this," he asked. "Oh, I guess these numbers that are staring me in the face. Five seconds should do it."

"Officers," JJ said with mock exasperation.

Mountie checked the position of the merc armor, then retreated until he could stand up. He took five large steps back, armed the toad, then ran forward, launching it high into the air before falling on his belly to watch.

Forty or fifty meters was a long, long throw, and the toad hit two switchbacks before the armor. It bounced high, then over the next level, and to his great surprise, clanked off one of the half-tracs. The toad skittered away, just reaching the next drop-off when it erupted into a small, burning star. Immediately the small scrub on the slope caught on fire, and black smoke mixed with the toad's white.

"Oh, man! Close!" JJ said.

All four vehicles immediately lurched into motion, retreating back down the trail. A tank and half-trac collided at the turn, but with no obvious damage. Each of the four made it all the way back to the start of the switchbacks.

"Well, you got their attention," Jasper said. "Wish you could have nailed one, though."

The toad petered out, and the bushes, no longer fed by the intense heat, started going out as well.

Mountie felt more than a little let down. He knew the chances of actually taking out a tank had been minimal, but to have the toad actually hit one of the half-tracs and then bounce off was disheartening.

"I think all the grunts that are coming are up here now," JJ said.

Mountie turned to where the merc infantry had climbed the slope. He couldn't see any of them. That meant that about 30 mercs were at their same elevation, moving towards them, and there was nothing they could do but wait. It was getting to be go-time.

"OK, no more messing around. JJ, I want you in as close to the wall as you can, aiming right at the edge where the face bends. The second you see anything, I want a full mag emptied. Let them know they're going to have to fight for every centimeter.

"Jasper, hang back out of the line of fire. When JJ or I tell you, throw those breaching charges at them; then you're weapons free with your merc rifle there."

Mountie hoped the breaching charges would do some damage. They packed a good punch, but they were not anti-personnel grenades. JJ had rigged them to override the minimum detonation time—they should explode four seconds after being thrown.

"Roger that, sir. Let them come," JJ said.

Mountie was expecting to wait twenty or thirty minutes, but almost as soon as JJ was ready, the first merc carefully stepped into view. He jerked back at the drone of JJ's M90, but not fast enough, tumbling head-first down the scree.

Immediately, the now-30 vehicles from below opened up, sending a barrage of heavy machinegun and 60mm fire up to them, rounds impacting over seemingly every square centimeter of rock.

"Shit!" JJ shouted slapping his neck where blood started welling.

Pieces of blasted rock stung Mountie's face as he stumbled back.

"Are you OK?" he shouted at JJ, who was also scrambling back.

"Fucking rock hit me!" he shouted to be heard over the cacophony of sound as he looked at his bloody hand where he'd wiped his neck.

"Do I throw the charges now?" Jasper asked.

"No, wait for a break in the firing," Mountie said, knowing that as soon as any of them exposed themselves, it would be over. "They can't keep going forever!"

But he knew that right now, when they couldn't fight back, the merc infantry was closing in, taking full advantage of the covering fire from their armor.

The crescendo of fire slackened only slightly to a more measured, disciplined rate. Pulverized rock filled the air in choking dust, and shards flew with stinging speed. Mountie knew he'd been cut several times, but he couldn't afford to think of that now.

He wasn't just going to sit there, lambs to the slaughter. He picked up one of Jasper's breaching charges, pushed the arming button five times, then without looking or exposing himself more than his arm, flung it blindly around the edge and towards where the mercs were advancing. He was rewarded with a low boom that overwhelmed the sound of firing for a moment, but he didn't know if he'd taken anyone out.

"OK, back up. They still have to come in here. We'll just retreat ten and let them have it," he ordered.

All three ran back, then fell on their bellies, weapons pointed to the opening. A round ricocheted off the rock face and hit the trail-bed by Mountie's side, but he ignored it.

The high rounds continued unabated, but there was a shift in the sounds; to their right, the firing slowed, then stopped.

"Get ready," Mountie told the other two, knowing the shift in the base of fire meant that the mercs were right there, ready to rush in.

A minute later, an arm came whipping around the edge of the opening, and a small object came at them, flying over to land behind.

"Grenade!" JJ shouted. "Get ready!"

Luckily, the grenade went too far, and it exploded with a whump that Mountie felt in his core, but without an accompanying sting of shrapnel.

Immediately, four mercs came screaming around the side and onto the roadbed, firing blindly. All three fired into the mercs, dropping them with a fusillade of darts and rounds.

"Push to the sides!" JJ shouted, with JJ and him scooting to the right and Mountie scooting to the left, all up against the mountain walls.

That exposed Mountie, and in the next group of five to charge out onto the road, one merc immediately saw him and started sweeping his Gescard down to spray him when one of the other mercs either pushed or stepped on his foot in his eagerness to get some cover, and the .370 cal slugs ripped in front of Mountie, missing his face by centimeters.

Two mercs fell to JJ or Jasper's fire, and Mountie hit one more, who fell onto his ass and tried to back out of the line of fire. Two more had escaped the large volume of Federation fire and had hit the deck. They were prone, firing at Mountie and the other two while all three of them were firing at the mercs, both sides only ten meters apart. Amazingly—impossibly—no one was hit. One of the mercs lost his nerve, and he bolted back, diving out of sight to the left. A moment later, the last merc shuddered and slumped, blood pouring from under his helmet.

Mountie took a deep breath, trying to regain his composure. Most of the support firing had ceased, and it seemed quiet in comparison. He was able to hear the whine of engines below. The Tenner armor would be climbing the trail. He could hear voices shouting to the right as the mercs shouted orders at each other. He couldn't tell if they would try to rush them again, or just wait for the tanks to get up to the pass and crush them.

"You OK," he called to the other two.

"Jasper's hit," JJ said.

"I'm OK," Jasper immediately added. "I'm still in the fight."

With the lack of firing, half-a-dozen drones hovered overhead. Mountie knew the feeds would be going to the infantry. They'd know exactly where the three of them were.

A merc voice reached out, clearly audible to Mountie, shouting, "In the pass now, everyone!"

"Shit, they're coming" Mountie yelled at the other two. "This is it!"

The first two mercs stumbled into sight, looking back, of all things. Both were immediately dropped before a mob, pushing and fighting each other, came around the east edge of the opening before they simply seemed to come apart with gouts of blood and body parts separating from each other.

"Their own armor is killing them!" JJ shouted, but Mountie knew different.

The whine he'd heard was not the merc armor. Only one thing he knew had that lovely sound—A Federation Navy Basilisk, known to those who flew them as the Lizard.

"It's a Lizard! It's a Lizard!" Mountie shouted, jumping to his feet and rushing forward, ignoring the pile of muck that had been living men only moments before.

There, pulling a beautiful Lin turn, the Lizard was swooping straight up, almost touching her belly to the rock face of the mountain. From below, armored vehicles fired, tracers reaching up to try and catch the Lizard. Slipping on guts and blood, his M90 at the ready, Mountie edged forward. The 150 meters between the opening and the bend in the mountain cliff had been almost swept clear. Two mercs were moving, but down and struggling to get back. Whoever else had been there was gone. Lumps littered the slope, but Mountie didn't look too closely at them.

"Ooh-rah, mother fuckers!" JJ shouted, M90 held high in one hand while he jumped up and down.

Mountie watched, oblivious to the merc armor below, as the Lizard reached apogee, then spun on its tail to swoop back down. Mountie could see the two mounted BV-G30's under the wings. These were not designed for armor, but they'd get the job done. Maybe not for 30 vehicles, but for a good number of them. The pilot still had his Forsythe vulcan, of course, the same weapon he'd used to scrape the mercs off the mountain, and he might get a few more that way.

Only the Lizard didn't dive at the armor. She came in directly for the pass. Mountie looked around for more mercs, spotting the one who'd retreated to the left, but he had his hands raised in surrender, looking at the Lizard.

Oh, shit! Our see-me's must be getting jammed!

"Let him see us!" he told the other two as he started waving his arms. "The pilot doesn't know we're Federation."

With the armor firing at him, Mountie wondered why he'd be wasting time with a handful of what he thought were merc infantry, but that's what it had to be.

There was a flash from the underside of the Lizard, and Mountie instinctively ducked, but it was a hit from one of the armored vehicles below. The Lizard is a tough frame, and she flew on, but she couldn't take too much of that kind of pounding.

A thousand meters out, the Lizard wheeled to the left, inverted, and then came back along the face of the mountain, cockpit facing it. She swooped right at their level, maybe 30 meters away.

Hell, that's Skeets! he realized as the Lizard buzzed past them, Skeets waving at them. *What they hell's he doing showboating like that?*

"I think he wants us to move," Jasper said.

"What?"

"He wants us to get out of the way. He's going to block the pass."

He's right! That's why the BV-G30's!

"Run!" he shouted.

All three immediately bolted as Skeets shot his Lizard up into the air.

"How far do we have to get?" JJ asked.

"A hell of a lot farther than this," Mountie answered, sneaking a peek back.

Ten meters behind them, weaponless and catching up fast, was the lone remaining merc. He caught Mountie's eyes and said nothing.

"Keep running," Mountie said, as Jasper started faltering, blood staining his side.

Mountie closed in to help, but the merc brushed him aside, putting an arm around Jasper's waist and pulling him along.

This isn't right, Mountie thought, then let it go for the moment.

He'd sort it out later.

He wasn't sure how far they'd gone when a huge roar reached them. All four men slowed to a stop and turned just as the concussion reached them. Back at the opening to the pass, some 300 meters back, clouds of smoke obscured their sight. Rocks, thrown up into the sky, came back to earth, landing all around them.

One, bigger than the rock that JJ had sent down onto the Pecker-3, landed 15 meters from Mountie, making the ground shake.

No one said a word as the smoke billowed higher and higher, maybe reaching the mountain peaks. As it began clear, the sight of rock and rubble began to emerge. Hundreds, if not thousands of tons of mountain had collapsed to block the pass. It didn't take an engineer to know that nothing would be getting through that for a long, long time.

A lone Lizard cut through the smoke cloud and came low, flying over the cliff walls. Skeets waggled his wings at them before heading back north.

"Um, I guess I'm your prisoner?" the merc said, the first to break the silence.

JJ started to raise his M90, but Mountie pushed the muzzle back down with his hand.

"What's your name?" Mountie asked.

"Infantry Specialist Three Waterson, sir."

"Well, Spec Waterson, I accept your surrender. Why don't you help Private van Ruiker there? We've got a long hump to get out of here."

The four men turned to the north and started walking.

Epilogue

Mountie ran through his checks. The Basilisk, so maneuverable in an atmosphere, was a pig in space with little room for error, and he couldn't afford any problems. It wasn't unheard of for a pilot to survive a fight, only to buy it on the way back to the carrier.

"Buddley, I'm getting a 92 on the right oxypack."

"All you need is 90% for an up-check," ADR2 Baron said.

"I know what we need, but it's not your ass on the line, is it. You'll be heading up to the *Andaman Sea* in one of the shuttles, all nice and comfy."

"Sucks to be an officer, huh, sir? Anyways, that's about all we've got left. I've got three worse than that, and one Cat 4'd. If you want to get back, it's this one or nothing."

Mountie stepped back and looked across the tarmac, heat waves rippling in the air. No, he wanted to get off this piece of crap world as soon as he could. If all he could get was a 92% on the right pack, he'd make sure he nursed it along. Even with only the left pack, he should still be able to make rendezvous with the carrier, up there in low orbit, even if the SOP for a one-engine approach meant being tractored in—and that was mortifying for any plane-jockey.

Of course, Skeets had brand new packs clamped over his engine intakes. Rank had its privileges, something he was used to, and with Mutt gone, he was the junior pilot in the squadron.

The thought of Mutt made him pause. He'd spoken with Mutt's parents on the starsat once since getting back from being shot down, but he knew he had to make a personal visit as soon as he could. Mutt was from Earth, so it might take a while for him to schedule it, but it was something he had to do.

"Miss you, Mutt," he said, slamming his fist to his chest, then extending a forefinger as he raised his hand to the sky.

The squadron had lost three aircraft during the fight, a Lizard and two Kangaroos: one of those 'Roos had 12 Marines onboard. Three lost while fighting a sophisticated enemy was better than they might have hoped for, but that didn't make the pain of losing his friend any less. And for what? Why had six sailors died, why had the Marines lost over 200 men? They hadn't won the fight. They hadn't lost the fight. They'd been merely a sideshow in the war, an afterthought.

After the Battle of the Black, where Navy ships slugged it out at tremendous ranges, the powers that be had decided that enough was enough. Both sides met on St. Barnabas, the homeworld of the Brotherhood of Servants, and after a month, had hammered out a peace. The Federation declared victory, of course, and from a military standpoint, they had won. But the Tenners managed to wring out concessions, most of what they had initially demanded from the Federation only to be turned down at the time.

Mountie still hadn't gone over all the details of the treaty, but he had a sneaky suspicion that the only real winner in the war was the Brotherhood of Servants. In the midst of the negotiations, they somehow came out with an independent world and rights to a good chunk of empty space in which to colonize.

What really pissed Mountie off was that they could have won. The enveloping force at Spirit Lake had been a Tenner afterthought, an opportunity that they'd jumped on. When it had been blocked, they'd gone ahead with their major thrust up through Elena Pass—and been stopped in their tracks by the militia. Yes, the militia had suffered heavy casualties, far more than the Tenner mercs, and the Marines' Charlie Company with them had almost been wiped out, but together, they had dug in and pushed back the mercs. That was the last major operation of the war on this planet, at least. For the next four months, it had been raids and patrols without any major change in control over the ground. General Corning, the planetary militia commander (and former FCDC sergeant first class) had pushed for a major offensive, but it had soon become clear that the war had entered its final phase, and both the Federation and Tenner commanders were hesitant to waste lives and seemed willing to let the top-level negotiators decide on the outcome.

Mountie, though, had wanted to pursue this little corner of the war and end it. The ghosts of the dead farmer and his family still haunted his dreams, begging for revenge and so their release into the long sleep.

Last week, after the armistice, he'd watched shuttle flares as the Tenners evacuated from one of their forward bases, only 80 klicks away. One quick flight, five minutes in his Lizard, and ground support craft or not, he could have blasted one of the shuttles out of the air. The weird thing was that Mountie couldn't tell if he was merely daydreaming or if he was truly tempted.

Not all the Tenners were gone. Mountie looked over to the squadron command where he knew a Tenner liaison officer was monitoring their retrograde. Some of the other pilots had gotten into conversations with him, but Mountie couldn't bring himself to talk to the man.

Snap out of it, man. It's over. Let it go!

He turned back to his aircraft maintenance chief, who was patiently waiting to set the *Pretty Gabby* to green.

"OK, Buddley, I accept the plane."

"Roger that, sir," he said quickly, punching his code into his PA. "See you back here at 1700!"

He watched Buddley dash off, obviously happy to get this last task done. In six hours, he'd be riding the shuttle back to the ship with a clean bunk, a full night's sleep, and real chow.

The thought of the welcome-back meal lifted Mountie's dark mood. Besides being a tradition, the *Andaman Sea*, or rather Master Chief Pious-Strength, put on a feast that was known throughout the division if not the fleet. His mouth started watering at the thought.

"Sir! Respectfully request your attention, sir!" someone shouted out from behind him.

Oh, what now? he wondered as he turned—to see one Lance Corporal Javier Julio Gregory Portillo, United Federation Marine Corps, and Private Jasper van Ruiker, Nieuwe Utrecht Militia, in a Marine uniform with the white tulip patch of Nieuwe Utrecht instead of the Federation patch on his sleeve, both standing at an exaggerated attention, right arms up in a rigid salute.

"Oh, my God, look who they let on the base," he said after automatically returning the salute and then stepping forward to hug JJ and pound him on the back.

"We heard you Navy-types were bugging out first, so we thought we'd come to send you off," JJ said.

"Yeah, we're anxious to get back to decent company, you know. Civilized folk and all," he answered as he released the Marine.

"And what's this?" he asked the militiaman as he enveloped him as well. "You joining the Marines?"

"Oh, good God, no! I'm too old for them. But I've been a militia liaison to the Corps, ever since Spirit Lake. See the patch?"

"I see something else," Mountie said, touching the nametag sewn into the older man's utility blouse. "Gyver?"

"Well, why not?" JJ asked. "He earned it. He's also getting a Battle Commendation First."

"Really? Congrats, Gyver."

"And JJ's been put in for a Bronze Star."

They both looked at him expectantly, but he didn't say anything. Getting shot down was not something taken lightly in the Navy, so despite his squadron recommending him for a DFC, Fleet was going to look long and hard at that. And the wing being the wing, whatever he'd done on the ground with the two standing in front of him wouldn't be worth a warm bucket of spit with his seniors.

It didn't really matter much to him. As much as he lived to fly, he cherished his time behind enemy lines with these two. They would be part of his life forever.

"Well, look. I'm off in four hours, but the squadron commander has opened up the bar. I'm flying, so I can only have one, and I've got to take a Jolt-Sober after, but I'd be honored to lift one with your two in memory of Mutt and Sergeant Go."

"I'm not leaving for four more days, and our battalion commander has not opened the bar, but as I'm with a real live Navy 'ossifer,' if he'd make that an order, I'd be honored as well."

"Well, then consider it an order there, Marine. You, too, Marine liaison. I think I've still got authority over you."

"Aye-aye, sir," the two chorused as the three headed off the tarmac and into the field-expedient club.

****

"Sergeant Gary James Go, Engineer Platoon. 4 March 138," the sergeant major intoned.

JJ stepped one foot forward and placed the helmet on top of the M90 that was driven muzzle first into the ground.

He came back to attention, refusing to wipe the tear that had formed in his left eye and threatened to run down his cheek.

He barely heard the sergeant major continue the honor roll with, "First Lieutenant Shareef Koudra-Miyako, First Platoon, Charlie Company. 7 March 138."

March 7th was the date of the merc offensive, so JJ knew he'd be standing at attention for a long time. He didn't care. Honoring the fallen was something every Marine treasured. Traditionally, this was done on Founding Day, where each of the Marines who'd fallen during the year was so honored, but the Marines in the battalion had requested a separate ceremony on Nieuwe Utrecht soil, and the commanding officer had readily agreed. Two-hundred and ten M90's were driven into the ground of the planet in 21 rows of ten, one for each of the 206 Marines and four Navy corpsmen who had fallen. In front of each one, a friend stood, helmet in hand, to place on the weapon.

Most of the dead had already been shipped back to division before they'd be sent to their homes for burial or cremation. Fourteen of the 206 fallen Marines, however, would be left on the planet when the CO stepped into the last shuttle, including the four recon Marines who'd died at the bridge with him. Recovery teams would be sent later to try and find the bodies, but for now, this was their resting place, and the Marines wanted a ceremony here.

July on Nieuwe Utrecht was close to the planetary equinox, but the day was hot, the sun beating down the gathered Marines. The sweat rolled down his back as JJ stared at the small brass nameplate attached to the stock of the M90 with Sergeant Go's name engraved on it. He'd come to terms with the sergeant's death, but the ceremony was a time for remembrance. The image of the sergeant, the door of the truck opening, the flash of the merc's handgun going off invaded his thoughts. Sergeant Go was a Marine's Marine, and to be taken down by some limp-dick driver seemed like a travesty.

He wondered whatever happened to the driver, if he'd survived the war, if he was in some bar right now, recounting how he single-handedly took out a Federation Marine. Despite himself, he almost smiled as he thought of others calling bullshit on him, not believing a word.

He wasn't even really angry at the merc anymore. He'd done what he'd had to do, nothing more. What the merc did had a personal impact on him, but he had to admit that he'd done far more damage, killed far more mercs than most Marines, certainly more than any other engineer.

"I hope I did you proud, Sergeant," he whispered.

"Private William Sanderson, 2 July 138," the sergeant major said almost half-an-hour later. Bill was the last Marine to die, killed when his M-180 turned over in a ditch and crushed him, a week after the armistice was signed.

And the ceremony was over. There were no speeches, no attempts to rally the troops. The ceremony was the names, and the names were the ceremony. Nothing more was needed.

JJ broke his position of attention, looking around. Staff Sergeant Inca, his platoon sergeant, walked up and gave his shoulder a pat.

"Good job, Portillo. Go-man would have been pleased."

It hadn't been a good job. He'd just stood there until it was his turn to put the helmet on the M90. Hell, it hadn't even been the sergeant's helmet, just one drawn from supply for the ceremony. And JJ wasn't sure Sergeant Go would be pleased. Wherever he was now, if he could see them, he'd probably be pissing and screaming his displeasure. But JJ also knew that was what Marines said to each other in times like this.

"Thanks, Staff Sergeant," he answered.

He looked up, scanning the line of spectators before he spotted his target.

"Excuse me; I need to go take care of something."

"First formation for standing by to stand by is in an hour. Make sure you're there," the staff sergeant said.

"Roger that."

JJ passed through the milling Marines, finally reaching Jasper, who was standing in the transport bullpen.

"So, you're ready to leave, too, Gyver," he said, holding out a hand.

"Aye-yah. Not much use for me here with you boys gone."

"I told you, you don't have to leave. I've talked with the first sergeant, then with the sergeant major. The CO--the battalion CO, not the company—will approve the age waiver for enlistment. You can be a real Marine."

"And I appreciate it. I can't say I'm not tempted, too. But there's an age limit for a reason, and I'm old and slow now. Being a Marine is a young man's game."

"Old and slow, yeah, right. You forget, I humped all over behind merc lines with you. You're tougher than 90% of all the Marines I know. And you are bes-bes in a fight."

"'Bes-bes?' I'm guessing that's good, but that just goes to show that I'm in the generation that's passing. Our time for making a statement has gone and past."

"You're wrong, and you know it. I've watched you, and you're living large here, enjoying life."

Jasper looked up at the sky for a moment, then back at JJ, saying, "I won't deny it. But I've got my wife back at home. We've got the grandkids, too, and then there's the farm. It'll take a lot of work to get it back on its feet again."

"You don't have to leave now. Go home, see your wife, spend some time decompressing. But your waiver is on record, so when you want, you head down to the capital and the Federation building, and they'll take care of you."

"Thanks, JJ. I'll think about it."

"That's all I ask," JJ said, before changing the subject to, "So you're heading to Lassen now?"

"Aye-yah. They're taking all of us there, then giving us tickets for our follow-on destinations."

"A ticket to Donkerbroek?"

"That's the plan. I told them we're out in the boonies, and there's no public transportation yet, but they say they'll find something."

"And you believe them?" JJ asked.

"Not in the slightest."

"Ha! See you do know the Big Suck, after all. You're already one of us."

"Alpha Stick, load up," a civilian contractor yelled out.

"That's me. We liaisons got priority, don't you know," Jasper said.

"Yeah, and I need to get back. Staff Sergeant Inca's getting paranoid that some of us will miss the lift."

"Well, that's it, I guess. You've got my connector. Don't be a stranger, and give me a call sometime, let me know how you're doing."

"And you've got mine. You know where to reach me," JJ said.

"Well . . ."

"Shit, Gyver. No reason to be shy now," JJ said, pulling the older man into a back-breaking embrace. "I'm going to miss you, brother."

"Alpha Stick. That means now, unless you want to walk to Lassen," the contractor shouted out.

"Take care, JJ," Jasper said as he broke the embrace.

"You, too. Horatius forever, Jasper!"

JJ watched as Jasper got in line and climbed into the transport van. He didn't see where his friend took a seat, but he waited until the van pulled out and onto the road.

"Go with God, Gyver," he said before turning around and heading for his own assembly area.

****

"Thanks for the ride," Jasper said, hopping out of the cab.

"Sure thing. And thanks for your service," Gerrick, the truck driver said. "Take care."

He watched the big blue Sinotruk rise on its blowers, then smoothly head off, Gerrick waving through the driver's window. Jasper didn't know if there had been any hovertrucks on the planet before the war—the unimproved roads made the cheaper wheeled and half-tracked trucks more practical, but all the latest and greatest equipment and machinery had been brought in along with the invasion of contractors, both private and those hired by the government. Thirty percent of the populated areas of the planet had been devastated, and that meant a lot of corporations were going to make a lot of money in the reconstruction.

Jasper wasn't sure what he thought of the gold rush. It felt almost obscene in some ways, like piranhas swarming a dead cow that had fallen into a stream. On the other hand, he knew the planet needed help if it was going to get back on its feet. Besides, he'd been able to hitch a ride from Lassen, saving him time and effort in getting back to Donkerbroek.

He was surprised at how much progress had been done since he'd last seen his hometown. Most of the buildings were gone, but the debris had been removed, and he could count at least eight new buildings in the center of town alone, with bright and clean wall panels, untouched by the elements, screaming out their newness.

On the other hand, that was sobering. A simple HD home could be erected in a day once the panels were delivered. The fact that there were only eight was a reflection of how few people had returned.

Of the 28 men on Koltan's Hill during the fight, only four were still alive. Three other men had survived the battle, to escape and hide out in the nearby forest. Lyon Helsing had been badly wounded and was still in the hospital at Lassen.

Of the 72 women and children, only 41 had survived. Twenty-two were with Keela at Spirit Lake. Three others had been found at one of the terraforming projectors, and 16 had been captured by the mercs and held in a detainment camp. Other than the two children who had been swept away by the river and four whose bodies were turned over by the Tenners after the cessation of hostilities, no sign of the rest had yet been found.

Nine of the survivors had not wanted to return to the town, choosing to put the bad memories behind them. Donkerbroek, which had a pre-war population of exactly 100 souls, was now down to 31.

Make that 32, he thought, now that he was back.

As he started to walk into town, Tyler Portois backed out of a pile of rubble, pulling a wheelbarrow. He did a nice three-point turn and started pushing it forward when he caught sight of Jasper.

"Oh! Hi Mr. van Ruiker!" he said. "Welcome back home!"

"Thanks, Tyler. How're you doing? How's your mother?"

"I'm great. We're great. We've moved into the Mr. Brussie's old home, up on the Estate."

The Estate was a small ledge overlooking the center of town with three homes. The fact that they were in Maarten's home was a reflection that neither he nor Carrie had survived.

"It didn't burn?"

"No, sir! None of the three did. I'm just helping Ms. Teussel now, scrounging, you know, for their farm."

Jasper marveled at the development of the boy. He'd never been shy, but he was now brimming with confidence. Both he and Greta had become minor celebrities after Spirit Lake. Their run up the pass and to the small settlement there, and calling for help had kept the mercs from pushing an enveloping force out onto the plateau. The fact that it had also certainly saved Mountie, JJ, and his life, simply added to their acclaim.

"I've got to go, now, sir. But if you need anything, you just call me, OK?"

"I sure will, son."

He watched the boy dig in his feet and start to sprint away, pushing the wheelbarrow. He owed the young man, and he wasn't sure if he could ever repay him, but he wanted to give him a token of his appreciation.

"Wait!" he shouted.

He unslung his Gescard, took off his pack, then pulled out one of his utility blouses.

"Do you know what this is?" he asked.

"That's a Marine combat uniform," Handel answered, his eyes alight.

"Yes, it's the same. But different. Look here. See this tulip? That's for us, for everyone on the planet. So, this blouse is both, a Marine and a Utrechter, understand?"

"Oh, wow. That's toppers," he said, reaching out and stroking the fabric.

"I'd like you to have it, if you want."

"Really? Like for me?"

"Aye-yah, you earned it."

He yipped an excited yell, then grabbed the blouse and put it on. He was almost lost in it, and Jasper stepped forward, rolling up the sleeves.

"Don't worry; you'll grow into it soon enough."

"I gotta go show everyone! Thanks, Mr. van Ruiker! Thanks!" he shouted, grabbing his wheelbarrow and sprinting off.

He gave another inarticulate yip, bringing a smile to Jasper's face. He marveled at the flexibility of children. They can be traumatized, they could lose their homes and their lives as they knew it, but they still bounced back.

He, on the other hand, was looking 80 dead in the face. He should have another good 40 years or so left in him, but was he ready to start from scratch again? Did he have a child's resiliency?

It was noon, and lunch would be the order of the day, but still, the lack of people on the street depressed him. He passed empty lots, most cleaned, but stark reminders of what the town had been. Turning on Red Oak Lane, he prepared himself for his return home. Keela had already told him what to expect and had sent holos. The house itself had only partially burned. It had taken nine panels to repair the structure. It didn't look pretty, but it was shelter.

The farm was something else. Of course, the entire crop had been lost, both starter and harvest. The tubes had been damaged, as had the control system. It would take hard work, money, and time if it could even be salvaged.

Red Oak Lane climbed past what had been a row of houses, only one of which had been replaced.

A window pushed open on the new home, and Hette leaned her head out, shouting, "Welcome back, Jasper! I know Keela's waiting for you so I won't keep you, but please stop by for a visit later, OK?"

"Sure will, Hette," he said as he picked up his pace.

He dreaded what he'd find of the property, but he had to see his wife again.

Cresting the rise, he looked down into his 10 hectares. The house was just like the holos, but beyond the new barn, the tubes, were they cycling?

The front door burst open, and Keela came running out.

"Jasper! Hette just told me you're here! Why didn't you call me?"

She didn't slow, covering the 50 meters and plowing into him, almost knocking him down. He didn't care. He enveloped her, never wanting to let her go. He could feel hot tears on his shoulder as she wept.

An hour later, or possibly a few seconds—time didn't make sense anymore—Keela broke her grasp and said, "Welcome home, Jasper."

"Opa!" the two little ones shouted, their small legs slower in covering the ground. Within a few moments, he had his grandkids hanging on his legs, shouting with joy. In the doorway, he could see Radiant standing, looking terrible, Wevers holding her hand.

Keela had told him about their daughter-in-law. She wasn't doing well, and Keela thought she might need professional help.

And that was the major reason why they were all under the same roof. Radiant was not ready to run a household. And until she was, she and the grandkids were living with them.

"I got my Lil' Bunny," Amee said, holding the small PA up for Jasper to see.

"I told you that Tyler and Greta would give it back. Thanks for sharing," Jasper told her.

With the little ones chattering about anything and everything, Jasper and Keela made their way back to the house.

"Are the tubes flowing?" Jasper asked. "It looks like they are."

Keela broke out into a huge smile and said, "Radiant, take the children," then to Jasper, "Come on! Let me show you!"

"I want to stay with Opa!" Amee and Pieter shouted.

"We'll be back," Keela said. "Go finish your lunch, and then you can tell him everything!"

They walked around the corner of the house and past the new barn, but Jasper's eyes were locked on the rows of tubes. Tiny bubbles rose through the blue-green-tinted water.

"I don't understand," he said, flabbergasted.

"Henri, come here and meet Jasper," Keela shouted.

Jasper tore his eyes away from the tubes to see a small man, one side of his face scarred with burns, walk hesitantly up. Keela had told him that Henri had arrived from Wieksloot, one of the city's many refugees, and that she had hired him to help put the farm back in order, but in his wildest dreams, he'd never imagined this.

"Good to meet you, Henri," Jasper said, reaching out a hand.

Henri startled and took half a step back, then tentatively reached back and shook.

"I need to finish my lunch, ma'am," he said, then turned and went back to the barn, slipping inside and out-of-sight.

"He's, uh, he's damaged, Jasper. But he's been wonderful here. We've got 93% of the tubes running, we've got crop growing, and all because of him. We'll talk about it later, but I'd like for him to stay on. We can build him a small cottage, if we can afford it."

"Sure, we can talk about it, but 93%?" he asked, stepping up to the first row.

He put a hand up against the plastiglass tubes, feeling the vibration of nutrients and nitrogen flowing from bottom to top. The murkiness was a sure sign that algae were growing inside.

"This is the first crop," Keela told him. "I wanted one before you got back."

"But the starter? It had to be lost."

"It was."

"Then how did you get any more? I heard the government hadn't worked out a contract yet."

"You're not going to believe this. I got it from Donbury Ag last week."

Jasper was floored. He looked at Keela, his mouth hanging open.

"Donbury Ag? The Donbury Ag, one of the Tenner corporations?"

"Yes, the rep came by last week, making the rounds. The starter was free, and we don't even have to sell to them, but they promised a good price if we do."

"Donbury Ag? Who we've been fighting?"

Keela suddenly sounded unsure of herself as she said, "I hope that's OK. The government says it'll be at least ten months, and this, well, it was free, and they matched the strain. I just wanted, you know, I just wanted everything back to normal when you got home. I need things to be normal again."

Jasper looked at his wife, at the worried expression on her face, and he felt guilty. He'd been gone, but life as a Marine liaison had not been difficult. For the most part, it had been easy, to tell the truth. Meanwhile, Keela had been stuck trying to put their life together while dealing with the grandchildren and a daughter-in-law who was more of a burden than a help.

"Come here," he said, drawing her into his embrace. "I'm just amazed that you've done so much."

He kissed her, long and hard. She was stiff in his arms, then melted into him. He felt stirrings that had been absent for too long, stirrings that she noticed.

"Why Mr, van Ruiker, what do you want with me?" she asked with a throaty chuckle, her hands falling from his shoulders to squeeze his butt.

"I will show you, Ms. van Ruiker, this evening after the little ears are asleep."

"Promises, Mr. van Ruiker, promises. And I will hold you to them."

They walked arm-in-arm back up to the house, opening the back door and walking in.

"Opa, can you read to us?" Pieter asked, holding out a tablet. "It's *The Lion and the Elephant!*"

"Opa just got back," Keela told him. "He has to change and get rid of . . . why do you still have that gun?" she asked him, as if only now noticing it."

"I had to turn in the M90, but I kept this. I hope I never have to use it again, but better to have it than not."

She didn't seem convinced, but she said to the grandkids, "Let Opa get cleaned up, OK?"

Jasper had to kiss each of them before he was able to break away and get to the bedroom. Half of the exterior wall was new and still unfinished, but other than a few marks, the furniture was in surprisingly good shape. He dropped his pack and rifle, then sat on the bed, bouncing up and down a few times.

He looked up guiltily. Keela was death on being on the bed in dirty clothes, and his utilities were reeking. He dropped the trou and stepped out, then pulled the blouse off, leaving both in a pile on the floor. As he was stepping into the shower, he caught sight of his reflection in the mirror. He'd lost at least five kilos, and he looked, well, harder. With a shrug, he stepped into the shower and luxuriated in ten minutes of hot water, washing away the grime of over almost five months. The Marines had both sonic and water showers, but there's something about a man's own shower that simply cannot be matched.

Keela had his clothes hanging neatly in his small closet. His three pair of yodzhis hung in a row. He pulled them down and dropped them on the floor, images of the dead farmer and his son forcing themselves from the recesses of his mind where he'd pushed them. He kicked the pants to the back, then pulled out a pair of denims and a prince shirt. It had been a long time since he'd been in normal clothes, and it felt odd, almost like he was still naked.

That's weird. Seventy-eight years dressing like this, and I feel odd?

His Gescard was lying on the bed where he'd placed it. Keela wouldn't like that, he knew. He looked around the room, trying to figure out what to do with it. He'd get a lock for it later, but for now, he took it into his closet, up against the back wall and out of sight.

His pack was still on the floor, as were his dirty utilities, giving off more than a little stink that he noticed now that he was clean. The laundry room was next door, so he poked his head out the door, then tiptoed over. It only took two minutes to run them through the sonic, more dirt than he thought sifting to the catch-tray. He tip-toed back to the bedroom.

Jasper contemplated the pack, then decided he'd get to it later. He shoved it against the wall, then took the clean utilities and opened the closet and put them on a hanger. He hesitated a moment, his finger stroking the "Gyver" nametag, a smile creasing his face.

Being in the militia, going through what he did, had had a big impact on his life. Serving with the Marines as a liaison had been equally noteworthy. It had been horrible, but it had been great, maybe the best thing he'd ever done. He felt like he'd accomplished something, that he'd become part of history. Part of him wanted to go back, to look up JJ and get that waiver, to become a real Marine. The sirens were calling him, and not for the first time.

What was he here? An algae farmer, one of the hundreds of thousands if not more of them, all busily going about their lives like bees in a hive, producing mankind's honey. As a Marine, though, he'd be something special, someone admired and looked up to.

"Amee! That's mine! Give it back! I'm going to tell Opa!" Pieter screeched, his voice reaching up from downstairs.

And Jasper smiled. He was something, he was admired, and people looked up to him. And he had a good woman who loved him, one he loved right back.

He pulled apart the hanging clothes and hung the utilities on one of the hooks on the back wall. Hesitating only a moment, he pushed the other clothes back together, hiding the utilities out of sight.

"OK, who was it that wanted me to read them *The Lion and the Elephant!*" he shouted down the stairs as he walked out of the bedroom.

Thank you for reading *Behind Enemy Lines*. I hope you enjoyed it, and I welcome a review on Amazon, Goodreads, or any other outlet.

If you would like updates on new books releases, news, or special offers, please consider signing up for my mailing list. Your email will not be sold, rented, or in any other way disseminated. If you are interested, please sign up at the link below:

http://eepurl.com/bnFSHH

Other Books by Jonathan Brazee

The United Federation Marine Corps' Lysander Twins
Legacy Marines
Esther's Story
Noah's Story (Coming)

The United Federation Marine Corps
Recruit
Sergeant
Lieutenant
Captain
Major
Lieutenant Colonel
Colonel
Commandant

Rebel (Set in the UFMC universe.

Women of the United Federation Marines
Gladiator
Sniper
Corpsman

High Value Target (A Gracie Medicine Crow Short Story)
BOLO Mission (A Gracie Medicine Crow Short Story

The Return of the Marines Trilogy
The Few
The Proud
The Marines

The Al Anbar Chronicles: First Marine Expeditionary Force--Iraq
Prisoner of Fallujah
Combat Corpsman
Sniper

<u>Werewolf of Marines</u>
Werewolf of Marines: Semper Lycanus
Werewolf of Marines: Patria Lycanus
Werewolf of Marines: Pax Lycanus

To the Shores of Tripoli

Wererat

Darwin's Quest: The Search for the Ultimate Survivor

Venus: A Paleolithic Short Story

Secession

<u>Non-Fiction</u>
Exercise for a Longer Life

Author Website
http://www.jonathanbrazee.com

Made in the USA
Middletown, DE
21 April 2017